Olympia Dukakis and Laura Linney were made from the first three *Tales* novels. *The Night Listener* became a feature film starring Robin Williams and Toni Collette. Maupin lives in San Francisco with his husband, Christopher Turner.

For more information on Armistead Maupin and his books, see his website at www.armisteadmaupin.com

MICHAEL TOLLIVER
LIVES

Armistead Maupin

BLACK SWAN

TRANSWORLD PUBLISHERS
61–63 Uxbridge Road, London W5 5SA
A Random House Group Company
www.rbooks.co.uk

MICHAEL TOLLIVER LIVES
A BLACK SWAN BOOK: 9780552772938

First published in Great Britain
in 2007 by Doubleday
a division of Transworld Publishers
Black Swan edition published 2008

A CIP catalogue record for this book
is available from the British Library.

Addresses for Random House Group Ltd companies outside the UK
can be found at: www.randomhouse.co.uk
The Random House Group Ltd Reg. No. 954009

Typeset in 11/16pt Giovanni Book by
Falcon Oast Graphic Art Ltd.

11

Penguin Random House is committed to a sustainable future for
our business, our readers and our planet. This book is made from
Forest Stewardship Council® certified paper.

Printed and bound in Great Britain by Clays Ltd, St Ives plc

For my beloved husband,
Christopher Turner

"You are old, father William," the young man said,
"And your hair has become very white;
And yet you incessantly stand on your head—
Do you think, at your age, it is right?"

—Lewis Carroll

"People like you and me ... we're gonna be fifty-year-old libertines in a world full of twenty-year-old Calvinists."

—Brian Hawkins to Michael Tolliver, 1976

Michael Tolliver Lives

1

Confederacy
of Survivors

Not long ago, down on Castro Street, a stranger in a
Giants parka gave me a loaded glance as we passed each
other in front of Cliff's Hardware. He was close to my
age, I guess, not *that* far past fifty—and not bad-looking
either, in a beat-up, Bruce Willis-y sort of way—so I
waited a moment before turning to see if he would go
for a second look. He knew this old do-si-do as well as
I did, and hit his mark perfectly.

"Hey," he called, "you're supposed to be dead."

I gave him an off-kilter smile. "Guess I didn't get the
memo."

His face grew redder as he approached. "Sorry, I just
meant . . . it's been a really long time and . . . sometimes you just *assume* . . . you know . . ."

I did know. Here in our beloved Gayberry you can
barely turn around without gazing into the strangely

familiar features of someone long believed dead. Having lost track of him in darker days, you had all but composed his obituary and scattered his ashes at sea, when he shows up in the housewares aisle at Cala Foods to tell you he's been growing roses in Petaluma for the past decade. This happens to me a lot, these odd little supermarket resurrections, so I figured it could just as easily happen to someone else.

But who the hell *was* he?

"You're looking good," he said pleasantly.

"Thanks. You too." His face had trenches like mine—the usual wasting from the meds. A fellow cigar store Indian.

"You *are* Mike Tolliver, right?"

"Michael. Yeah. But I can't quite—"

"Oh . . . sorry." He thrust out his hand. "Ed Lyons. We met at Joe Dimitri's after the second Gay Games."

That was no help at all, and it must have shown.

"You know," the guy offered gamely. "The big house up on Collingwood?"

Still nothing.

"The circle jerk?"

"Ah."

"We went back to my place afterward."

"On Potrero Hill!"

"You remember!"

What I remembered—*all* I remembered after

12

nineteen years—was his dick. I remembered how its less-than-average length was made irrelevant by its girth. It was one of the thickest I'd ever seen, with a head that flared like a caveman's club. Remembering *him* was a good deal harder. Nineteen years is too long a time to remember a face.

"We had fun," I said, hoping that a friendly leer would make up for my phallocentric memory.

"You had something to do with plants, didn't you?"

"Still do." I showed him my dirty cuticles. "I had a nursery back then, but now I garden full time."

That seemed to excite him, because he tugged on the strap of my overalls and uttered a guttural "woof." If he was angling for a nooner, I wasn't up for it. The green-collar job that had stoked his furnace had left me with some nasty twinges in my rotator cuffs, and I still had podocarps to prune in Glen Park. All I really wanted was an easy evening with Ben and the hot tub and a rare bacon cheeseburger from Burgermeister.

Somehow he seemed to pick up on that. "You married these days?"

"Yeah . . . pretty much."

"*Married* married or just . . . regular?"

"You mean . . . did we go down to City Hall?"

"Yeah."

I told him we did.

"Must've been amazing," he said.

13

"Well, it was a mob scene, but . . . you know . . . pretty cool." I wasn't especially forthcoming, but I had told the story once too often and had usually failed to convey the oddball magic of that day: all those separate dreams coming true in a gilded, high-domed palace straight out of *Beauty and the Beast*. You had to have *witnessed* that long line of middle-aged people standing in the rain, some of them with kids in tow, waiting to affirm what they'd already known for years. And the mayor himself, so young and handsome and . . . *neat* . . . that he actually *looked* like the man on top of a wedding cake.

"Well," said Ed Lyons, stranger no more, now that I'd put a name to the penis. "I'm heading down to the bagel shop. How 'bout you?"

I told him I was headed for my truck.

"Woof!" he exclaimed, aroused by the mere mention of my vehicle.

I must've rolled my eyes just a little.

"What?" he asked.

"It's not that butch a truck," I told him.

He laughed and charged off. As I watched his broad shoulders navigate the stream of pedestrians, I wondered if I would find Ed's job—whatever it might be—as sexy as he found mine. *Oh, yeah, buddy, that's right, make me want it, make me buy that two-bedroom condo! That Century 21 blazer is so fucking hot!*

I headed for my truck (a light-blue Tacoma, if you must know), buzzing on a sort of homegrown euphoria that sweeps over me from time to time. After thirty years in the city, it's nice to be reminded that I'm still glad to be here, still glad to belong to this sweet confederacy of survivors, where men meet in front of the hardware store and talk of love and death and circle jerks as if they're discussing the weather.

It helps that I have Ben; I know that. Some years back, when I was still single, the charm of the city was wearing thin for me. All those imperial dot-commers in their SUVs and Hummers barreling down the middle of Noe Street as if leading an assault on a Third World nation. And those freshly minted queens down at Badlands, wreathed in cigarette smoke and attitude, who seemed to believe that political activism meant a subscription to *Out* magazine and regular attendance at *Queer as Folk* night. Not to mention the traffic snarls and the fuck-you-all maître d's and the small-town queers who brought their small-town fears to the Castro and tried to bar the door against The Outsiders. I remember one in particular, petitions in hand, who cornered me on the sidewalk to alert me that the F streetcar—the one bearing straight tourists from Fisherman's Wharf—was scheduling a new stop at Castro and Market. "They just can't do this," he cried.

"This is the center of our spirituality!" We were standing in front of a window displaying make-your-own dildos and dick-on-a-rope soap. I told him my spirituality would survive.

The dot-commers have been humbled, of course, but house prices are still rising like gangbusters, with no end in sight. I'm glad I staked a claim here seventeen years ago, when it was still possible for a nurseryman and a nonprofit preservationist to buy a house in the heart of the city. The place hadn't seemed special at the time, just another starter cottage that needed serious attention. But once my partner, Thack, and I had stripped away its ugly green asbestos shingles, the historic bones of the house revealed themselves. Our little fixer-upper was actually a grouping of three "earthquake shacks," refugee housing built in the parks after the 1906 disaster, then hauled away on drays for use as permanent dwellings. They were just crude boxes, featureless and cobbled together at odd angles, but we exposed some of the interior planking and loved telling visitors about our home's colorful catastrophic origins. What could have been more appropriate? We were knee-deep in catastrophe ourselves—the last Big One of the century—and bracing for the worst.

But then I didn't die. The new drug cocktails came along, and I got better, and Thack worked up the nerve to tell me he wanted out. When he left for a job in

Chicago in the mid-nineties, the house became mine alone. It was a tomb at first, filled with too many ghosts, but I exorcised them with paint and fabric and furniture. Over the next eight years, almost without noticing, I arrived at a quiet revelation: You *could* make a home by yourself. You could fill that home with friends and friendly strangers without someone sleeping next to you. You could tend your garden and cook your meals and find predictable pleasure in your own autonomy.

In other words, I was ready for Ben.

I met him on the Internet. Well, not exactly; I saw him on the Internet, and met him on the street in North Beach. But I would never have known who he was, or rather what he was looking for, had my friend Barney not modeled for a website catering to older gay men. Barney is forty-eight, a successful mortgage broker, and something of a muscle daddy. He's a wee bit vain, too. He could barely contain himself when he stopped me on Market Street one day to tell me that his big white marble ass was now available to World Wide Wankers for only $21.95 a month, credit card or online check.

Once upon a time, this would have struck me as sleazy, but the Internet has somehow persuaded half the world to get naked for the enjoyment of the other half. Barney is a fairly sexy guy, but I squirmed a little when I checked out his photos on the site. Maybe I've just known him too long, but there was something incestuous and unsettling about it, like watching your Aunt Gladys flashing titty for the troops.

At any rate, there was a personals section on the website, so once I'd fled the sight of Barney's winking sphincter, I checked out the guys who were looking for Sex, Friendship, or Long Term Relationships. There were lots of geezers there—by which I mean anyone my age or older—regular Joes from Lodi or Tulsa, smiling bravely by their vintage vehicles, or dressed for some formal event. Most of them offered separate close-ups of their erections, artfully shot from below, so that doubtful browsers could find their way past the snow on the roof to the still-raging fire in the furnace.

What surprised me, though, was the number of young guys on the site. Guys in their twenties or thirties specifically looking for partners over forty-five. The one who caught my attention, and held it—CLEANCUTLAD4U—was a sandy blond with a brush cut and shining brown eyes. His actual name was not provided, but his profile identified him as thirty-three and Versatile, a resident of the Bay Area. He was lying against a headboard, smiling sleepily, a white sheet pulled down to the first suggestion of pubic hair. For reasons I still can't name, he came across like someone from another century, a stalwart captured on daguerreotype, casually masculine and tender of heart.

So how did this work? Did I have to submit a profile or could I just email him directly? He'd want to see a photo, wouldn't he? Would I have to get naked? The young can keep a little mystery, it seems to me, but the old have to show you their stuff. Which, of course, is easier said than done. Sure, the right dick can distract from a falling ass, and some people actually get off on a nice round stomach, but who has any use for that no-man's-land between them, that troublesome *lower* stomach of sloppy skin?

Maybe I could pose in my dirty work clothes with just my dick hanging out? (I could call myself NICENDIRTY4U.) But who would take the picture? Barney was the logical choice, but I had a sudden gruesome flash of him directing my debut and thought better of it. Who was I kidding, anyway? CleanCutLad probably got hundreds of offers a week. It was wiser to stick to my monthly night at the Steamworks, where the goods were always on the table, and rejection, when it came, was instant and clean.

And that's the way I left it, aside from printing out the guy's webpage and posting it above my potting shed. It stayed there for ages, curling at the edges, a pinup boy for a war that would never be waged. I might not have met him at all if my friend Anna Madrigal hadn't called to invite me for dinner at the Caffe Sport.

The Caffe Sport is on Green Street, way across town in North Beach, a gaudy Sicilian cavern that dishes up huge creamy mounds of seafood and pasta. Anna had been going there for over thirty years and often used its peasanty charms as a way of luring me out of my complacent nest in the Castro. At eighty-five, she was convinced I was growing too set in my ways. I needed some excitement, she said, and she was the gal to provide it.

So there we sat, awash in colors and aromas, when the impossible happened. Anna was adjusting her turban at the time, consulting the mirror behind my back as she fussed with wisps of snowy hair. Yet somehow she *still* caught the look on my face.

"What is it, dear?"

"I'm not sure," I said.

"Well, you must have an idea."

A cluster of departing diners had moved toward the door, obscuring my view. "I think I saw someone."

"Someone you know?"

"No . . . not exactly."

"Mmm . . . someone you *want* to know." She shooed me with a large gloved hand. "Go on, then. Catch up with him."

"I don't know . . ."

"Yes you do. Get the hell out of here. I'll be here with my wine."

So I sprang to my feet and shimmied through the tightly packed crowd. By the time I reached the door he was nowhere in sight. I looked to the right, toward the fog-cushioned neon of Columbus, then left, toward Grant Avenue. He was almost at the end of the block and picking up speed. I had no choice but to make myself ridiculous.

"Excuse me," I yelled, hurrying after him.

No response at all. He didn't even stop walking.

"Excuse me! In the blue jacket!"

He stopped, then turned. "Yeah?"

"Sorry, but . . . I was in the restaurant and—"

"Oh, shit." He reached reflexively for his back pocket. "Did I leave my wallet?"

"No," I replied. "Just *me*."

I had hoped that this would prove to be an ice-breaker, but it landed with a dull thud, missing the ice completely. The guy just blinked at me in confusion.

"I think I saw you on a website," I explained.

Another blink.

"CLEANCUTLAD4U?"

Finally he smiled. There was a fetching gap between his two front teeth, which only enhanced the fuckable Norman Rockwell image.

"I could've sent you my profile," I told him, "but I

figured it was easier just to chase you down the street."

He laughed and stuck out his hand. "I'm Ben McKenna."

"Michael Tolliver."

"I saw you inside with that lady." He had held my hand a little longer than actually required. "Was that your mother?"

I chuckled. Anna would love to hear that. "Not exactly," I said.

"She looks interesting."

"She *is*, believe me." We were rapidly veering off the subject, so I decided to take the bullock by the horns. "I have to get her home, as a matter of fact. Would you mind giving me your phone number? Or I could give you mine."

He looked almost surprised. "Either way," he said with a shrug.

We went back into the restaurant for pencil and paper. As Ben scribbled away by the cash register I looked across the room and saw that Anna was watching this transaction with a look of smug accomplishment on her face. And I knew this would not be the end of it; something this juicy could amuse her for weeks.

"My, my," she said as soon as I returned. "I hope you carded him."

"He's thirty-three. Cut me some slack."

22

"You *asked* him his age?"

"I read it online."

"O Brave New World," she intoned melo-dramatically. "Shall we head down to the park, dear? Before we call it a night?"

"Thought you'd never ask," I said.

So I walked her down to Washington Square, where we sat in the cool foggy dark and shared a quick doobie before bedtime.

2

Hugs, Ben

I'll give you a moment to do the math. Ben is twenty-one years younger than I am—an *entire adult* younger, if you insist on looking at it that way. But I really haven't made a habit of this. My first lover, Jon, who died back in '82, was a year older than I was, and Thack and I are only months apart in age. It's true that lately I've gone out with guys who might be described as, well, less than middle-aged, but it never lasted very long. Sooner or later they would bore me silly with their tales of "partying" on crystal meth or their belief in the cultural importance of Paris Hilton's dog. And most of them, I'm sorry to say, seemed to think they were doing me a favor.

Before Ben I'd had little experience with daddy hunters. I knew there were young guys who went for older guys, but I'd always assumed that it was largely about money and power. But Ben claims he's lusted after older men since he was twelve in Colorado Springs and began jerking off to magazines. He remembers rushing home from school to search the latest issue of his dad's *Sports Illustrated* for the heart-stopping image of Jim Palmer in his Jockey shorts. And several years later, in the same magazine, he read a story about Dr. Tom Waddell, the retired Olympic decathlete who established the Gay Games. The very *fact* of this aging gay gladiator filled him with the hope that *some* of the men he wanted might actually want him back. And all doubt was finally removed when he moved to San Francisco after college. The daddies Ben met down at Starbucks or the Edge were sometimes slow to read the gleam in his eye, but given half a chance and a little encouragement, they could leap whole decades in a single bound.

God knows *I* did. Ben called me the very next morning, and I invited him over for dinner the following night. I told him I was making pot roast, just in case he didn't consider this a sex date. And just in case he *did*, I popped a Viagra half an hour before his scheduled arrival. He appeared at the door exactly on time in well-fitted Diesel jeans and a pale-blue T-shirt, bearing a bottle of Chianti that clattered to the floor as soon as I grabbed him. When we finally broke from the kiss, he uttered a sigh that suggested both arousal and relief, as if he, too, had worried that we might have to eat pot roast first.

"You should know," I said, releasing him. "I'm positive."

He looked in my eyes and smiled. "About what?"

"Don't get smart with your elders," I said, leading the way to the bedroom.

"You know," Ben said afterward. "I think I've seen you before."

He was lying in the crook of my arm, thoughtfully blotting the wet spot, his fingers arranging my chest hair with serene deliberation, like a Zen master raking sand.

I asked him what he meant.

"I think you do the garden at my neighbors' house," he said.

"No kidding? Where?"

"Out on Taraval."

"Not Mrs. Gagnier?"

"I don't know her name, really."

"French-Canadian, right? Prematurely gray. Makes jam out of her lavender."

"Well, I don't know about the *jam* part, but . . ."

"I do. She gave me some last Christmas. Tastes like shampoo."

He chuckled. "Do you always work with your shirt off?"

I scolded him with a playful yank on his ear. "Only when I think someone's *spying on me in the bushes*."

"I wasn't in the bushes, I was on my roof."

"Why didn't you yell down or something?"

"I dunno. I couldn't tell if you were queer from up there."

I gave him a puzzled frown. "How high is that roof, anyway?"

He laughed, snuggling into my side again. After an interval of uncomplicated silence he said, "So how do you know the lady you were with?"

I explained that she had been my landlady years ago when I lived on Russian Hill. I told him about her backyard marijuana garden and her huge collection of kimonos, and the rambling old house itself, tucked away in the alps of those high wooden stairs.

"How does she manage that now?"

"She doesn't. She had a stroke a few years ago, so she moved down to the Duboce Triangle. There are people who help out, you know, in the building, so there's a number of us to . . . share the load."

"Well, that's good."

"Not that it *is* one," I added. "I love being with her."

"Sure."

"She affects a lot of people that way, which is good.

She's still got it going, you know? She still gives a shit about things. Most trannies never make it that far."

He blinked at me for a moment. "You mean . . . ?"

I smiled in the affirmative. "She was the first one I ever knew."

"She pulls it off pretty well," he said.

I told him she'd had some practice, that she'd been a woman for over forty years, almost as long as she'd *not* been a woman.

Ben took that in for a moment. "I'd like to meet her sometime."

Already that sounded so right to me.

After that first pyrotechnic night, we saw each other about twice a week for three or four months. Ben was kind and bright and appreciative of everything about me I'd recoiled from in recent years: the thickening trunk and silky butt, the wildfire of gray hair sweeping across my chest. Some people think we finally become adults when both our parents have died; for me it happened when someone desired the person I'd become. For years I'd been in a state of suspended boyhood, counting every crow's foot as I searched for the all-loving man who would finally set things right. Ben made me think that I could *be* that man. Not as some father figure, if that's what you're thinking—Ben was way too independent for that—but simply as

28

someone who knew how it felt to be cheated of a father's comfort and tenderness. Someone who could give you all that.

Loving Ben would be like loving myself, long ago.

I tried to stay cool about it. There was very little to indicate that Ben was even in the market for romance. The emails he sent me from work usually closed with "Hugs, Ben"—a surefire sign, I felt, that he saw us as compatible fuck buddies and nothing more. True, Ben had been partnered several times already, and always to older guys, but there was something distressingly self-contained about him. My heart sank when he outlined his plans for remodeling his tiny one-man apartment, or rhapsodized about hiking in the Alaskan wilderness, where he'd perch on mountaintops for hours on end, reveling in his solitude. Even Ben's job with a South of Market furniture designer was a little troubling, since one day, he said, he hoped it would afford him the chance to live in Milan or Paris.

None of these scenarios left much room for me, I felt.

But all of them turned me on. I loved picturing Ben in that matchbox room on Taraval, making hibiscus tea before bed. Or swimming naked in a mountain stream, his jeans warming on a nearby boulder. I often fell hard for such manly free spirits when I was Ben's age or younger, though very few of them returned the favor.

That my prince should come now, desirous as he was desirable, was almost too much to believe.

So I took each day as it came, dutifully noting even the slightest sign of hope along the way. The day he showed me sketches of a sideboard he was designing. The night he brought us white peaches from the Farmers Market. A Sunday trip to the Headlands, where we lay all day on an army blanket, comrades-in-arms, without having sex at all. Little doubt remained, in fact, when "Hugs, Ben" became "Love, Ben" and the floodgates finally opened, inundating our emails with reckless Victorian endearments:

My Darling Boy
My Handsome Man
My Wonderful One
My Own

We were sitting on a bench at Lands End, watching a sunset exactly the color of the bridge, when he popped the question:

"I don't think I could ever be totally monogamous, do you?"

I was momentarily at a loss for an answer.

"I mean," he went on, "it's not like I'm a sex addict or anything. I don't want you to think that . . . but sometimes, you know . . . opportunities arise."

I laughed nervously. "That's one way of putting it."

"And if you really love the guy you're with . . . and you see yourselves as soul mates and all . . . then you should *want* each other to have those experiences, shouldn't you? I mean, shouldn't your love make that possible?"

"Mmm." It was more of a noise, really, than an actual reply.

"Everyone I know who agrees to monogamy just ends up sneaking around, deceiving the person who matters to them most. That hurts a lot more than just . . . adjusting the rules, so that your love for each other can just make things better. Men aren't designed to be monogamous, in *my* opinion, and the ones who force themselves into that mold either break each other's hearts eventually or just . . . completely neuter themselves. I don't mean a new playmate every week, or even every month *necessarily*, but . . . as long as it's out in the open and doesn't impinge upon . . . you know . . . your intimacy with each other, or becomes, like . . . *romantic* or something that's really . . . consciously hurtful, then I don't see why two people can't just agree to . . ." Flustered, he gave up the effort altogether. "Feel free to jump in any time, Michael."

I stroked his cheek for a moment. "You're too young to be monogamous," I told him. "And I'm too old."

He studied me seriously for a moment. "You mean that?"

I nodded, smiling dimly. "In some ways I wish I didn't, but I do. I know too much about life to think otherwise. Which is not to say I can't still get jealous—"

"Good," he blurted.

"Is it?"

"Well, yeah, because I can get jealous, too. And I could get *really* jealous about you."

Why did that make me feel so much better? "We'll work on that together," I said.

He was grinning broadly now, revealing that adorable gap again. "Could we take about thirty years?"

I counted soberly on my fingers for a moment. "That may be doable, yeah."

The next day he removed his personals ad from the website.

And that spoke more eloquently than any marriage license from City Hall.

3

Far Beyond
Saving

Okay, thirty years might be stretching it, given the virus
I've lived with for the past twenty. I'm still in the Valley
of the Shadow—as Mama would put it—but at least it's
a bigger valley these days, and the scenery has improved
considerably. In my best moments I'm filled with a
curious peace, an almost passable impersonation of
how it used to be. Then my T cells drop suddenly or I
sprout a virulent rash on my back or shit my best
corduroys while waiting in line at the DMV, and I'm
once again reminded how fucking *tenuous* it all is. My
life, whatever its duration, is still a lurching, lopsided
contraption held together by chewing gum and baling
wire.

And here's the kicker: the longer you survive the
virus, the closer you get to dying the regular way. My
current recipe for continued existence, a fine-tuned

mélange of Viramune and Combivir, now competes for shelf space in my medicine cabinet with Lipitor, Wellbutrin, and Glucosamine Chondroitin, remedies commonly associated with age and decrepitude. (Well, maybe not Wellbutrin, since even the young get depressed, but that was no big deal in my own youth.) There are plenty of ironies in this, lessons to be learned about fate and the fickleness of death and getting on with life while the getting is good, but you won't read them here. I've had enough lessons from this disease.

Strange as it seems, I can remember a time when I was sure I wouldn't outlive my dog. I acknowledged this to Harry, the dog himself, one drizzly winter night when Thack was away on business. As Harry lay curled in my lap, I told him I'd be leaving soon but not to worry, that I'd be in a better place. I don't know what got into me; I don't even *believe* in a better place. But there I sat, morbid with fear, soft-pedaling oblivion the way parents do with their kids. And five years later my little white lie blossomed into black comedy when I laid Harry to rest under a stepping-stone in the garden.

I made the same assumption about my mother. Back in the days of night sweats and endless fatigue, it was reasonable to believe that I'd beat Mama to the grave. In fact, Mama herself argued energetically for my exportation to "a nice Orlando memorial park just down the road from Disney World." My father had been buried there several years earlier, so Mama was bound and determined to launch a tradition: a family reunion of sorts, without the dirt bikes and Jell-O salad. I turned her down gently, but my brother Irwin caved in and bought a plot that could comfortably accommodate his entire family, even the daughter who'd moved to St. Pete to work for the Home Shopping Network. Irwin is fifty-seven, a Chris-tian and a realtor, and so thoroughly committed to both disciplines that he belongs to an organization of Christian realtors.

I'm not fucking with you here; they have a website and everything.

It was Irwin who called to tell me that Mama was feeling poorly and that I might want to think about coming home soon.

"I don't wanna scare you, Mikey, but I thought you should know."

"That's okay, Irwin. I appreciate it."

"It could be six weeks or six months, but . . . it's not looking good."

As hard as it was to hear this, I wasn't surprised. My mother's emphysema, the result of decades of liberation by Virginia Slims, had already confined her to a Christian-run convalescent home in Orlovista, Florida, where, for the past six years, between walls of yellowing family photos, she'd been convalescing her way to death.

"Is she hurting?" I asked.

"Not really," said Irwin. "Just kinda . . . wheezy, ya know. And her color isn't good. She's been asking about you a lot lately."

"Well . . . tell her I'll be there soon. I've got some miles saved up."

"Great . . . that's great, Mikey."

I asked him how Mama had liked the birthday present I'd sent several weeks earlier: a silver-framed snapshot of me and Ben, taken just after the wedding, standing beside a waterfall at Big Sur. I hadn't a word from anyone, so I'd been wondering.

He thought for a moment. "Oh, yeah . . . the picture."

"Right."

He chuckled nervously. "Good one, Mikey. You had me going for a while."

"What do you mean?"

"C'mon. He works for you, right? Or he's a friend or something."

"No," I said evenly, as if talking to a three-year-old. "That's Ben. That's my husband. The one I've told you about."

"Oh . . . sorry . . . I just . . . he looked so—"

"No need to be sorry."

"But wasn't that annulled or something?"

I had no choice but to torture him. "What do you mean?"

36

"You know . . . the state court made a ruling, didn't they?"

"You're shitting me!"

"No. They revoked it. It was big news, Mikey . . . even in Florida."

You bet your ass it was. Singing and dancing in the streets no doubt. Might even be a state holiday by now.

"This is awful," I said glumly.

"I can't believe you didn't hear about it."

"Do you know what this means?" I said. "We've been living in sin!"

After a moment, the light dawned and he groaned in exasperation. "You see," he said, "this is what I mean. Always jerkin' my chain. Can't trust a darn thing you say."

"Or even a damn thing," I added, laughing.

Now he was laughing, too. "I mean, c'mon, bro. You send us this picture of . . . I dunno . . . Huckleberry Finn or somethin' . . . and you tell us he's your *husband* . . ."

"If it helps any," I said, "he's older than he looks."

A silence, and then: "How old *is* he?"

"How old was Jesus when he rose from the dead?"

"Mikey, if you're gonna be disrespectful—"

"I'm giving you a reference point, Irwin."

"Oh."

"Ben is a grown man, is all I mean. He's had a life already. There's no training required."

"He's thirty-three, you mean?"

"Very good. Big gold star on your forehead."

"Well . . ." Irwin cleared his throat in preparation for a brave leap into the abyss. "He does look nice . . . I mean he looks like a nice guy . . . from the picture."

"He is, Irwin. He's got a heart and a conscience and there's a really solid bond between us. There's stuff to talk about, you know. The age thing isn't an issue." I was trying to be straight with him now, since I wanted him to understand the gravity of what had happened to me. "I'll be bringing him with me," I said, "if he wants to come."

It took him a while to respond. "Well . . . that's good. I mean . . . it's good to have support, isn't it? . . . at a time like this."

Not bad, Irwin.

"I'd ask you to stay with us," he said, "but Lenore's got her puppets spread all over the guest bedroom. You never seen such a mess."

"Look, we really don't—"

"And . . . I almost forgot . . . we're having the floors redone, so the whole place will be . . . you know, pretty much of a disaster area."

"Well, thanks for the offer, but . . . I think we'll look for a motel. I kinda *like* the idea of a motel,

38

actually. A neutral place, you know. And some privacy."

"You sure now?" Irwin's relief was all but spewing from the receiver. "I could find y'all a condo at least. I think we've got an empty demo over by the Gospel Palms."

The Gospel Palms was Mama's rest home.

"That's okay," I told him. "We'll just find some place near." (Even in Orlando, I figured there had to be a decent gay bed-and-breakfast.)

"All right, then."

"I'll call you when we've set a date."

"Mama's gonna be mighty happy, Mikey."

"Well, give her a hug for me, when you see her."

And the picture, big brother. Give her the fucking picture.

Let's put this in perspective: My family has known I'm gay for going on thirty years. I wrote a letter to my mother in 1977 when she joined Anita Bryant's Save Our Children campaign, hoping against hope to save her own two sons from recruitment by homosexuals. The news that I was beyond saving—and happy as hell about it—was met first by silence, then by a lone pound cake that I chose to regard as an awkward step toward enlightenment.

But, hey, it was just a pound cake. My folks still loved me all right, but they saw that love as cause for forgiveness, not acceptance. And while Mama and Papa eventually met Thack—and made a damn good show of liking him—they saw no reason whatsoever to modify their stance. My life had been conveniently reduced to a "lifestyle" by then, something easily separable from me, that they could abhor to their heart's content without fear of being perceived as unchristian. By the time the Berlin Wall fell and queers replaced commies on the big TV screens at my brother's church, I knew not to expect a miracle anymore; my family was as far beyond saving as I was.

"And your brother's an actual deacon in the church?"

This was Ben, calling from the bathroom across the hall, where I could hear him rummaging in a drawer. It was just after eight that evening and I was already on the bed, flat on my stomach with my new Lucky jeans shoved down around my ankles.

I twisted my head in his direction. "More like a Sunday school teacher, I think. I don't understand the hierarchy. They've all got *something* to do."

"No shit?"

"Last year Lenore—that's Irwin's wife—was in charge of the fetus key rings."

"C'mon!"

"No . . . they were selling these little plastic fetuses that were supposed to be the *exact* size of an early fetus. You know . . . so you can carry it around with you and

. . . get to know it better. Sort of . . . 'Fetuses are people, too.' "

Ben came into the room and sat down on the bed next to me, tearing open a foil packet. "You're creeping me out," he murmured.

"You should see the *really big one* they put up on Halloween."

"What do you mean?" Ben removed the alcohol swab from the packet. "Put up where?" He drew a line with his finger from the top of my ass crack to the mound due east of it and began swabbing the target area briskly.

"In a haunted house," I explained. "You know . . . like they have for kids. Only it's not spaghetti guts and eyeballs in a bowl, it's the Big Giant Aborted Fetus."

Ben groaned.

"And right next to the Big Giant Aborted Fetus is the Gay Man With AIDS."

"Don't tell me they actually *took* you to this thing?" There was barely a tingle as the syringe hit its target. And *target* is the word, too, since Ben is a kind soul and thinks he's less likely to hurt me if he just gives the syringe a jaunty toss, like a dart.

"Well, I didn't actually *see* it," I said, "but I met this queen at a local bar who did. He said they used iridescent-purple lipstick for the lesions."

Ben swabbed my butt again. "Stay there a second, sweetheart. You're bleeding a little."

41

"Never mind that. Are my balls shrinking?"

Ben laughed and reached between my legs. "All present and accounted for, Captain."

"I know *that*. But are they shrinking?"

"Well, not in my expert opinion."

My doctor had warned me about the shrinking thing when I started testosterone therapy two years ago. The stuff can give you energy, restore your libido, lift your spirits, and make you grow hair like a Chia Pet, but it can also shrink your balls. Apparently, if your testicles wise up to the fact that someone else is on the job, they can lose interest in the job altogether. The meat may be sizzling, but the potatoes have taken a hike.

"How do they seem to you?" asked Ben. "You handle 'em more than I do."

I chuckled. "We'll have to work on that."

Ben patted my ass. "You're good to go, honey."

As I pulled my jeans up Ben dropped the syringe into an empty Ragu jar we had saved for that purpose. "You know," he said, screwing the lid on, "we should start a Liberal Haunted House. We could have oilmen bombing kids . . . and fags being tied to fences . . . and black men being dragged behind trucks . . . and maybe those Abu Ghraib guys, you know, with the hoods and the wires and all."

I said that was a nice twist but too unsubtle for liberals.

"That's the problem," he said. "We're *always* too subtle." He gave me a long, tender look. "I'm sorry, babe . . . about your mom. "

"Thanks," I said, looking back.

"I'm glad I'll get a chance to meet her."

Poor guy. Little did he know.

4

Our Little
Grrrl

Several times a month I pick up fruit trees at a nursery on Clement Street called Plant Parenthood. That always makes me nostalgic, since I ran the place for twelve years before selling it to my business partner, Brian Hawkins. My T cells had begun to climb by then, and I was sick of pushing Tuscan flowerpots to bored house-wives. I wanted to plant something serious for once, to leave my mark on the earth before somebody planted *me*. I've never regretted that decision. I'm now tending at least a dozen mature gardens that I myself created years ago: lush green kingdoms seeded from my own imagination.

Not that it's getting easier. My arthritis seems to be here for good, and the sheer grunt work of the job can put me out of commission for days on end. I'm my own boss, of course, so I can adjust my schedule accordingly, and I do have an assistant now—the aptly named Jake Greenleaf—who helps me with the trimming and hauling. But the big question remains: *How long can I keep this up?* The topic is almost unavoidable at Plant Parenthood, since Brian turned sixty-one this year, and retirement is his chief preoccupation.

On a recent visit I found my old friend hunched over his laptop with a crazed gleam in his eye, like a zealot planning a people's revolution. Brian Hawkins, hippie-turned-radical-lawyer-turned-waiter-turned-nursery -man, was poring over a website for motor homes. "What do you think of this one, Michael? It's still a class C, but it's got most of the amenities of a class A, without the bulk. It's a little more eco-friendly."

"I hate the name," I said.

"What's the name got to do with it?"

"You're not seriously gonna hit the road in something called a Minnie Winnie?"

"Hey," he said, "I'm secure in my wussyhood."

I laughed. "Have you thought about where you'll have to *park* the damn thing? Your neighbors will all have bumper stickers that say 'Baby Jesus On Board.' "

Brian spun around in his chair. "That's a gross generalization."

"Is it?"

"Damn straight. All kinds of people have RVs."

"Like who?"

45

"Well . . . this sculptress I met at Burning Man, for one."

"Ah . . . this sculptress."

Brian grinned. "Don't start with me, man—"

"You got some New Age pussy in a Winnebago, and now it's the only way to travel."

"You missed something, that's all."

"What do you mean?"

"Burning Man, buttwipe! The desert! There were sandstorms whipping up all around us, and the stars were so bright you could see by them. The Winnebago made me feel . . . I dunno . . . so *self-contained* out there in the middle of nowhere. I haven't felt that way since . . . Wounded Knee, maybe."

I smirked as benignly as possible.

"I'm ancient, aren't I?"

"Pretty much," I said.

"Next thing you know I'll be wearing Sansabelt slacks." He wrinkled his brow in thought for a moment. "Do old farts even *wear* those anymore?"

"I think they wear jeans," I said.

"I think they do, too."

We exchanged rueful looks, sharing our pain. We've done this for almost thirty years now, since the day we met, in fact, in the courtyard at Anna Madrigal's apartment house on Russian Hill. We were both in swim trunks at the time, both bronzing our bodies for a night

46

at the bars, though the bars were as different as the objects of our lust. We were just a couple of guys talking about guy things, cheerfully enslaved to our dicks yet secretly, deeply, romantic. And those ever-warring instincts drew us ever closer.

Like me, Brian is at least twenty (or so) pounds heavier these days, but that architectural cleft in his chin is just as fetching as it ever was, especially under a sandpaper beard, though the sand is now white as Daytona Beach. It's been ages since I've felt anything like lust for Brian—that would be way too incestuous—but Benjamin, my beloved, finds him eminently fuckable. And Brian *loves* knowing that.

I walked to the window and looked out at the latest shipment of fruit trees. "I need something tall for a courtyard on Townsend. That lemon tree is pretty, isn't it?"

"Yeah," Brian deadpanned, "and the lemon flower is sweet."

"*But*," I said, playing along in a dry professorial tone, "I've always found that the actual *fruit* of the poor lemon is . . . very nearly . . . *impossible* to eat."

"I couldn't agree with you more."

We laughed with idiotic abandon, terribly amused by ourselves, until a voice in the doorway told us we were no longer alone. "You guys are way weird."

It was Shawna, Brian's daughter—an assault of

dark-red lipstick beneath crow-black bangs and Harlequin glasses—addressing us tartly with hand on hip. She had stopped by to bring her father a brown-bag lunch from Cowgirl Creamery at the Ferry Building. "If this is early Alzheimer's or something, I need a little warning."

Brian laughed. "We were riffing on a song."

Shawna made the open-mouthed "Huh?" expression that's so popular with the young people today.

"You know," I said, and began to sing for her: "'Lemon tree, very pretty, and the lemon flower is sweet . . .'"

Brian joined in, giving it a saucy Caribbean beat: "'. . . but the fruit of the poor lemon is impossible—'"

"All right . . . fine," said Shawna. "I'll take your word for it."

I turned to Brian, slack-jawed. "She's never heard of it."

"God," he said, "I'm a fucking Neanderthal."

"It's from Peter, Paul, and Mary," I told Shawna. "Tell your father you've heard of them before he self-immolates."

"Oh . . . well, I have," she said.

"Thank God," I said.

"Those old guys on PBS, right? With the fat blond chick?"

Brian groaned.

48

"Oh, you poor, poor Boomers," said Shawna, rolling her eyes. "Life is always so hard for you."

"I'm not a Boomer," I said. "I was born well into the fifties. And Brian's too *old* to be one."

"Bite me," said Brian.

"Listen, guys," said Shawna. "I'd love to stick around and get truly pathetic with you, but I've gotta get back to work."

Brian faced off his daughter like a soulful spaniel. "Dare I ask?"

"It's the same thing, Dad—the Lusty Lady—I've only been there two days."

"Oh, yeah." Brian remained lackluster. "Seemed like more somehow."

I laughed, ushering her out of the room. "C'mon. I'll walk you to the car."

"Ah," said Brian. "Now you're gonna talk about me."

We did talk about him. Or, more accurately, his discomfort over his daughter's budding literary career. Shawna, who's twenty-two and a Stanford graduate, writes a widely read blog called "Grrrl on the Loose" in which she chronicles her escapades in the pansexual wonderland of San Francisco. She'd just signed on for a week of work at the Lusty Lady, a peep show in North Beach that recently became the nation's first worker-owned strip club. This is journalism for Shawna—a big thrill, sure, but mostly fodder for her site. She has no inhibitions about sex. She's breezy and unapologetic about her own desires and her willingness to explore them in others. Previous columns have dealt with latex fetishists, foot worshipers, and people who like to fuck in clown costumes. Shawna isn't always a participant, much to Brian's relief, but her curiosity remains vigorous and laced with scrappy irreverence. Our little grrrl is nothing if not modern.

I say *our* because I've felt like her uncle since 1988, when her mother, a local television anchor, left Brian and Shawna for a career in New York. Brian was a fretful single father but ended up, ironically, establishing his first successful relationship with a female. He lived with Shawna far longer than he has with anyone else, and even though she now rents a studio in the Mission, the two of them are still something of a couple.

There are other ironies, too. First among them being that Brian, the longtime horn dog of the West, has bred a daughter so unashamedly free-spirited that she makes him feel like—and sometimes behave like—my fundamentalist brother in Florida. And it's somehow poetic that Shawna's vocation incorporates both her mother's love of media exposure and her father's love of . . . well, pussy. Not that Shawna's a dyke. She likes dick as well. And lots of other stuff, believe me. They're all just gadgets in her toy box.

As far as I can tell, Brian rarely, if ever, visits his daughter's website. He wants her to succeed and be happy, but he'd rather not know the particulars. Clearly this less-than-blissful ignorance will become more and more difficult to maintain, since Shawna has already signed a book deal, and the talk-show circuit can't be far behind.

"I need to talk to you about something," she said outside the nursery.

"Talk away," I told her.

She glanced at her watch. "Shit. I'm gonna be late. Raven's gonna be pissed. Look, Mouse . . . why don't you come meet me later?"

That nickname always feels like a shout from the past. Shawna learned it as a child from her mother—the one who split for New York—and no one else calls me that now.

"Where?" I asked.

"What's wrong with the club?" she said.

"The Lusty Lady?"

"Sure. We can talk in my booth."

I'm sure I must have winced. "I dunno," I said. "I'd be there under false pretenses."

She chuckled. "Everyone's there under false pretenses. We aren't even allowed to use our real names."

I made a note to remember that. It would come as a comfort to Brian.

51

I found the Lusty Lady on Kearny Street between Columbus and Broadway. I've passed the place for years, big queer that I am, without wasting a moment's thought on what actually happens inside. A brightly backlit plastic sign now spelled it out for me in quaint Victorian block letters—PRIVATE BOOTHS—OPEN 24 HOURS—as if to invoke the halcyon days of the Barbary Coast. Women, after all, have been shaking their moneymakers at the foot of Telegraph Hill since the streets were sloppy with mud and the girls were paid in gold nuggets. The only new twist is unionization. The Lusty Ladies were recently seen picketing the club in pink T-shirts reading BAD GIRLS LIKE GOOD CONTRACTS while they chanted "Two, four, six, eight, pay us more to stimulate!"

Shawna, I knew, was intrigued by this collision of the city's two magnificent obsessions, sex and social justice. She liked the idea of women who embrace their libidos yet refuse to accept exploitation. The dancers had unionized when management installed two-way mirrors through which the girls could be videotaped for porn movies without their knowledge or consent—and certainly without compensation. They wanted the mirrors removed and new carpet installed and a guaranteed pay rate of twenty-seven dollars an hour. The money was crucial, the strikers insisted, since unlike lap dancers and other strippers, the girls who work the main stage are physically unable to receive tips; the Lusty Ladies (some of whom are domestic lesbians in real life) are shrewdly separated from their feverish customers (like Jodie Foster from Hannibal Lecter) by walls of protective Plexiglas.

Shawna had already told me her *nom de porn*, so once inside the club I asked the door person where I might find Mary Margaret. I'd dismissed the preposterously dowdy name as Shawna's way of being subversive in a strip club until I was directed to a Private Pleasures booth and Shawna appeared, moments later, grinning at her anxious gay uncle behind a sheet of streaky Plexiglas. She was done up like one of the schoolgirls over at Saints Peter and Paul, in a pleated skirt, knee socks, and pigtails. And neatly arrayed behind her, like treasured dolls awaiting playtime, was an unnerving selection of dildos.

I tried to mask my discomfort with a joke: "I didn't know you were Catholic, Mary Margaret."

She cocked an eyebrow wickedly. "I'm anything you want, mister."

"Okay, don't do that. You're creeping me out."

She laughed. "Sorry, Mouse."

"Can we go out for coffee or something?"

She shook her head. "This is my shift. I don't want them to think I'm frivolous."

"Oh, right . . . can't have that."

She smiled indulgently. "It's cool just to talk here. A lotta customers do, believe it or not."

I asked her what the other ones do.

"Masturbate," she said brightly, "or watch me play with myself. Or both. It's not a terrible gig, when you get right down to it."

"Right." This was all I could manage. I had just noticed the handrails flanking the window, apparently enabling the ladies to grind against the Plexiglas. There was also a slot through which cash could be crammed when things really got going.

"It's been a revelation, Mouse. You guys are such funny whimpering creatures."

"Can we make that straight guys, please?"

"No, we cannot. You're *all* all about visuals. Every single one of you. Give you something juicy to look at, and you're set for the evening." The sweet, inquisitive kid I'd taught to roller-skate and taken to nearly every Cirque du Soleil bounced onto a large crushed-velvet cushion and crossed her legs with childish zest, as if I were about to tell her a bedtime story. "It's not sticky over there, is it?"

"I don't wanna look," I told her.

I had already entertained a graphic fantasy about attacking that Plexiglas with a family-sized spray bottle of Simple Green.

"I've only got three more days," Shawna said, trying

54

sweetly to reassure me. "Then I'm moving on to Heirloom Tomatoes."

"Thank God," I said. "Simple wholesome produce."

"Actually, it's a group of old broads in West Marin. They're into lingerie. Heirloom Tomatoes . . . get it?"

I told her that was cute, and meant it, comparatively speaking. It was a whole lot cuter than this unionized mastabatorium, that's for sure.

"Once I'm outta here," Shawna went on, "Pacifica takes over this booth. She's seven months pregnant, and that's the bomb with some of the customers. I'm thinking about doing a piece on it."

"You're kidding me?"

"Well, why not?"

"You mean she—?"

"Don't make that face. Lotsa people find pregnant women hot. Lotsa guys, in fact. That's good news in any woman's book."

There's justice, I know, in the fact of an aging gay libertine being made to squirm about sex. Shawna is my karma, I suppose, my just deserts for banking too blindly on the power of my own liberation. There's plenty I don't know about, or care to know about, in my comfortable, vagina-free existence, and Pacifica the Pregnant Lady and her devotees are just the tip of the iceberg. I'm not proud of this; it's just so.

My friend George felt stifled by his own limitations

and made up his mind upon turning forty to eat pussy at the next available opportunity. It was not a success, he said, and the woman who had volunteered for this noble experiment had freshened up with a cinnamon douche, so George was left only with a lasting distaste for breakfast rolls. He worked as a ticket agent for Southwest, so the smell of warm Cinnabons wafting through an airport could undo him completely. Some things are better left alone, he said.

Shawna, as it turned out, had decided to move to Manhattan when her book was published and wanted my take on how Brian would react to the news. She's always been this way, anticipating her father's feelings like a devoted but anxious wife, desperately afraid of hurting him—of betraying him, really, as strong as that word may seem. The considerate children of single parents often seem to carry that additional burden.

"I think he's got plans of his own," I told her.

"You mean the RV?"

"Yeah."

"He's not serious about that."

"Yeah. You're probably right."

"He's Mr. Inertia," she said. "And he's happy that way as long as nothing else changes."

I remembered Shawna's mother saying something similar when she left Brian and her little girl to launch her career in New York. She had found Brian's mellow passivity intolerable, a serious obstacle to her own ambition. Shawna loves her father as is—down to the last tie-dyed T-shirt and Neil Young album—but she's leaving town just the same; she must worry a little about reconstituting that earlier trauma.

"He'll be all right," I told her. "He always is."

"I guess so," she said, fiddling with a tassel on the pillow. "Will you and Ben come visit me once I'm settled?" She seemed almost waifish at that moment.

"Of course, sweetie. Ben's crazy about New York."

"I know *you* aren't," she said, "but I'll make things fun for you."

"You always have."

I felt tearful all of a sudden, sitting there in that fuckless brothel while the apple of my eye laid out her dreams for my approval. She looked a little wistful herself.

"Don't let him grow a ponytail," she said. "He always does that when he gets depressed."

I laughed. "Don't worry."

"I hate ponytails on old dudes."

"I hear you."

"A guy was in here yesterday who had the greasiest ponytail and every time he—"

"Can we talk about something else?" I said.

"All right, Auntie," she said with an impertinent grin.

5

The Family
Circle

It occurred to me recently that this is probably the last
house I'll ever own. (It was the first as well, come to
think of it.) The endless possibilities of my youth have
been whittled down to this little plot on a hillside, this
view of the valley, this perfect lamp, this favorite chair,
this flock of wild parrots breakfasting in the hawthorn
tree. I'm still enough of a Southerner to love the notion
of my own land, my own teacup Tara.

It's not unimaginable that Ben and I could one day
pick up and move to a condo in Palm Springs or
Hawaii, but I wouldn't bank on it. This is my home on
the deepest level; it comforts me in ways I've forgotten
how to measure. And were we to leave for momentarily
greener pastures, I know we'd harbor the fear of all San
Franciscans who leave—that the real estate market, that
cruelest of sentinels, would never let us back in.

So I concentrate on what I have and where I am. I take pleasure, for instance, in the way the house is aging—the shingles in particular, which have moved so gracefully past tan and tarnished silver to a rich dark brown. Some of this is just dirt, of course, left there by the vagrant fog, but the effect is enchanting. The shingles have grown as rough and mossy as bark, so the house seems more organic, like something rooted in the earth that will have to return there, sooner or later. To my overly romanticizing eyes, shingles are most beautiful when they're closest to collapse.

On my better days, I try to see my own weathering this way. I rarely succeed. I'm not ready to discolor and rot, no matter how charming the process might seem to others. I'll have to get over this, I know, since I'd rather not leave the planet in a state of panic and self-loathing. I'd rather there be peace and a sense of completion. And I'd like Ben there, of course, cuddling me into the void with the usual sweet assurances. I know that's not original as fantasies go—and impossible to ordain—but a boy can dream.

In the meantime, I tinker with our home in a way that Ben finds comical, if not a little pathetic. I arrange objects like talismans in a tomb, carefully balancing according to color, texture, and motif. I could show you, for instance, how the rivets on the bowl on the coffee table are repeated in the frame of the dining room mirror and the base of an Arts and Crafts candle-stick. I know where every spot of Chinese red can be found in the living room. I never add anything to the decor without considering the metal-to-wood ratio and the need for the sheen and color of ceramics. "Have nothing in your houses," William Morris decreed, "that you do not know to be useful, or believe to be beauti-ful," and I can show you a wastebasket that fills that bill to a tee. I bought it off eBay for $385. This house will be perfect by the time I'm committed.

A case in point: one night Ben and I were watching *Six Feet Under* when I sprang from the sofa and began rearranging the art pottery on the shelf above the TV tansu. Ben indulged me sweetly as I swapped the purple Fulper ginger jar for the light-green one and offset them both with the large bronze Heintz vase.

"That's been bothering you, has it?"

"I couldn't put my finger on it," I told him, "but it's better, don't you think?"

"Oh, absolutely."

"Don't look at me like I'm Rain Man," I said.

"Come back," he said. "Keith is about to get naked."

As we settled in again for the show, Ben's head warm-ing my chest, my gaze began to creep away from the television screen and back to that shelf of now perfectly composed pottery. And Ben somehow sensed this with-out looking up.

"Stop that," he said, slapping my belly. "Watch the damn show."

If I'm a stickler for perfect interiors, Ben is our tech support, our resident troubleshooter. He's practically a dyke in this regard, so I'm lucky to have him, since I've never troubleshot anything beyond a snail-infested garden. Anna, my octogenarian friend, is much the same way and has learned to tap Ben for his expertise in thorny matters of the new millennium. She's always been good about asking for help.

"They're turning off my email," she told him bleakly one night. The three of us were eating Thai delivery food in her garden apartment off Duboce Park.

"Who's turning it off?" asked Ben.

"The people at Wahoo," she said.

Ben smiled faintly but didn't correct her. "Have you paid your bill?"

"Certainly," she replied, "but they found a virus on an email someone sent me. It was called 'Your Doom.' Can you imagine? Like a Gypsy curse out of nowhere."

"Sounds fishy," Ben said. "They don't cut off your email because of something that's been sent to you. Did you click on any attachments?"

"Well, no. The mention of my doom scared the hell out of me. Was I wrong? Should I have clicked?"

"No, just delete it. It's probably carrying a virus

itself. They're trying to scare you so you'll do what they want."

"How wicked," she said. "Like the president."

"Yes," said Ben. "Except no one's dead yet."

Anna smiled at him appraisingly, then turned and looked at me, widening her eyes. "This boy's a treasure, dear."

I told her I knew that already.

"Well, aren't you glad I made you go after him?"

"Oh," I said, teasing her. "You want credit now?"

"It certainly wouldn't hurt." She dunked her chicken skewer into the peanut sauce.

"Well, *I'm* grateful," said Ben.

"Thank you, child. You get some more Pad Thai."

"It's delicious," I said, grateful for a chance to change the subject. I've always been uneasy about proclaiming my bliss too confidently, for fear of it deserting me—as fucked-up as that sounds. "Where did it come from?"

"A new little place down the street. Shawna told me about it."

"God," I said. "What *doesn't* that girl know about?"

"She's just *interested*," Anna said. "That goes a long way in this world."

She meant it only as a compliment to Shawna, but somehow I felt reprimanded for my failure to be more adventurous.

"Michael went down to the Lusty Lady," Ben offered.

Anna blinked at him in confusion.

"You know," said Ben. "The strip joint Shawna's writing about."

"Oh, yes!" Anna crowed. "I can't wait for that one. She's always so sharp and funny. And she gets so *involved*, doesn't she?"

"I'll say," I muttered.

Anna dabbed the corners of her mouth with a napkin. "You sound like you don't approve, dear."

"It's not a question of approval," I told her. "I'm just concerned."

"Oh dear, that was Brian's line, too. You boys are being silly. She's an extremely sensible girl. What she's doing now is just . . . raw material . . . not a way of life."

"Gimme a break," I said. "She's diddling herself in a plywood cubicle."

"Oh," said Anna, remaining deadpan. "And you never did that, I suppose?"

Ben chuckled. "She's on to you, baby."

"That wasn't for money," I shot back. "And I wasn't dressed as a Catholic schoolgirl."

Both of them were laughing now, and not entirely *with* me. "Oh, well," said Anna, winking at Ben. "Thank God he has standards."

It's awful when young and old alike can team up to mock you.

After dinner Jake Greenleaf joined us in the garden. Jake, you may recall, is my sometime assistant. He's a short, stocky bear of thirty or thereabouts with a trim little beard and soulful gray eyes. I brought him into the family four or five years ago, when I was still single, having picked him up at the Lone Star Saloon one night. Though he lives upstairs from Anna in another apartment, he comes and goes freely as a helpmate.

Appearing on the terrace that night, Jake looked like someone from another era—my own, in fact—in loose khakis with wide suspenders and a flannel shirt. The effect of this mining-camp getup is just as deliberate as Jake's rusticated name. Both were chosen to suggest the strong, earthy, no-nonsense person he intended to become.

"You guys wanna vaporize?" he said, holding up a wooden box from which a plastic hose dangled like an umbilical cord. Vaporizers, for the uninitiated, are designed to heat cannabis just enough to release its psychoactive ingredients but not enough to create harmful respiratory toxins—i.e., smoke. They're all the rage now among the health conscious and the elderly. The ordinary kind is sold for a hundred bucks or so at shops in the Haight, but this wacky contraption was Jake's own creation. He was proud as he could be of it. He had built it out of barn timber from Sonoma and adorned it with eucalyptus pods.

"Your timing is perfect," said Anna. "Come sit down, dear."

So Jake joined the family circle and plugged the vaporizer into an outlet in the terrace. Soon we were passing the tube around, sucking up the smokeless, pot-flavored air like Alice's caterpillar. Ben, as usual, abstained. By his own account, he did too much speed and ecstasy in his youth (way back in the mid-nineties), so he limits himself to wine and the occasional mojito. He would never be so sanctimonious as to say that he's high on life, but he is, the little bastard; he's his own source of intoxication.

"What is that smell?" he asked, when the rest of us were pleasantly buzzed.

"Can you smell it?" asked Jake. "Your nose must be really sensitive."

"No. That floral smell. It's so intense."

"That's the datura," said Anna. She lifted her wobbly blue-veined hand and pointed to the tree at the end of the garden. "It releases its scent at night."

Ben turned and looked at this preposterous plant with its dozens of pendulous trumpet-shaped blossoms. "It has psychotropic qualities," I explained. "Shamans have used it for centuries to see spirits and induce trances."

"It's also a poison," Jake added. "It can drive you insane."

Anna was already lost in recollection. "We had a lovely one at Barbary Lane. A golden one. In the corner next to the garbage cans. Mona was always threatening to make tea out of it." She turned and looked at me sweetly. "Do you remember it, Michael?"

I wasn't sure I did, but said so, anyway.

"The more I trimmed it back," she said, "the more blossoms it grew. All year long. I thought it would never stop entertaining us."

There was a distinctly bittersweet ring to these words, so Ben, bless his heart, leaped gallantly into the silence that followed. "Michael's told me about Barbary Lane. It must've been wonderful. Your own little secret world up there."

"It was nice," said Anna, keeping it short and sweet. She seemed on the verge of tears. "You should see for yourself, dear. It's an actual city street. They can't keep you out. Just walk up the stairs and act like you belong there."

Later that night, when we were done with the vaporizing, I told Anna and Jake that Ben and I would be visiting my family in Florida the following week.

"Well . . . that'll be nice," said Anna. "For how long?"

There was a trace of anxiety in this question, so I tried to minimize it. "Just three or four days. No more than that. My mother's not doing very well."

"I'm sorry to hear that," said Anna. "Would you give her my best?"

Anna met my mother no more than twice, and well over twenty years ago, but she never stopped sending her best to Florida. My mother had little use for it. She rarely ever remembered who Anna *was*, unless I broke down and referred to her as "my colorful landlady." That always nailed it for Mama, and I'm pretty sure Anna's "color" was what made her suspect in Mama's eyes. I don't think she had a clue about Anna's sex change, but the instinct that "something ain't right" was deeply embedded in her DNA. "When it comes to folks," Mama always said, "you can't be too careful."

"When were you last home?" asked Jake.

"You mean in Florida?" I said. "Two years, I guess."

"Have they met Ben yet?"

"No, but they've torn up his picture."

Ben flashed his sexy jack-o'-lantern smile. "You don't know that."

"Well, they aren't showing it around, that's for sure. Unless they're praying over it at an Ex-gay meeting."

"Don't be naughty," said Anna. "You're frightening Ben." She turned to the object of her concern. "I'm sure they're lovely people, dear. I've met his mother and she's the salt of the earth."

"Salt of the wound is more like it."

"*Michael!*" This was Anna and Ben, scolding me in

unison. Jake, I noticed, was leaning back in his chair, legs crossed, arms folded, chuckling manfully under his breath. He knew what I was talking about. He has a mother like mine in Oklahoma.

The evening didn't last much longer. Anna was getting tired, and Jake had to get up early to help me thin a clump of bamboo at a house in Parnassus Heights. Ben and I kissed Anna goodbye, and Jake, as usual, escorted us down the passageway to the street. It was a tight squeeze between the houses, but it was strung with colored lights year-round—a nod to the full-scale fantasia Anna once orchestrated at 28 Barbary Lane. This little studio in the flats with its lone datura and its two potted azaleas was a touching distillation of everything Anna had left behind. It seemed to make her happy, though; it seemed to be all she needed.

"She looks good," I told Jake, once we were out of earshot. "She's over that flu, I guess?"

"Pretty much," he replied. "Notice her new nail polish?"

"Nice," I said. "Very Sally Bowles. I should've said something to her. Are you responsible for that?"

"Yeah, right," Jake snorted, reminding me that he was strictly the heavy-hauling dude in the building; the seriously girly shit was left to his flatmates.

"Who's Sally Bowles?" asked Ben.

I turned and looked at my younger, less theatrical half. "She used to be married to Ansel Adams."

"You're kidding?"

"Yes, I am," I said.

Jake clapped Ben on the shoulder, brother to brother. "Don't let him fuck with you. I don't know who the hell she is, either."

"What is happening to queers?" I said.

Jake chortled and opened the gate for us. "I'll see you in the morning, boss. You guys take care." He turned to Ben. "You're the one doing the driving, aren't you?"

"Oh, yeah," said Ben.

"Good."

They exchanged a knowing look that, more than anything, made me feel loved.

6

A Guy Without Trying

The night I met Jake at the Lone Star the place was almost empty. He was sitting alone at the bar, this sturdy little Shetland-pony-of-a-guy with a Corona in his fist. Every time he took a swig from the bottle, he'd set it down and regard it intently, as if about to say something terribly important to the lime wedge at the bottom. It was quite a brave show of independence, so I was fairly certain he was looking for company.

I pulled out the stool next him. "You mind?" I would not have asked that in a crowded bar, but it seemed polite under the circumstances.

"Nah, buddy, it's cool."

So I sat down and ordered a beer. Jake's little swig-and-stare ritual seemed to intensify, but he didn't gaze in my direction.

"Kinda slow tonight, isn't it?" I said.

"Yeah, I guess. I'm new to here."

"The bar or the town?"

"The bar," he replied. "And the town, too, more or less. I moved here from Tulsa a year ago."

I asked him if San Francisco agreed with him.

"It's okay." He shrugged.

"But?"

"I dunno. The guys are either totally married or ordering each other like pizzas off the Internet. Or both. I'd like more of the stuff in between."

"Like?"

"You know, just hangin' and talkin' and . . . takin' it from there. I'm into buddy sex, I guess. It doesn't have to be romantic or anything, just . . . you know."

"Intimate," I said, providing the dreaded word.

Those gray eyes were fixed on me now, almost lupine in the darkness. "Yeah."

"Nothing wrong with that," I said. "But you can say all that online, you know. That's the great thing about the Web. You can ask for exactly what you need."

"I know that," he said, "but I'd rather not ask the whole world if I can help it."

I turned and smiled at him. "I know what you mean."

At the time, I thought I did.

* * *

Ten minutes later Jake suggested we head out for something to eat. I was ready to take him home by then, having already imagined the feral heat of that furry little body, but I thought it better to let him set the pace. He seemed like a certainty, and buddy sex was sounding pretty good to me, so why the hell *not* take our time about it?

I went to pee before we left, and while I was standing at the trough, a guy in tribal tats and a grimy canvas Utilikilt was peeing like a fire hose at the other end. I'd noticed him earlier, watching me from across the room, so I wasn't surprised when he spoke.

"Listen," he said, gazing straight ahead. "It's none of my business, but . . ." He shook his dick a few times, then returned it to its Bat Cave under the Utilikilt. "If you're looking to get fucked tonight, you're looking in the wrong place."

"Excuse me?" I stiffened on the spot—and not in a friendly way, either. *The nerve of this asshole*, I thought. I had barely even glanced at him.

"That guy you're talking to," he said, "is a transman."

I must have taken a little too long to answer.

"He used to be a girl," he explained.

"I know what it means," I said quietly.

"No offense, dude. Just thought you should know if you didn't. I met him once at the Sundance Saloon. There's nothing down there."

He clapped his hand on my shoulder as he left.

"Just doin' you a favor," he said.

Leaving the toilet, I had a creepy sense of déjà vu. I remembered another guy, another total stranger, who once "did me a favor" by tipping me off that a potential playmate was HIV positive. I should have told him I was positive myself and had no use for his health warning. I should have said I found him ridiculously old-fashioned, since anyone in his right mind these days—especially around here—presumes *everyone* to be positive, and takes responsibility for his own fucking health, because there is no free ride anymore, you sorry-ass gossipy old leather nancy. I should have said all of that, but I didn't. I just stood there gaping while he dropped his little stink bomb and sashayed off like a spiteful teenage girl. All he'd wanted, anyway, was to see the look on my face.

Not unlike the queen in the kilt.

Jake hopped off the stool as soon as he saw me returning from the rest room. He was about five-six or thereabouts, somewhere in the Tom Cruise range.

"What'll it be, buddy? Burritos or burgers?"

"Either's fine," I said.

As we left the Lone Star together, the kilt queen turned and watched us in undisguised horror.

I gave him a thumbs-up, just for the hell of it.

I won't pretend I wasn't walloped by the news. Jake's masculinity was the very thing that had drawn me to him in the first place. It wasn't some phony butch overlay; it came from deep inside, and it was totally devoid of irony. He didn't even seem queer to me; he was more like some easygoing straight guy, a guy without trying.

Except.

I stole quick glimpses of him as we sauntered toward the taqueria. Under the streetlight his jaw looked just as strong and square as it had in the dark. I tried like hell to see a woman there, but couldn't. His gait was a little studied, I guess, like a boy rehearsing his swagger on the first day of camp, and I towered over him considerably, but all of that just added to the charm.

I wondered if his chest was bound or if he'd had surgery. I wondered if his nipples were funny-looking. I wondered if he'd had a penis made out of whatever the fuck they make penises out of. I wondered how often he picked up gay men and if he'd always preferred them to women and if he was scared shitless right now, wondering if I'd already guessed, wondering what I'd do when the other shoe dropped.

At the taqueria we talked about gardening and the war in Iraq and the nifty new copper-clad museum rising in the park. He tried to talk about the Forty-niners, poor thing, but gave up the effort when it became clear that sports banter was not in my manly repertoire. When our talk turned to where we lived, I knew where we were heading.

"I'm in the Duboce Triangle," he said, "but I have roommates."

"Ah," I said, realizing exactly what that "but" meant.

"How 'bout you?" he asked.

"I'm up on Noe Hill."

"No partner or anything?"

"Nope." I smiled at him. "Not for a few years now. I'm just out for fun these days."

He nodded solemnly for a moment. "I'm really into giving head," he said.

"Is that so?" I gave him a crooked smile.

"I'm pretty good at it, too. You could just kick back."

There was no easy response to this, nothing glib that could rescue me. I liked Jake well enough, and he was still a hot little bear cub in my mind's eye, but what would happen once we got down to business? Would the illusion still hold? Would I embarrass myself completely, or, worse, hurt his feelings? I bought time by asking a question I'd rarely asked before in my fifty-five years of existence: "Aren't I a little old for you?"

Jake just shrugged. "Age is no biggie, if I like the guy."

"And there's something else," I said, reminding myself of Jack Lemmon in the last scene of *Some Like It Hot*, when he's up against the wall and desperately searching for all the reasons he can't marry Joe E. Brown. "I'm HIV positive."

That just made him shrug again. "Then I won't floss," he said.

When I laughed at that, Jake laughed, too, almost in relief, realizing that he'd won that round out of sheer audacity. It was a moment of brotherly bonding, so the pressure was off for a full five seconds before he turned serious again.

"There's something I have to tell *you*," he said.

I'd been ready for this, so I looked him squarely in the eye. "No, you don't," I said. "You really don't."

He gazed at me solemnly for a moment. "You're cool with it, then?"

"I'm new to it," I said. "Let's put it that way."

"We could talk about it, if you want."

I shook my head. "I'll spare you the after-school special. I'm sure that gets old."

"Oh, man," said Jake.

"The thing is," I offered, "I'm sort of an old dog. And you're sort of a new trick."

Jake smiled at my inadvertent pun. "Do you mind if I ask how you knew?"

I decided to banish the kilt queen once and for all. "It doesn't matter," I told him. "It had nothing to do with how you look, if that's what you mean."

"For real?"

I nodded. "You're a handsome guy from where I sit."

Jake was blushing furiously now, a tide of scarlet surging beneath his five-o'clock shadow. He plunged a fork into his burrito. "Can we go to your place, then?"

I nodded. "As long as you understand—"

"You won't have to do anything to *me*, all right?"

"That wasn't what I—"

"And don't worry," he added. "I'll keep my jeans on. I don't like that thing any more than you do."

Jake followed me back to Noe Hill in his car. Once inside the house—and the proper lighting was established—I retrieved my hammered-copper pot tray from the drawer by the sofa. As I rolled a joint, Jake just stood there, bouncing on his heels and socking his fist into his palm like an anxious delinquent. He reminded me of myself, over thirty years earlier, all bluster and bluff, when I first went home with a stranger.

"Sit down," I said, patting the sofa.

Jake sat next to me, but not especially close.

I lit the joint and held it out. He took it and toked expertly.

"Did you get stoned in Tulsa?" I asked.

"Are you kidding? I worked at Wal-Mart."

"Does that mean yes or no?"

"It means what the fuck *else* is there to do."

He passed the joint back to me, and I dragged on it

fiercely, hoping it would give me the nerve to face the uncharted territory ahead. I took courage from the memory of a hot night in Chicago when I smoked a doobie on Navy Pier, then went back to the Drake and whacked off to straight porn on Spectravision and got off on it fine, especially with poppers, because sex, I was learning, is a place where all of us go, regardless of gender or sexuality. No matter where we begin, it's just one big steamy locker room in the end.

Which is the scary part, of course.

"You wanna take off your boots?" I asked.

"That's okay, buddy, I'm cool." Jake was sitting forward, elbows on his knees, rocking a little as he gazed at me sideways. "You wanna kick back?" he asked.

I took a last drag on the joint, then stubbed it out in my little Roycroft ashtray. I scooched back into the nubby cotton bolster as Jake knelt between my legs and got to work with quiet efficiency, still wearing his jeans and a loose gray T-shirt. He popped the top button of my 501s, mercifully liberating my belly, but didn't pull my jeans off right away, just fingered me studiously through the denim as if fitting my dick for a custom suit. When I started to get hard, he looked up. "Are you okay?" he asked.

"What does it look like?" I said.

He grinned and popped the other five buttons.

I said the first thing that came to mind: "You remind

78

me a lot of a scoutmaster I used to have."

"Oh, yeah? Did you guys do stuff like this?"

"Oh, hell, no," I said. "He was straight as they come. He took us to the Everglades once, and I saw him in his boxer shorts. I never got over it."

I felt the brush of Jake's beard against my thigh as his tongue swabbed its way along my dick. *This is not his first time*, I thought. When he was finally free to speak, he gazed up at me intently.

"You got any?" he asked.

I wasn't sure what he meant.

"Boxer shorts," he explained.

I smiled. "Yeah."

"Want me to wear 'em?"

"Sure."

He hopped to his feet. "Where?"

"Straight back and to the left," I said. "Second drawer from the top."

He was gone less than a minute. When he returned he stood in the doorway for a moment, legs apart, to give me the full scoutmaster effect.

"Very nice," I said.

It wasn't a faithful reproduction of Mr. Ragsdale, but it was close enough.

The sex was pretty much as advertised. Mostly he went down on me, and that was nice, I have to say. He was a

79

good kisser, too, though he seemed less interested in that. I felt kind of selfish, to tell you the truth, just lying back like a sultan, so I moved my leg up into those boxer shorts, thinking that a little pressure there might be appreciated. My leg was promptly redirected, so I returned to my passive state and took the rest of my cues from Jake. He wanted to see me come, he said, so I jerked off while he worked my nips with the efficiency of a seasoned safecracker. I left my load, as directed, on the front of his Nature Conservancy T-shirt. "All riiiight," he growled. "Good one, buddy."

We lay there side by side, limbs overlapping, until my breathing had subsided and I felt called upon to break the silence.

"Do people always ask you—?"

"—what my name used to be?"

I laughed. "Guess they do."

"I never tell them," he said.

"Why? Was it Myrtle or something?"

It was a calculated risk, but he did crack a smile. "It's nothing to do with the name."

"You just don't know that person anymore."

"Right," he said. "Close enough."

"I hear you," I said.

"You ever need a hand, by the way?"

I wasn't sure what he meant by this.

80

"You said you were a gardener, right?"

"Yeah. Sure."

"Well, if you need help ... I'm really into horticulture."

"Great."

"I grew up on a farm. I don't mind a little work."

"I'll remember that," I told him. My usual practice was to hire one or more of the Mexican guys hustling for day labor down on Cesar Chavez, but it was like buying a pig in a poke, as my mother used to say. Lots of the guys are incredibly hardworking and sweet, but others can be falling-down drunk or homophobic or both. I don't speak a bit of Spanish, but the word *maricón* has a way of leaping out at you, believe me. I've heard it so often on the job, you'd think it was a species of plant. Who the hell needs that?

Jake reached into his jeans and handed me a crumpled card with his cell-phone number. The card was khaki-colored and JAKE GREENLEAF was written in dark-green letters intertwined with ivy. Below, in smaller letters, it said: New Man.

I thought that was cool and told him so.

By mutual choice, Jake and I never played again, but several weeks later I asked him to help me with a job near Buena Vista Park. He was all I'd hoped he'd be: dependable, cheerful, and not too chatty on the job.

Best of all, he seemed to enjoy tackling the tougher stuff—digging out roots, say, or hauling flagstones, or working in the rain. Heavy labor was apparently a kind of fulfillment to Jake, a necessary stop on his path to completion—if not completion itself. I could hand him the nastiest job in the world and feel almost noble about it. Ours was a match made in gardening heaven.

One day at lunch, when we were both eating yogurt in a client's backyard, I noticed how the hair on my arms had grown and realized in a moment of shivery solidarity that Jake and I were probably *both* shooting testosterone. We'd never really talked about his pharmaceutical requirements, but this seemed like a logical opening, so I showed him my lushly foliated forearms and told him what had caused them.

"Yeah," he said, smiling. "It'll do that."

"It's amazing stuff," I said. "It really boosted my spirits . . . *and* my energy."

He nodded. "Same here."

"I worry sometimes about prostate cancer, but . . ." I didn't pursue this thought since it wasn't an issue for him, I presumed, and I was wary of destroying our cozy commonality. "Everything's got its risks, I guess."

Another nod. "That's why I'm against surgery."

I thought he meant surgery in general, which puzzled me.

82

"You know," he said. "The operation. The addadictomy."

"Oh," I said. "Is that what it's called?"

He grinned. "That's what *I* call it, anyway."

It took me a few more seconds to get it. "Oh, fuck," I said, laughing. "Addadictomy."

Jake looked pleased with himself. "A little tranny humor," he said.

I'd never heard him use that term to describe himself, so I was emboldened to press further. "Have you always felt like a gay man?"

He thought for a moment, then shrugged. "I've always felt male. And I've always wanted to be with men."

"Isn't that the same thing?" I asked.

Jake lobbed his yogurt can into a trash barrel like a kid shooting hoops. "I don't feel very gay most of the time."

It wasn't hard to grasp the alienation of a guy who wants to chase dick without having one himself. Jake had spent most of his life feeling betrayed by his anatomy, but even now that he'd relocated to Queersville he was still too queer for the queers. *He just needs a nice girl*, I thought, reminding myself of my mother when she learned I was gay. But it was true. Men are hung up on visuals, as Shawna had recently observed, but women give weight to the heart and the mind when measuring attraction. If Jake identified as a butch lesbian—or even as a straight man—some woman would find reason to love him.

"There's someone I want you to meet," I told him.

Three weeks later, when Anna was recuperating from her stroke, that meeting finally occurred. I took Jake by St. Sebastian's Hospital one day after work and introduced him to my former landlady. She was thrilled to have company beyond her regulars, and I could tell that she saw in Jake a potential protégé. Jake, in turn, found a sort of spiritual grandmother, someone who understood him without effort or condescension. He would visit on his own after that, bringing her chocolate and magazines, then just sitting by her bed while she read. "He doesn't have much to say," Anna once told me, "but there's a lovely little light in there."

At that point Anna was just another tenant at 28 Barbary Lane, having sold the building in the early nineties to a Hong Kong investor. When her stroke made it clear that she could no longer manage that precipitous climb, it was Jake who proposed a solution. There was a vacancy in his building, he told her, a sunny garden apartment surrounded by level terrain. His own place was upstairs, so he could lend her a hand whenever she needed it. Anna accepted this invitation but only if Jake would agree to be paid for his services.

She had a decent nest egg from the sale of the building, and she needed assistance from someone, so why shouldn't it be Jake? She knew he needed the money, and he already felt like family.

She got a good deal more family than she bargained for. Jake's flatmates, an investment counselor and a teacher at the Harvey Milk School, were also trans-gendered folk—MTFs like Anna—and they regarded their new downstairs tenant with something akin to reverence. Anna, after all, had affirmed her woman-hood well before either one of them was born, so it was almost like having an ancestor around—or so they once told me.

I was invited to a cocktail party in the upstairs flat shortly after Anna took up residence. There were several dozen trannies in the room, hovering around her like acolytes. I couldn't help remembering that Anna had struck me as the rarest of birds all those years ago, yet here she was now, just one among the many. She had never aspired to being ordinary, of course, but it must have been awfully nice to have a little company.

7

Footnotes to a Feeling

Every six weeks or so Ben takes off for an afternoon of hunting and gathering at one of the local bathhouses. He invariably tells me this a day or so before, since he wants me to know he's not sneaking around, and I do my best to receive the news as casually as he delivers it, since I want him to know that I'm cool with it. Such is the nature of our open relationship (modified plan), and so far it's working. It's a tricky little dance sometimes, but it's preferable to the perils of endless monogamy or constant whoring.

I've seen too many male couples who have either neutered each other with enforced exclusivity or opened the relationship so wide that they turn into quarreling roommates and make their own sex life superfluous. In either case, romance dies on the spot. We don't want that to happen. We've chosen to walk the middle road of full disclosure (minus details) and primary consideration for the feelings of the other. For the moment, that means no frolicking with mutual acquaintances and no sleeping over anywhere and no bringing guys back to the house at any time of the day. Our bodies may be shared from time to time, but our bed is just for us, the temple of our California King–sized love.

The first time Ben went to the tubs in Berkeley I drove down to the one in San Jose to show my solidarity with our plan, but this lame little tit-for-tat proved unsatisfying. I wasn't even horny at the time, and my morbid preoccupation with Ben and some nameless beast across the bay turned my lone encounter into a lackluster foursome. I was done in half an hour and ended up next to the snack machines, boring some poor guy half to death with tales of my happy May–September marriage.

Since then, I'm more likely to be found cavorting with guys via my DVD on the occasional afternoons when Ben's out playing. That's fine with me. When it comes to sex, I'm happy to receive the occasional windfall, but I just don't have the spirit for the hunt anymore. It's enough to know that Ben will call as soon as he's done, proposing plans for the evening and downplaying his fun. "Boy," he'll say, "they must've been having a special on little dicks," and I'll laugh at that and love him for it, whether it's true or not, because, at the end of the day, I'll have another eight hours of holding him in my arms.

At my suggestion Ben had a bathhouse afternoon just before we left for Orlando. I was paying penance-in-advance, I guess, for inflicting my family on him. (My *biological* family, that is—as opposed to my logical one—as Anna likes to put it.) So Ben took off for the Steamworks at noon, and I stayed at home to wash the truck and curl up in the window seat with a glass of chocolate soymilk and the latest issue of *American Bungalow* magazine. There was an article on Bisbee, Arizona, and its funky little bungalow neighborhoods, and I wondered if that would make a good destination for us; we'd loved our recent road trip through the Southwest and had talked of returning.

I laid down the magazine and glanced at the clock. It was almost one.

He's bound to be there by now, already undressed and wrapped in a towel, already cruising the hallways. He's searching for daddies, of course, preferably with fur, politely deflecting the young and the smooth, the ones who inevitably regard him as their natural birthright. But it won't be long before he finds what he wants . . .

I picked up the magazine again, losing myself in the Southwest. In Monument Valley we hired a Navajo guide named Harley, a chummy twenty-seven-year-old in a Metallica sweatshirt who, for a few dollars more, drove us into sacred territory, a roadless landscape of blood-red monoliths reserved for tribal ceremonies and the occasional Toyota commercial. I don't know if Harley knew we were a couple—he may well have mistaken us for father and son—but he gave a sweet little spiel about the Navajo nation's reverence for androgyny and later played his flute for us and sang while we lay on our backs in a cave, goofy with peace, staring up through a hole at a perfect circle of sky.

By now he's spotted someone—across the steam room, maybe, or loitering in a corner of the labyrinth. He's a bearded history prof at Berkeley, Jewish possibly, or a black Amway salesman from Oakland with silver at his temples, or some beefy working-class Irish brute. Whoever he is, he's reaching for my husband right now, cupping those clean-shaven balls in his hairy hand as he smiles with avuncular assurance.

The gutters, I realized, were in serious need of cleaning, so I dragged the extension ladder from the truck and propped it against the house. I have just the slightest touch of acrophobia, so the climb left me woozy. I steadied myself at the top, catching my breath for a moment as I gazed across the valley at the television tower on Mount Sutro. It's a gangly *War of the Worlds* monstrosity, but sometimes—like that particular afternoon—the fog erases everything but the top three antennae, creating the ghostly effect of a galleon sailing above the clouds, the Castro's own *Flying Dutchman*.

They've gone to the guy's room, no doubt. Or maybe to Ben's, if he rented one this time. The terrycloth has hit the deck by now, and somebody's blowing somebody. Or maybe they're even fucking already. Right. This. Very. Moment.

I began scooping handfuls of leaves out of the gutter. It's a handsome gutter, as gutters go: copper beginning to show traces of green. I installed it ten years ago, right after Thack moved out, partly to reassert my dominion over the house. The downspouts were badly clogged with leaves last winter, inundating the terrace at one point and threatening to do the same to the house. This year I'd be ready for the rain.

When the gutters were clean, I climbed down from the ladder and returned it to the truck before raking the rotten leaves from the terrace. There was still space left in the green recycling bin, so I crammed in a few dead fronds from the tree fern at the end of the driveway. The rest of the garden looked okay, but I figured there were chores aplenty in the kitchen. Sure enough, the grime under the sink had reached crisis proportions, so I pulled out all the rusting cleanser containers and Simple Greened the hell out of the place.

Are they done yet? Or have they started all over again? Are they lying somewhere together now, catching their breath, explaining themselves to each other?

By four o'clock I was on the sofa watching a Netflix movie. Normally I save them for the two of us, but this one was a thriller, and Ben's never been crazy about the creepy stuff. Besides, I required serious distraction, and I'd run out of stuff to clean.

In the midst of the movie the phone rang. I hit mute and picked up the receiver. "Hello."

"Hi, babe. It's me. I'm on the bridge."

"Hey, sweetie."

"What are you up to?" he asked.

"Just a movie," I said. "Sharon Stone in a big house with snakes dropping from the chandeliers."

"Glad I missed that one."

"How were the tubs?"

"Okay," he said with a comforting lack of enthusiasm.

"Just okay?"

"It was pretty slow for a Sunday."

"Ah. That's too bad."

"There was this guy from San Leandro who was kinda hot, but he had awful dragon breath."

"Ugh," I said, but of course I meant Thank You, Jesus.

"He knows you, in fact," Ben added. "Or of you, anyway. You worked on his ex's backyard in Pacific Heights."

"It's not ringing a bell," I said.

"It was back in the eighties, I think. He remembered your name, that's all. It doesn't matter."

He was right. All that mattered was that Ben had brought up my name to this foul-smelling stud, making it patently clear that he already belonged to someone else.

"Do we need anything?" he asked.

I did a quick mental inventory. "We're out of laundry detergent, if you feel like stopping at the corner."

"Okay. What about for dinner?"

"I thought we'd do some chicken on the grill. I got this great new finishing sauce with apple and chipotle. Fuck!"

"What?"

"We're out of propane."

"No we're not. There's a spare tank in the shed."

"Oh, you're right," I said. "What would I do without you?"

He chuckled. "Watch Sharon Stone movies, I guess."

We lay on the sofa after supper, intertwined and swapping endearments. I won't bother to repeat them here. Whoever named them sweet nothings was right. They really are nothing; they're little more than foot-notes to a feeling, almost useless out of context.

"You know what?" said Ben, idly caressing my chest.

"What?"

"I'd sort of given up believing this could happen. I thought I was being unrealistic."

"C'mon," I said. "You're thirty-three."

"So?"

"So that's too early to have given up." I realized this was bullshit the moment it came out of my mouth. I spent most of my twenties feeling unrealistic about love.

"You don't know," said Ben. "It's not that easy to find an older guy who isn't already fucked up."

"Why, thank you, Colonel Butler!"

He laughed. "I mean it."

"I know," I said, kissing the top of his head.

"Your generation has a lot of baggage."

I said that's why I preferred not to date them.

"They think of themselves as liberated, but there are so many wounded old tarts out there. Sex inside a relationship scares the holy shit out of them."

"Well, I'm grateful for them," I said. "They were saving you for me."

He snuggled closer and pecked me on the ear. We were silent for a while.

"I saw Anna at the Bi-Rite," he said at last. "She was there all by herself, just humming away over the produce bins."

I told him that Anna liked to walk to the market sometimes, that she usually referred to it as her "constitutional."

"I hope I'm still that vigorous when I'm her age," Ben said.

"I hope you are, too," I replied. "I'll be a hundred and five, so I won't much feel like getting the groceries."

He laughed. "Did she ever have . . . you know . . . anybody?"

"Anna, you mean?"

"Yeah."

I thought about that for a moment. "One or two, I guess. A long time ago. She had an affair with a married businessman back in the seventies. His wife was a major drunk and he was dying of something, and . . . Anna gave him a real life for a while. He was dead in a year, but she still keeps his picture around. And there was this guy in Greece in the late eighties. On Lesbos." I chuckled at the thought of that. "He was an actual Lesbian."

"What was she doing on Lesbos?"

"Vacationing with her daughter. . . the lowercase lesbian."

"Oh, yeah," said Ben. "So what happened to this guy?"

"Nothing. He's still there, I guess, if he's even alive. He was this stocky little guy with white hair and twinkly eyes. He wanted her to come live with him. They were really hot for each other . . . soul mates even, but . . . she turned him down."

"Why?"

I heard myself sighing. "I think it was me, actually."

"What do you mean?"

"I'd been positive for a couple of years, and everybody just assumed I was about to get sick and die. I assumed it myself. That's the way it was back then."

"And she didn't want to leave you, in case . . ."

". . . she never saw me again."

Ben muttered a reverential "Wow."

"She never said that, of course, but I'm sure it was the reason."

He petted the side of my head, having already arrived at where I was heading. "You shouldn't feel guilty about living, honey."

I told him I felt guilty about not insisting that Anna go back to Greece, that I could have made that my dying wish, that she had been my rock when my lover Jon was dying and it was time for me to return the favor, to place her best interests above my own, especially if I thought I was near death. Anna had waited until she was almost seventy to find a satisfying love, and I had effectively stood in the way of that great happiness.

"She wouldn't have gone," said Ben. "Even I can tell that."

"Maybe not," I said, "but I should have tried. I could have shown her what she meant to me. I could have been a grown-up about it and not just a needy child. I think of her walking down to the market all by herself . . ." I started to tear up, surprising myself.

"C'mon. I told you she looked happy. And she's surrounded by all sorts of people who love and respect her."

"She doesn't have this, though." I meant, of course, a warm body next to hers.

"Well, no, but you didn't either after Thack left. You thought it was the end of love . . . you told me so yourself. You can't control these things, Michael. Life hands you shit, and you have to take it. And nobody can fix that for anybody else."

Then why do I feel so fixed? I thought.

8

Darn Straight

My brother's living room in Orlando is two stories high, a cathedral of drywall with portholes high up that look out into the tops of palm trees. Ben and I found five such houses on that cul-de-sac, but Irwin had made a point of telling us that the Tolliver residence would be the only one with a speedboat in the driveway: "There's no way you can miss it, bro." There was no way you could miss it from the living room, either, thanks to a strategically positioned sofa. Irwin's latest toy was perfectly framed in the window as he sang its praises from a big leather armchair shaped like a catcher's mitt.

"She's a hottie, ain't she?"

At fifty-seven Irwin was just too old to be using the word *hottie*. Even to describe a boat. *Especially* to describe a boat. But it gave him something safe to talk about beyond that *other* hottie under scrutiny—the man I'd just introduced as my husband.

"That's quite a color," I said. "What do they call that?"

"That's your citron yellow."

I thought about that. "Guess *lemon*'s a word they try to avoid."

Typically, Irwin mistook ironic observation for criticism. "She's no lemon, I can tell you that."

"No . . . I didn't mean . . . That color must look great on the water."

"And lemme tell you, that baby turns on a dime. She's a Cobalt 240 with all the extras . . . reversed chines and everything."

I had no idea what a reversed chine was and had no intention of asking, since Irwin was obviously testing me. All he's ever required to be boring is the frank admission of anyone else's ignorance. "Irwin really knows his boats," I told Ben pointedly.

Ben was a gentleman and led us elsewhere. "Did you guys have boats when you were little?"

"Darn straight we did!" Irwin said, and I realized then exactly how low he had sunk in his recent effort to Christianize his cussing. *Darn straight? Who the fuck says that?*

"It was really Irwin's boat," I told Ben. "I was just crew."

98

"Hey, remember the night we snuck down to Lake Tibet?"

The name of that lake, I explained to Ben, was spelled like the Himalayan country but around these parts usually pronounced "Tibbit."

My brother confirmed this oddity. "Our granddaddy called it that, too. I had this dinky little rowboat hidden down there in the reeds. The folks didn't even know about it. They thought we were at the movies. Remember, Mikey?"

How could I have forgotten? I had waited all goddamn year to see *Mary Poppins*, starring my favorite person in the world, when Irwin, newly licensed and hormonally imbalanced, had hijacked me to the swamps. "I remember," I told him.

"Boy," he murmured, "we hunted us some gators that night."

Ben gave me one of his looks. "*You* hunted gators?"

"Is that so hard to fathom?"

"Well, yeah," he said, smirking.

"We didn't really hunt 'em," my brother admitted. "It was more like . . . harass 'em." He chuckled, warming to the memory. "We'd shine our flashlights around until we could see their eyes . . . sometimes there were hundreds of 'em shining out there in the dark . . . but we were lookin' for the eyes that were closest together."

Ben was obviously confused.

"That meant they were little," I explained, "and couldn't hurt us."

"Ah."

"Then," said Irwin, "we'd stun 'em with an oar and toss 'em in a bucket."

Ben turned to me with furrowed brow. "Why would you do that?"

"To play with them," I said. "They were . . . you know . . . more docile when they were stunned."

"Well, I guess so." My beloved's jaw was slack with horror. He looked like he was on the verge of reporting me to PETA.

"We didn't hit them that hard," I told him, "and we always put them back."

That did nothing to fix his expression.

"It wasn't *my* idea," I said.

They both laughed, but it was the truth. *Nothing* had been my idea back then. Irwin had been the architect of every folly, the guy who taught me how guys become guys and beat the shit out of me in the process. The tide didn't begin to turn until I was admitted to the university that had rejected Irwin two years earlier. Though he later enrolled in a business college in Tallahassee, he was expelled after a string of drunken misdemeanors, causing a major parental hissy fit at home. When, at twenty-six, I finally told my folks I was gay, Irwin received the news so unhysterically that it took me a while to realize that what he felt, more than anything, was relief. To him, my coming-out meant he was no longer the disgrace of the family; he could go about breeding kids and selling houses, being the man again.

That was decades ago, of course, and Irwin, like George W. Bush, has long since proven that even serious fuckups can make a go of it. But sitting there in that bland suburban hacienda, I tallied the score of our ancient rivalry and realized that I envied nothing about my brother's life. Not the boat or the four thousand plus square feet or the wife or the grandkid, either—none of the things I once worried I might be missing if I committed fully to a life of homosexuality. That life hasn't been perfect, but it has been *my* life, tailored to my dreams and safely beyond the reach of God's terrible swift sword.

My brother can't say that. Never could.

Irwin's wife, Lenore, was at Children's Bible Study, he told us, doing her puppet ministry with one of the grandkids. He expected her back by four o'clock, at which point we could discuss where to go for dinner. There were several malls nearby, offering a plenitude of choices, including an Outback whose steaks, Irwin assured me, were far superior to the Outback steaks on the West Coast. Except, of course, Irwin said *Left* Coast, since that's been his favorite zinger ever since he learned it on *Rush Limbaugh*.

"So y'all had a good flight?" Irwin was already running out of conversation, but I liked the sound of that second-person plural, since *y'all*, in its way, implies a couple, and Irwin, of course, knew that I knew that. It sort of sanctified our union. Sort of.

"It was okay," Ben answered. "Lousy legroom, but . . . you just have to deal."

"Oh, man, you got that right! I fly business or first these days, but I know what you mean." He banged his palm rhythmically against the leather of that giant catcher's mitt as he scrambled for something to say. "So . . . where are y'all staying?"

"Just a little B&B," I replied. "It's basic, but it's all we need."

It was, to be more specific, a little gay B&B we'd found in the *Spartacus Guide*. We'd been attracted to the name—Inn Among the Flowers—but the flowers had proven to be everywhere but in the garden. The owners, a pair of retired Italian queens from Queens, had lovingly floralized every surface: from the sheets to the upholstery to the toilet paper.

"You shoulda checked with me," said Irwin. "I coulda got you a discount at the Ramada. Many Mansions meets there every Monday."

I translated for Ben. "That's his Christian realtors group."

"Ah."

I couldn't resist the urge to elaborate. "The name comes from the Bible. You know . . . 'In my father's house are many mansions.'"

Ben nodded. "Right."

My brother chuckled. "Some people think it's because we *sell* mansions. We do sell a few . . . some of us . . . but that's not what it means."

Ben smiled back. "It means the different races, right?"

"Well, not so much *races* as . . . it just means rooms, really . . . that there's plenty of room for everybody in God's house."

"And you wouldn't believe the low low down payment," I said.

Ben shot me a chastising look.

"It's okay," Irwin told Ben. "He's always been a smart-mouth."

Lenore arrived home on schedule, a whirling dervish in a pink tracksuit and careful hair. Well into her fifties, she had remained girlish and petite, a feat made all the more dramatic by the presence of her grandson, a delicate doe-eyed seven-year-old named Sumter who had volunteered to help with her burgeoning puppet ministry. As I watched from the porch, they emerged from Lenore's Chevy Tahoe and began pulling plastic poles from the rear door like a team of well-seasoned roustabouts. It was curiously touching.

I hollered at her. "Need a hand with that?"

She looked up with a start. "Oh, Mikey, you're here! I wondered whose pretty car that was. Come gimme a hug, but don't look, I'm a mess. Shoot, I was gonna change for you. I hate lookin' this way. Sumter, you remember your Great-Uncle Michael."

It was more of a command than a question, so the boy issued a dutiful "Yes, ma'am," but there's no way he could have remembered. I hadn't seen him in at least four years, when his mother (my niece Kimberly, divorced last year from her meth-addicted husband) spent the night with her family at Fisherman's Wharf on their way to a Pleasant Hawaiian Holiday. Sumter shook my hand with somber courtesy and began to tug folds of blue fabric from the back of the SUV.

My sister-in-law embraced me fragrantly. "You look so *good*, Mikey!"

"Thanks, Lenore. You too."

"I mean, you really do. You've got some nice ruddy color in your cheeks."

Yep, some of those meds have lovely side effects.

"Where's Ben?" Lenore asked, looking around.

"Inside," I said, pleased that she'd remembered his name. "With Irwin."

"Oh, no. Gettin' an ear fulla boat, I bet."

I laughed. "I think that's over with now."

Sumter was almost staggering under the weight of that bunched blue curtain. "Just leave that, honey," his grandmother told him. "We'll get it later."

"Is that your puppet theater?" I asked the boy.

"Yes sir," he replied. "It fits on the these here poles." I'd forgotten about that "sir" business. I had to do that myself when I was Sumter's age.

"So it works like a tent," I said. "That's pretty cool." (I don't know why I insist on saying "cool" around the young; it only makes me feel older.)

Sumter crawled into the vehicle and laid his hand reverently on a cardboard box. "This is where we keep the puppets." He pulled out a yarn-haired Muppet-style creature and held it up for my scrutiny. "These sticks here make the arms move, see?"

Lenore gave me a grown-up-to-grown-up look. "He's *real* into this."

"Nothing wrong with that," I said, smiling, taking the puppet in hand. It was a Bert or possibly Ernie look-alike with the letters GAP imprinted on his sweatshirt. I didn't get it. "Is the Gap sponsoring you or something?"

"Oh, no." She chuckled at my ignorance. "That stands for God Answers Prayers."

"Oh . . . okay . . ."

105

"All the puppets have little sayings on their clothes. It's the best way to teach kids the Bible. Keeps 'em interested, you know."

Sumter had removed another puppet for my inspection, a female in flowing Middle Eastern garb. "This one here's a Foolish Virgin."

"So I see," I said.

Lenore took my arm. "You know that story, don't you? The Five Foolish Virgins?"

I shrugged. "Maybe I did once but—"

Sumter piped up. "Their oil ran out. They weren't ready for the Bridegroom."

Their oil ran out?

"That's right, Sumter. They weren't prepared, so they didn't have enough oil to light their lamps." She turned back to me. "It's a parable about readiness. Preparing our souls for the Kingdom of Heaven."

"Well . . . you can never have enough oil for that."

I made that joke purely for myself, knowing it would breeze past Lenore. Ben and I had already agreed not to confront the biologicals about the war in Iraq unless they brought it up first. My dying mother was waiting to meet my true love at a Christian old folks' home in Orlo-fucking-vista; there wasn't *time* for all-out holy warfare.

Sumter slid out of the SUV and posed by its side. "I wanna be the Foolish Virgin next time."

106

"Well, you can't," his grandmother said, slamming the tailgate.

"Why not?"

"Because . . . you're perfect as the Bridegroom. And boys don't get to be Foolish Virgins. That's just plain silly, honey. I've told you that before. Don't give Nor-Nor a hard time about this." She turned, gathering the plastic poles in her arms as she widened her eyes at me. "And not a peep out of you, mister."

"I wasn't even—"

"I know it's a silly name, but one of the kids picked it, and . . . I can't be Granny yet. I'm sorry, I just can't."

I gave her a smile and a salute. "As you wish . . . Nor-Nor."

Lenore heaved a sigh. "Sounds like a creature from *Star Wars*, doesn't it? That's what Irwin said." She readjusted the poles and began striding toward the house. "Did he offer y'all somethin' to eat? No, of course not. What am I talkin' about? You look wonderful, Mikey. You really do. Mama Tolliver's gonna be so happy to see you."

She charged ahead of me into the cluster mansion—hell-bent for the first sight of Ben, I guess—leaving me and Sumter to fend for ourselves. The boy looked up at me pleasantly, blinking once or twice, then rubbing his nose with the back of his hand.

"Wanna see the rest of my puppets?" he asked.

9

Uppity

With Lenore in the house the menfolk relaxed a little.
Ben and I welcomed the enlivening effects of a
woman—even this one—and Irwin seemed much more
at ease with the proof of his normality fluttering
nearby. Sumter, meanwhile, had taken an instant shine
to my husband, heaping puppets at his feet like
offerings to a fair-haired god.

"This one here's a lion who's scared all the time," the
kid announced. "And this one's a witch, even though
her dress is way too pretty for a witch, if you ask me."

"Well, she's the good witch," Ben explained. "That
green one over there is the wicked one."

"He's never seen the movie," Lenore said, smiling at
Ben. "A neighbor brought those over for him."

"Well, we'll have to fix *that*," said Ben. "Do you watch
DVDs, Sumter?"

"Sometimes," said the boy. "I watched *The Princess Diaries* and *Cheaper by the Dozen* and . . . *The Passion of the Christ*."

"We watched that with him, of course," Lenore said *sotto voce*. "It's real inspirational, but it takes . . . you know, a grown-up to explain things."

I asked her, somewhat wickedly, if she understood Aramaic.

"Oh, no. I meant . . . the suffering part."

"Oh, I don't know," I said with a shrug. "It's no worse than . . . say . . . *The Texas Chainsaw Massacre*."

Lenore missed this impertinence—or chose to ignore it—but Irwin shot me a scowl from the depths of the catcher's mitt.

Don't get righteous with me, I thought. *You're the one showing S&M snuff movies to a seven-year-old.*

"And this one's my favorite," Sumter was telling Ben, ignoring the old folks altogether. "Her name is Ariel. I can make her tail wiggle, see? I've got this cool underwater backdrop that I made from Mama's shower curtain, only that's back at—"

"Listen, sport," Irwin interjected, "the grown-ups are fixin' to talk, so why don't you take your toys up to Nor-Nor's room? Your mama'll be here soon—"

"They're not toys," said Sumter. "They're puppets."

Irwin, it seemed to me, was already in a state over his grandson's passionate theatricality and in no mood to

109

split hairs. "Take them upstairs, Sumter. Right this minute, you hear? Or Granddaddy won't take you to the Dolphins game next week."

Sumter, so help me, rolled his eyes. "I'm so scared."

Seeing her husband's color beginning to rise, Lenore tactfully interceded. "Sumter, honey, what did I tell you about sassing your granddaddy?"

Solemnly, and with dramatic deliberation, the boy filled his arms with puppets and left the room without another word.

"He's such a funny little fella," Lenore said.

"He needs a man in his life," said Irwin. "Somebody to smack some sense into him. He's got way too smart a mouth on him."

"Oh, now . . ."

"And I don't mean one of those wimps that Kimberly's been datin' on Match.com. That boy could use a nice long summer camp with a drill sergeant."

"Oh, Irwin, for heaven sakes." Lenore sighed at her husband, then gave me a crooked little smile. "He's kidding."

"The heck I am," said my brother.

"I envy him those puppets," I offered, changing the subject. "They're so much better than they used to be. I had to make my own out of old socks and papier-mâché. Remember, Irwin? I did *Jack and the Beanstalk*, and I made you be the giant."

Lenore gaped in delight. "I never knew you liked puppets when you were little!"

I nodded. "I made stages out of cardboard boxes from the Piggly Wiggly."

"Well, goodness," said Lenore. "I guess it runs in the family."

"I guess it does," I agreed.

What exactly *it* was remained discreetly ambiguous, but the air was electric with subtext. I didn't dare look at Benjamin. Or Irwin, for that matter.

I knew what they were thinking, though. Both of them.

Sumter's mother—my niece Kimberly, who works for Florida Citrus Mutual over in Lakeland—came to fetch the child a few minutes later. She stayed to make chitchat and give Ben a brief, voracious once-over, then left the four of us to our various discomforts and a tin-foil tray of deviled eggs Lenore had picked up from the deli at Publix.

"I figured y'all would wanna rest tonight," she said, passing the eggs to Ben. "We can head over to Mama Tolliver's in the morning."

"That's fine," I said.

"She's fresher in the morning."

I wasn't sure what that meant but thought it better not to ask. "Is there some place we can pick up an azalea or something?"

"Oh, sure. There's a nice mall right outside of Orlovista."

There's a nice mall right outside everywhere, Lenore. It's nothing BUT malls anymore.

"So . . . Ben . . . Mikey says you're originally from Colorado." It was the safest possible approach she could have taken, but at least she was making an effort.

"Right," Ben replied pleasantly. "Colorado Springs."

"Colorado's beautiful, I hear."

"It is, actually. Magnificent. It taught me to love the outdoors."

Her brow wrinkled in thought. "Oprah has a house there, doesn't she?"

"I think she does." Ben nodded. "Up near Telluride."

"They were redoin' it one time on her show. You know that decorator of hers? Nate?"

"Well, not personally." Ben grinned crookedly, offering a glimpse of that seductive gap. "I think I've seen him, though. Sort of . . . compact and handsome, right?"

"That's him," said Lenore. "I like him so much. He's just the nicest person."

"He seems to be," said Ben, casting a sideways glance at me.

"He really is," said Lenore. "And he has wonderful taste."

I found this endorsement touching. Lenore wanted my young swain to know that she'd had some exposure

112

to queers. If only the ones she'd seen on television.

After a moment she added: "His friend died in the tsunami, you know."

Ben's smile wilted. "No . . . I hadn't heard that."

It was news to me, too. "His partner, you mean?"

Lenore neither confirmed nor denied. "They were in Thailand in this little hut on the beach, and they woke up one morning, and the roof came clean off the hut, and this big wall of water just carried them away. Nate grabbed on to a telephone pole, but his friend didn't make it. It was the most awful thing. He talked about it on the show."

I was mildly unnerved. I'd seen Nate once or twice myself and could picture him tangled in 600-thread-count sheets with his boyfriend—a taller guy, I imagined, and darker, and just as gorgeous—when the unimaginable ripped them from their idyll. But, even thrusting Ben and me into the same situation, I couldn't get a handle on the horror and the loss. "At least he was out," I said. "He could be totally open about his grief."

"Out of where?" asked Lenore.

"You know . . . the closet."

Lenore frowned. "Well, I don't think he's one of those activists, if that's what you mean."

Irwin was squirming in his chair. "Would somebody please pass the eggs?"

Ben got up and handed the tray to my brother. "They're delicious, aren't they?"

"You know," I told Lenore as evenly as possible. "I think of myself as an activist."

"Oh . . . *now*," she said dismissively. "You know what I mean."

I did know what she meant. She meant there were good homosexuals and bad homosexuals, and she would never think of me as a bad one. My parents, I remembered, had once categorized black folks in much the same way. They didn't disapprove of *all* Negroes. Just the uppity ones. The ones who insisted on *special rights*.

Why do I even bother with this? I thought. I couldn't remember the last time I'd had a meaningful exchange with these people—one that didn't focus on scenery or television as a handy means of avoidance. The list of what we *couldn't* talk about grew larger all the time. Phony Florida elections. Secret American torture camps. "Intelligent design." A far-from-intelligent president who wanted to amend the Constitution to insure that wicked folks like Ben and me would never receive equal treatment under the law.

The truth was that I had long ago stopped caring what the biologicals thought about me, but I had never stopped accommodating their nonsense. It was a nasty old habit not easily broken—making them all feel as comfortable as possible. I gazed around the room, looking for an easy route back to the banal. I found it in a large kitschy print over the fireplace: a woodland chapel at night, its windows ablaze with a golden glow.

"That's very nice," I said. "Is that a new acquisition?"

Lenore beamed with pride. "It's a Thomas Kinkade. You know, the Painter of Light? Irwin gave it to me for Christmas."

Irwin puffed up like a partridge. "*That* one set me back big time," he said. "Lemme tell you."

That night, after dinner at the Outback, we returned to Inn Among the Flowers and decided to hit the sack early. The day had been draining for both of us. Ben was toweling off from a long shower when he tossed a low-grade thunderbolt my way:

"Why didn't you tell me your brother was hot?"

I took that in for a moment, stretched out on the bed, then looked up from a pamphlet on Disney World and the Epcot Center. "Because he's not," I said evenly.

"C'mon. I know he's your brother, but you must be able to—"

"What exactly is it that turns you on? The comb-over? The beer gut? The Banlon shirt?"

Ben laughed. "His gut's no bigger than yours."

"Well . . . technically maybe."

"He's just a big rugged guy, that's all. Sort of a Suit

115

Daddy. A countrified Suit Daddy. There are whole websites for those guys."

"I'm sure," I said. "Countrified Suit Daddy dot com."

He flopped on the bed next to me, naked and spicy-smelling. "He looks like somebody you'd see at an interstate rest stop looking for a little Brokeback action."

"Well, thank you for that," I said, rolling my eyes at him. "Thank you for that truly revolting new spin on my brother."

Ben waggled his eyebrows. "I'd like to have a truly revolting spin on your brother."

"Oh, for God's sake!"

He laughed and kissed my shoulder. "All other things being different."

"Thank you," I said grimly.

"But if I met him at a bar, say—"

"He doesn't drink," I shot back. "He doesn't even cuss anymore. Lenore has dragged his sorry ass to Jesus."

"Apparently," said Ben.

"He used to be kinda fun, you know. I mean—an asshole sometimes—but fun. Now he reminds me of our father at his worst. Especially when he was talking to Sumter."

Ben looked at me dreamily, rubbing my belly in silence for a moment.

116

"You think he's one of us?"

"Who? *Irwin?*"

A chastising swat. "No . . . Sumter."

I rolled on my side and grinned at him. "He is kind of a flamer, isn't he?"

Ben grinned back. "Pretty much."

"That would be a hoot, wouldn't it?"

"Not for Sumter," Ben observed. "Not in this family. Did you see the look on your brother's face when the kid was showing me his puppets?"

"Oh, man, how could you not?"

"He's obviously worried about it."

"Well . . . fuck him."

"Is that what you were like when you were nine?"

I feigned indignation. "No! Are you kidding? I ran a very butch puppet show."

Ben laughed. "I'm sure."

"Strictly cowboys and Indians. And the cowboys always won."

Ben moved closer, entangling his legs with mine. "I'd love to see where you lived. The orange groves and all. Just to be able to picture it."

"There's not much to see anymore," I said. "There's no home there now. Just a Home Depot."

He smiled. "But what did it look like?"

"Oh . . . dirt roads through the groves . . . white

frame houses with lightning rods. Granddaddy was in walking distance."

"Like a Disney movie."

"More or less." I gave him a dark little smile. "Before Disney got here."

Ben smiled and sighed.

"There were these wooden stands out on the highway," I told him. "This two-lane blacktop that ran along our grove. They sold orange-blossom perfume to the Yankee tourists. We hated those stands back then . . . Mama said they looked common . . . but I'd love to see one now . . . the way it was then, I mean. I'm sure I'd think it was wonderful."

"You wanna go look for one," Ben asked, "after we visit your mother?"

"After we visit my mother," I replied, "I wanna find a gay bar and get shit-faced and stick my tongue down your throat."

"That would work, too," said Ben.

118

10

A Little Bit
Blue

The Gospel Palms was located, not surprisingly, within spitting distance of a mall. The building was low and modern, the grounds modest but well tended. It might have passed for a small resort if not for the droning gray Muzak of the freeway and a Radio Shack visible through a tangle of palms and light poles. As Lenore turned the Little Witnesses Puppet Wagon into the parking lot, a pair of kids in Mickey Mouse ears were dodging the lawn sprinklers with lunatic glee. I had a terrible urge to join them.

"Listen," said Lenore, turning off the engine. "Before we go in. Do y'all know about the blue bloater thing?"

"Nooo . . ." I said, frowning in Ben's direction.

He shrugged. "Me neither."

"Well . . . with emphysema patients, you know, they divide 'em up into pink puffers and blue bloaters." She tilted her head and blinked her eyes in ladylike apology. "I know that sounds gross, but those are . . . you know . . . the actual terms they use."

She seemed to be waiting for a response, so I said: "Okay."

"Mama Tolliver's been a pink puffer for a real long time. They call 'em that because they take these short little puffs when they breathe . . . and, you know, because of the color they get. Real . . . *rosy* in the face. The way she's been until now, you know?"

I nodded. *Until now?*

"So," sighed Lenore, drawing out the suspense, working me like one of her puppets. "Sometimes the people who have it are just pink, and sometimes they're just blue, and sometimes . . . when it gets worse . . . they can change from one to the other."

Perversely, I found myself thinking of a home pregnancy test. Or one of those sticks you pee on for the Atkins diet. "So," I said, losing patience with my sister-in-law's theatrics. "I take it she's a blue . . . whatever . . . now?"

"Bloater," she said. "Yes."

"And what does that mean exactly?"

"It means that the arms and legs get all puffy and—"

"Bloated," I said.

"Yes." She wrinkled her nose in distaste. "And the skin gets sorta bluish."

120

"Right."

"Don't worry," Lenore said. "She keeps it covered up when she's got company."

"With makeup, you mean?"

She nodded ominously. "I'm afraid so." She widened her eyes as if to suggest, ever so nicely, that I should brace myself for a major cosmetic atrocity. Then she climbed out of the Puppet Wagon and fussed briefly with her hair in the rearview mirror. "Don't forget your pretty flowers," she said, meaning the hydrangea in the backseat.

Spotting that plant on a table at Publix, I'd remembered how much Mama loved hydrangeas. There were half a dozen bushes blooming in our backyard every summer, some of them the size of pup tents. Mama would pull up a lawn chair when the sprinkler was on, just to smoke her Slims and watch those thirsty blue globes bobbing in the spray.

To a boy of seven—Sumter's age, come to think of it—Mama seemed nothing less than a sorceress when it came to hydrangeas. I remember watching in amazement as she knelt in her cotton sundress to crucify the ground with rusty nails—a trick that she assured me would turn blue blossoms into pink ones before the year was out.

My love of gardening had come from this woman.

Her and Anna Madrigal.

121

* * *

The lobby of the Gospel Palms was tiny but efficient, presided over by a sweet-spirited portrait of a blue-eyed Christ delivering the Sermon on the Mount. There was an alcove for visitors and a mini florist's cooler—more like a vending machine, really—that dispensed carnation corsages in several unnatural colors. Behind the reception desk sat a balding Middle Eastern man who nodded at Lenore as we passed, though she didn't even bother to slow down. I noticed the bumper stickers on his file cabinet—PROUD AMERICAN and SUPPORT OUR TROOPS—strategically positioned for the benefit of anxious visitors. *Poor bastard*, I thought. *Guantánamo Bay must seem awfully close.*

Outside Mama's room we held a brief powwow, where Ben, bless his heart, offered to take Lenore over to Starbucks so I could have some time with Mama before introductions were made. She was sitting up in a chair when I entered. Her face was made alien by a bulbous nebulizer mask, and her hair was a meticulous helmet of lavender blue, obviously done that morning. She'd been waiting for me, I realized.

Seeing me in the doorway, she yanked off the mask in embarrassment. "Mikey," she said, her voice more gravelly than I'd ever heard it. "Lenore was spose to warn me."

"It's all right," I said, smiling at her. "I've worn one o'

122

those myself." I was relieved to see that her makeup, while a little on the goopy side, was not nearly as gruesome as Lenore had suggested. It seemed to cover the blue, at any rate.

I set the hydrangea on the bedside table and knelt to hug her, entering the faint mist of her nebulizer. She was wearing an old polyester pantsuit, and her legs did seem to be swollen. She pulled my cheek against hers, then released me with a brisk pat.

"When did you get to be so gray?" she asked.

I smiled at her. "About the time you got to be heliotrope."

This was only meant to be affectionate, but a cloud passed over her face. "Did Lenore tell y'all . . . ?" She stopped to suck air through pursed lips as if—God forbid—she were toking on a joint. "Did Lenore . . . ssss . . . tell y'all I was turning colors?"

I was mortified. "Oh, no, Mama! I just meant your hair color."

"Oh." She patted the side of her Easter-egg do, almost girlishly proud of it. *When nothing else can be done*, I thought, *you can always do your hair*.

"I like it," I told her. "It's very becoming."

"Patreese did it. My new hairdresser . . . ssss . . . Black as the ace of spades . . . ssss . . . but very talented."

In the old days, I would have taken issue with her phraseology—and she would have accused me of

123

overreacting—but it was way too late for all that now.

Mama shot a nervous glance toward the door. "She didn't . . . ssss . . . come with you, did she?"

I was confused. "Your hairdresser?"

"No . . . ssss . . . Lenore."

"She's over at the mall," I said. "I wanted this to be just us."

"I hope she didn't . . . ssss . . . bring those puppets!"

I chuckled. "No . . . well, they're in the van, but . . . I think we're safe."

"She liked to bore us silly last week. . . ssss . . . Set up the stage in the dining room without so much as . . . ssss . . . a pretty-please to anyone . . . ssss . . . Then she went and . . . ssss . . . told the whole blessed world I'd turned blue."

"Well, that's not very discreet." I could have been a lot more supportive, but I hadn't been expecting an open invitation to lay into Lenore.

A sly light came into Mama's eyes. "I never had so many . . . ssss . . . visitors in my life . . . ssss . . . all of 'em lookin' for the Famous Blue Lady . . . ssss . . . I think the young'ns . . . ssss . . .. were expectin' a Smurf."

When I laughed hard at that, she looked rather pleased with herself. Mama had gotten sassier in these last two decades without Papa. I'd always assumed she was trying to channel him a little, thereby taking up the slack in the pissing-and-moaning department.

She shook her head slowly. "I've never understood it."

"What, Mama?"

"What Irwin sees in that . . . ssss . . . *Jesusy* woman!"

"Well," I said, dragging up a chair and sitting down, "it's a damn good thing *we're* not married to her, isn't it?" I reached for her hand and held it for a while. It was small and unnaturally plump and—yes—a little bit blue.

"Some of us don't need puppet shows," Mama declared with a righteous scowl. "Some of us would like to . . . ssss . . . worship the Lord in silence."

I gazed down at her nebulizer mask, that ugly Muppet nose, lying abandoned in her lap. "Shouldn't you be wearing that thing?"

She shrugged. "I can . . . ssss . . . take it or leave it."

"Well, take it, then."

She resisted.

"C'mon, lady. Humor me."

She looked at me wearily for a moment, as if on the verge of saying something, then picked up the mask. "It's just medicine . . . ssss . . . it doesn't do anything."

"Be that as it may . . . let me do the talking for a while."

So Mama stayed on the nebulizer while I rattled on about the gardening business and the nice weather in Orlando and the landscaping at the Gospel Palms. My eyes, meanwhile, roamed the room for evidence of anything more substantive. I found it on a shelf by the window: the framed snapshot of Ben and me at Big Sur that I'd mailed to Irwin for Mama's last birthday. I'd apparently shamed him into giving it to her.

She caught me looking at the photo and pulled off the mask. "So where did you hide . . . ssss . . . the young feller?"

Normally, she wouldn't pronounce the word that way; she was being cute. She was doing her best Granny Clampett, to let me know she wasn't nearly the rube I took her for. It was a sweet gesture but unconvincing; somewhere beneath all that white makeup and blue skin, the same old red-state heart was beating. Mama was a proud member of the Greatest Generation—or at least its ladies' auxiliary—and those folks don't *have* to approve of you to love you. They can forgive you until the cows come home.

I gazed back at her calmly for a bit. "What bothers you more?" I asked. "The young part or the feller part?"

"Well," said Mama, "we'll just . . . ssss . . . have to see, won't we?"

Ben returned from Starbucks minus Lenore. She had some shopping to do, he said, but she'd be back in an hour to pick us up. I figured she knew the limits of Mama's energy and thought it best to give us a deadline.

126

That was fine with me; I wasn't even sure how well I could fill up the time. Ben made a valiant effort by dumping a handful of cellophane-wrapped cookies on the bedside table as soon as I'd introduced him to Mama. "I thought we should try these," he said. "They're madeleines. Ever had one?"

"Not from *Starbucks*," I said, giving him a jaundiced look as I took one.

Ben mugged at me and turned back to my mother, who seemed to be studying his face for some killer final exam. "How 'bout you, Alice?"

Jesus fuck! He called her Alice.

Mama blinked at him for a moment, then reached primly for a madeleine. "Don't mind if I do," she said.

"Madeleines seemed appropriate," Ben said, looking hopefully from mother to prodigal son as we nibbled away. "They're for remembering, right?"

"Only if you've had one before," I replied. "Only if you're Proust." I shared a private grin with him. "My madeleine would be a Moon Pie."

Ben laughed.

"That's a big fib . . . and you know it." Mama was eating and talking at the same time, which was something of a stretch. Madeleine crumbs had assembled unlawfully in the corners of her mouth. "I never . . . ssss . . . fed you boys Moon Pies in my life."

I chuckled. "I didn't say you fed us. I said I ate them."

"I'll tell you another thing . . . ssss . . . I know who Proust is . . . ssss . . . so don't you get snooty with me."

"I didn't mean—"

"Where'd you get 'em?"

"What?"

"The Moon Pies."

"The Esso station down on the highway. Mr. Grady with the drool rag. Same place I got the key ring with the wiggly naked lady inside."

Mama was fierce. "I don't remember any . . . ssss . . . key ring."

"I don't know why not," I said. "You confiscated it. You said you never wanted to see me with a naked lady again as long as you lived."

Her mouth went slack. "I never said . . . ssss . . . any such thing!"

"Well," I said darkly, "it's how *I* heard it."

"Michael." Ben was using the careful intonation of a kindergarten teacher. "Stop with the Norman Bates, please."

"She knows I'm kidding," I said, slipping my arm around Mama's shoulders.

Sulking, Mama smoothed the front of her blouse. "Don't think you can . . . ssss . . . blame me for your"— she searched for the right word—"good times."

"My good times," I echoed to Ben. "Blame her for my good times."

128

"Give it a break," he said. "Who's Mr. Grady with the drool rag?"

"He worked at the gas station," I said.

"He had a condition, " Mama added.

"So I gathered," said Ben.

"He was sort of a popular freak show for us kids," I said. "He had this long string of drool—"

"Ugh," said Ben.

"I know," said Mama, looking slyly at my husband. "You could never buy a blessed thing out of a wrapper."

It took him a moment to recognize her humor, but he finally smiled. "You're a pistol, aren't you, Alice?"

He could not have pleased her more. She smiled at him faintly, then turned back to me. "How did you ever meet . . . ssss . . . such a gentleman?"

I was feeling so comfortable by then that I almost brought up the website, but I thought better of it. "Just lucky, I guess."

"I was lucky, too," Ben told her.

Mama caught the look that passed between us. "Is that so?" she asked him.

He returned her gaze. "Yes, ma'am. It is."

Their eyes stayed locked for a while before she turned back to me. "Why don't you . . . ssss . . . go out and play?"

"What?"

"You heard me," she said, shooing me with a plump pastel hand.

I spent the time in something called the Prayer Gazebo, which was just what it sounds like: a gazebo in the form of a miniature chapel. It wouldn't function well as either, it seemed to me, but there were nice cushions that kept me comfortable while I was killing time. I was still killing it, by the way, when Lenore came back to pick us up.

"What happened to Ben?" she called.

"He's inside with Mama." I rose and walked toward her out of the gazebo.

I caught the raw scent of new-mown grass and felt suddenly, curiously buoyant.

"What are they talking about?" Lenore asked.

"I have no idea."

"Oh . . . *now*."

"I'm serious," I said. "I'm clueless."

Lenore pursed her lips. "Mikey, listen, I don't know what y'all are up to, and I don't wanna sound like some rhymes-with-witch, but Mama Tolliver can't take any stress right now . . . and just because y'all's political agenda means tellin' the whole blessed—"

"It was *her* idea, Lenore!"

Lenore looked satisfyingly blank.

"Mama *asked* to be alone with Ben."

"She did?"

"Yes. And lay off that agenda crap, Lenore. I hear a lot more about *your* agenda than you ever hear about mine."

"Oh, hush," she said. "We need to figure this out."

"Why?"

"Because she's up to somethin' . . ."

I just shrugged. "I think it's kinda sweet."

"Listen, if you think for one minute that she's in there givin' him her blessing on your . . . let's just say it, Mikey . . . cradle robbin'—"

"Oh, please," I said. "We're not asking for her approval. Or yours, for that matter."

Lenore's faced clouded with thought. "What is it, then? She just met him, didn't she? Doesn't that make you a little nervous?"

"I'd be more nervous, frankly, if it were Irwin."

Lenore frowned. "Irwin and Mama Tolliver?"

"No. Irwin and Ben."

I gave her a grin to let her know that I wasn't serious, but it didn't seem to help. "What are you talking about?" she asked, her frown growing deeper.

"Ben thinks he's hot."

"*Hot?*" She drew the word out to at least three syllables. "*Irwin?*"

"I know," I said. "There's no accountin', is there?"

131

Lenore was dumbstruck, somewhere just short of laughing or screaming.

"It was just a remark," I added. "He's not trying to bag him. Don't worry."

"Well . . ." She started to say something but stopped.

"What?" I asked.

"Nothing. You made me forget. You always do that." She turned and started striding toward the building. "C'mon, I gotta be at Curves by two."

11

The War at Home

While they'd never been close, Mama and Lenore had been confidantes for decades—a paradox that's not uncommon among Southern women. Lenore had been Mama's wailing wall in the matter of her gay son—and later, of course, her *dying* gay son—and they had borne those crosses together like good Christians. So I couldn't imagine what could possibly have driven Mama to find her daughter-in-law too "Jesusy" these days. I had a feeling Ben might know already, but I didn't dare pump him until Lenore had dropped us off down the block from our B&B and rounded the corner out of sight.

"So what did your girlfriend want?"

Ben's smile was more careful than I expected. "Just to talk."

"I thought that's what we were doing."

He took my arm sweetly, naturally, and walked us to Inn Among the Flowers. I've lived too long not to fret about displays of male tenderness when they happen in ... oh, say ... the South, so I took note of the trio of baggy-panted teens slouching toward us down the palm-lined sidewalk. They passed without comment, though, causing me to wonder if this was actual progress—or if they'd just seen a guy being nice to his dad.

"So what's going on?" I asked Ben, returning to the mystery at hand.

He hesitated. "She needs your help with something."

"And she couldn't ask me herself?"

Arriving at our room, he slipped the key into the door. "She thought you'd be more likely to listen to me." He pushed open the door, turning to me with a crooked smile. "Plus she thinks I'm a gentleman, remember?"

(That's another thing that annoys me about Southern women: they always work through the spouse.)

"Don't get too grand about it," I said, following him into the room. "That was her backhanded way of saying that I'm *not* a gentleman."

We sat on the edge of the bed and, almost simultaneously, tore at the Velcro of our Tevas. Ben turned and gazed at me soberly, then sighed and took the leap. "Here's the deal, sweetie: she wants to give you durable power of attorney."

I blinked at him for a moment, totally un-comprehending. "What do you mean? For a will or something? There can't be much of an estate."

Ben shook his head. "For health care."

"But Irwin and Lenore have always—"

"I know . . .. but she wants *you* to handle it now . . . and to sign something to that effect."

"But . . . why?"

Ben hesitated, assembling his words. "Her lungs are pretty much shot. They won't get any better. She could last for another few months, but . . ."

He didn't finish, but none of this was news to me. I couldn't understand why he was still treading so lightly.

"Once her lungs go," Ben went on, "they could put her on a respirator indefinitely, but . . . she doesn't want to be around at any cost. And she's afraid that . . . left to their own devices . . . your brother and Lenore . . ."

I finished the thought for him: ". . . wouldn't let her die."

He nodded slowly. "Yep."

"Jesus," I murmured.

"Pretty much," he said.

A long leaden silence.

"Has she *told* them that?" I asked. "What she wants, I mean."

"No."

135

"Why not? It's worth a shot. You never know if—"

"She's sure they wouldn't go for it. Especially Lenore."

"She asked her specifically, then?"

Ben shook his head. "They used to watch Terri Schiavo together."

"Motherfucker," I said. "Of *course*."

You must remember Terri Schiavo, the woman in the "persistent vegetative state" whose parents were fighting to keep her that way. Her husband had petitioned to have her feeding tube removed, and fundamentalists everywhere were outraged, Governor Jeb Bush among them. When permission was finally granted, the faithful gathered around their sets for a protracted deathwatch, a sideshow that proved so popular that the network tried it again several days later with the pope. But an old man shuffling into oblivion, however cute he might be, lacked the sheer gladiatorial drama of a good plug-pulling.

"Lenore would bring lunch to the Gospel Palms," Ben explained, "and her and your mom would watch Fox-TV every afternoon. It was sorta their soap opera. Lenore would get so worked up she'd talk back to the set. She said that letting someone die like that was worse than abortion. Even if they want to die. Even if they requested it."

I could feel my face burning. "And how does she feel

about slaughtering children for oil? Does that offend her Christian principles?"

Ben was waiting indulgently for me to return to the war at home.

"So all I have to do is sign something?"

He nodded. "She had a lawyer draw it up. She asked me to be one of the witnesses. She wants you to sign before Irwin and Lenore get wise."

"This doesn't mean . . ." I just couldn't find the right way to put it. "I mean . . . she'll be comfortable, won't she?"

Another nod. "They can make it that way." He reached over and held my arm. "Nothing different will be happening, sweetie. Things will just . . . take their course naturally. She just doesn't want the respirator."

"Gotcha."

"Are you okay?"

I nodded. "I guess I should call her."

He shook his head. "I told her you'd do it. We're gonna sign the papers on Thursday."

I raised my eyebrows. "You're way ahead of me, aren't you?"

He leaned closer and kissed me on the cheek. "Just beside you."

I smiled at him. "This could get sticky, you know."

"You think?"

"Well . . . they'll put up a fight if they get wind of it. I'm sure of that."

"Maybe," said Ben, "but there's nothing they can do about it. Once your mom's made her wishes known."

"I suppose." I had a sudden, macabre image of Lenore brandishing her puppets at the Gospel Palms while Mama breathed her last natural breaths. I could hear those loathsome Little Witnesses accusing me, pointing their little felt arms at the sinner from Sodom-by-the-Bay as the righteous assembled at Mama's bedside to sing hymns of devotion.

"She must hate it," I said, "that she has to turn to me."

"She doesn't have to," said Ben. "She wants to."

No, I thought, she *has* to. Everyone else has drunk the Kool-Aid.

12

Camouflage

Orlando's oldest gay bar, the Full Moon Saloon, was a few blocks from our B&B down Orange Blossom Trail. The place had been a hunting lodge when I was a kid, but now it catered largely to bears—specifically the Bears of Central Florida—whose headquarters (and hindquarters) could be found there. On certain nights of the week patrons were encouraged to wear leather, latex, or uniforms. This particular night was a Wednesday, so men in camouflage could buy domestic beers for $2.25.

In my youth, and many years thereafter, camouflage would have meant the jungle-green Vietnam variety, but most of these guys were decked out in the muted buffs and grays of the troops in Iraq. One of them, a solid-looking black bear nearing fifty, was sporting that new computer-generated camouflage on which random pixilated shapes have replaced the old swirly shrubbery patterns.

"He might be real," I said to Ben.

"A real what?"

"Soldier. I don't think that pattern has hit the thrift shops yet."

Ben gave me a dubious look. "Why would he wear it here? I don't think that outfit is much of a fantasy for people who have to wear it for real."

"I guess not." I smiled at him, appreciating his practical wisdom. "I'll get the drinks. What'll you have?"

Ben, as you know, is alarmingly moderate when it comes to substances, so "What'll you have?" is always a challenge. "How 'bout a Lemon Drop?" he said.

"Is that what our brave men are drinking now?"

He goosed me. "You can skip the pansy-ass glass."

"Yes sir." I gave him a smart salute. "No pansy-ass glass, sir."

I wriggled my way to the bar, where a chunky bartender in a camouflage tank top obliged by serving the cocktails in whiskey glasses rimmed with sugar. "There ya go," he said, setting them down. "Two butch Lemon Drops for the general."

He was just teasing, or maybe even flirting, but, proud old queer that I am, I didn't want him to think that I had masculinity issues about glassware—

especially in a room full of faux soldiers. "The short ones are easier to handle," I said. "In a crowd."

"Gotcha," said the bartender. "You from around here?"

"No," I replied. "Well . . . yes . . . but not lately."

"You sounded like you might be."

"I grew up out on Abbot Springs Road. My family had some orange groves out there."

The bartender shook his head. "Don't think I know it."

I gave him a crooked smile. "Don't think I do, either."

"Say what?"

"Nothing." I left him a ten-dollar bill, then lifted the Lemon Drop glasses in a double toast. "Keep the troops happy," I told him ruefully.

Two drinks later, the Full Moon was jammed, and, as usual, I was feeling both claustrophobic and disconnected. You wouldn't think those two would go together, but they do for me, especially in a bar, where it's all too easy to feel suffocated by nothingness. I was never a bar person, even as a young man; I preferred the wide-open spaces of the bathhouses, where willing members and stoned cuddling and a seven-grain sandwich with sprouts were never that far away. A noisy bar, on the other hand, is all posing and chaos; sooner or later I reach my limit and have to make a break for it, find some stars, breathe some clean night air, get Christina Fucking Aguilera out of my head.

So Ben and I retreated to a bench under a big live oak that must have been there when I was a boy and the place was exclusively dedicated to the joy of killing animals. From this distance the pounding music in the Full Moon sounded almost bittersweet, like an orchestra heard across a lake. The actual moon was far from full—just a little nail paring caught in the branches—but it was lovely. My body was starting to remember the precise feel of a balmy Florida night— that easy, velvety containment.

Ben slid closer, tucking a palm between my thighs. "This is better," he said.

"Ain't it?"

"Are you okay?"

I didn't speak right away. "You know what gets me?"

"What?"

I searched for the best way to frame it, the best way not to sound like a monster. "People always say, '*Of course* you love her, you have to, she's your mother,' but that kind of love can die as easily as any of the others. It has to be fed by something."

"She loves you, Michael."

"Not enough to question her preachers."

"Well—"

"You know they hauled her to the polls . . . oxygen

tank and all . . . so she could vote for Bush one more time? The guy who wants to protect marriage from you and me. And they expect us to act like everything's fine, like they're not *really* waging a holy war against us. And what do I do? I make it easy for them. I'm a good boy and joke about speedboats and alligators and Mr. Grady with the drool rag."

Ben smiled benignly, letting me vent.

"I've had thirty years of forgiveness," I said. "I'm fucking over it."

Ben nodded. "I'm sure."

"She's spent all that time trying not to know who I am, and now she's entrusting me with her death. I should feel touched or something, but I don't. I don't feel much of anything. I let her go a long time ago. I've done my mourning already."

Ben kept his eyes on the moon. "Wouldn't that be nice?"

"I mean it," I said. "I wish I didn't, but I do."

Ben just shrugged and smiled. "There is no fifth destination."

This takes some explaining. Last year I bought a Prius, one of those cute, high-butted hybrids that are multiplying like rabbits in the streets of San Francisco. As you might imagine, I love how it saves on gas and cuts pollution. I also love its eerie silence at stoplights and its wacky rearview camera and that disembodied voice—female, elegant, and a little bossy—who can somehow lead us back to Noe Hill (beguilingly labeled HOME) from anywhere in the country. During our trip through the Southwest, Ben and I grew so familiar with that voice that we named her Carlotta—well, all right, *I* did—after "the mad Carlotta" from *Vertigo*, because our own lady of mystery can sound downright loony sometimes.

One night, for instance, when we were driving home from a trip to Tahoe, there was a serious chill in the air, so Ben poked the little face on the steering wheel to call Carlotta.

"After the beep," she said, "please say a command."

So Ben said: "Seventy-two degrees."

And Carlotta replied: "There is no fifth destination."

"What did she say?" asked Ben.

"She said there is no fifth destination."

He chuckled. "Well, that's real helpful."

"I don't think you waited long enough after the beep."

"Well, okay," said Ben, "but why was that in there in the first place. *There is no fifth destination?* If that's the answer, what's the question?"

Intrigued by this conundrum, I told him to push the button again. He did so, reluctantly, and Carlotta returned. "After the beep," she said, "please say a command."

I leaned toward the steering wheel. "Go fuck yourself," I said.

"Pardon?" she replied.

"I said, eat a big one!"

Her voice, I swear, grew starchy: "System is showing beauty-shop icons."

Ben hooted. "I think she just called you a queen."

"I think she did, too . . . the tart."

"Well, talk nice to her, then."

"Push it again."

"No, Michael. That's enough."

"C'mon. I wanna see how freaky she gets . . ."

"Honey, you can't just sit here harassing machinery."

"Why not? It's a rare opportunity."

From that moment on, "There is no fifth destination" became our all-purpose pronouncement. It sounded important, like something Gandalf might have uttered, yet it was patently ridiculous at heart. It became our way of saying "Big deal" or "Who the hell knows?" or "Lighten up, for God's sake, you won't get out of this alive."

Maybe we only get four destinations in life, and Carlotta's trying to tell us not to be banking on the fifth, not to be wasting precious time on pipe dreams of eternity.

That's the way I hear it, anyway.

* * *

"Do you smell something?"

We were still sitting on the bench under the oak tree, and Ben's nose was tilted skyward. I followed his lead and noticed the same thing: the sweet, teasing pungency of marijuana. Tracking it to its source, I found a couple of bar patrons wreathed in smoke, standing in the shadows next to a Dumpster. "Man," I said, "the scent of home."

"Go get a hit," Ben whispered. Since I haven't traveled with grass—except sometimes by car in Northern California—since the "heightened security measures" of 9/11, my husband seems instinctively to feel my pain when I'm potless in a foreign city.

"I can't," I told him.

"Why not?"

"Because it's rude, when they're strangers. And they haven't offered it."

"Let's just stroll by, then. I need to go to the bathroom, anyway."

So we proceeded to stroll, ever so casually, until one of the tokers—the shorter of the two—was startled by the sight of us and palmed the joint with guilty efficiency.

"It's okay," I told him. "We're from San Francisco."

They laughed uneasily. They were both in their forties, both in polo shirts and chinos, both gazing carnivorously at Ben. I'm used to this, of course, and

146

these two weren't in the least threatening, since neither one of them was exactly embracing his daddyhood. Their highlighted hair and fake tans (visible even in the dark) betrayed just how hard—and how long—they'd been clinging to the conceit of youth. And it's not Peter Pan who makes little Ben's heart beat faster; it's Captain Hook.

These guys seemed pleasant enough, though—especially when the shorter one held out the joint. "Would you care to partake?" His voice was Southern and smooth as sorghum. I found it familiar and comforting and deeply repellent.

"Don't mind if I do," I said, matching his Victorian formality before sucking the blessed weed into my lungs.

"What about you?" the taller one asked Ben.

"No, thanks," Ben said. "You guys go ahead."

I handed the joint back to the taller one. "He's disgustingly clean."

The shorter one locked his eyes on Ben. "Well, good for you. You stay that way." His tone was slightly patronizing, as if he were addressing someone's teenage brother. He flashed an empty Tom Cruise smile. "Are y'all friends or something?"

"No," I said evenly. "We're a couple."

He blinked at me for a moment. "Well," he said, raising an eyebrow as he took the joint from the shorter one. "Didn't *you* hit the jackpot."

Before I could compose a sufficiently punishing answer, Ben had taken care of things. "I think we both did," he said.

"Of course," said the taller one, scolding his partner with a glance.

"We were married at City Hall," I told them, changing the subject.

"That's great," said the taller one. "We couldn't do that, of course, but . . . our pastor gave us a commitment ceremony."

I was surprised—and impressed—to hear that. "Around here, you mean?"

"Yep. Tully Memorial Baptist."

"Well, I'll be," I said. Three days back in Central Florida and I was already sounding like Mammy Yokum.

The shorter one sucked on the joint with a vengeance, making almost the same noise my mother made with her nebulizer. "We quit that congregation."

"Why?" asked Ben.

"Well, the pastor started preaching about how all religions are the same and how (ssss) they're all just guidelines for goodness and the Buddhists are just as good as we are and shit like that. Well, call me old-fashioned, but (ssss) when I accepted the Lord Jesus Christ as my personal savior (ssss) I didn't sign up for no Buddhism." He handed the joint to the taller one, then turned back to us. "I mean, can you imagine such a thing?"

I didn't dare catch Ben's eye for fear of uncontrollable smirking. "Oh, well," he said, struggling for something to say, "I can see how . . . so it was sort of . . . a question of—"

He was floundering pitifully, so I helped in my usual way—by interrupting. "I think I see what you mean," I said to the shorter one. "If you join a spiritual discipline . . . whatever it is . . . you expect to be given the purest version of it."

"*Thank you*," said the shorter one. "I told that pastor we wanted all Jesus all the time or he could just keep his damn collection plate. We'd rather spend it on shoes."

This time he'd meant to be funny, so Ben and I laughed, grateful for the release.

"He really did say that," said the taller one, terribly proud of his tell-it-like-it-is partner.

"Do y'all live around here?" I asked.

"Not far," said the taller one. "Winter Garden. We've got a condo there."

The shorter one nodded. "We're moving to Naples, though, just as soon as we've got the cash."

"Lucky you," said Ben. "Italy's wonderful."

"This one's in Florida," I explained with a crooked smile.

"Oh. Right. Of course."

"On the Gulf," said the taller one. "It's real pretty there, and the beaches are fabulous. White sand as far as you can see."

"And white *people*," said the shorter one. "It's the whitest place in the state. Call me old-fashioned, but I could use some of that right now."

There was dumbfounded silence from the two of us, so the taller one looked at me earnestly and attempted an explanation. "Our Miata got broke into last week."

Another long silence.

"You know what," Ben said at last. "I've really gotta pee."

Back in the bar, we finally released a barrage of groans and giggles. "Damn," said Ben, "what you won't do to get high."

"Hey. You're the one who told me to do it."

"Where do they make queens like that?"

"I dunno." I thought about it for a moment. "The Drama Club at Bob Jones University?"

Ben laughed. "Guess there has to be one, huh?"

"I swear, if it weren't for Mama I'd be on the next plane out of here."

"You don't like it here?" This question came from somewhere behind us, startling us both. We turned to find the burly black bear in the pixilated fatigues,

150

smiling broadly. The name JOHNSON was stitched in black above his breast pocket.

"Oh, sorry," I said, "no offense."

"None taken," he said.

"We just met some assholes," Ben put in. "It's nothing to do with Orlando."

"That camouflage is trippy," I said, changing the subject. "That's the real deal, isn't it?"

The guy nodded. "Yeah."

"So your name is really Johnson?"

"Yeah, but that's not—"

"Don't ask, don't tell, right?"

He chuckled. "Hell, no, honey. I'll tell you anything you want. That's my name, but I don't do war—I do hair."

Okay, shoot me for stereotyping, but I would never have taken him for a hairdresser. Aside from his offhanded use of "honey," there was nothing especially fey about him. He was more like some languid, gum-chewing UPS man whose forearms make you weak in the knees while you're trying to sign that little Etch-a-Sketch thing.

"Good," I told him. "Then we don't have to worry about you."

"What do you mean?"

"You know . . . dying in that asinine war."

He regarded me for a moment, as if composing a

response, but apparently thought it better to head in a different direction. "Y'all are partners, right?"

"Right," said Ben.

"But you go to bars together?"

Ben shrugged. "It feels good to cuddle in a crowd." His arm was already around me, so he pulled me closer for emphasis. I knew what he meant, of course. A public display of affection—in the right place—can feel like a public benediction.

The guy appraised us both, looking from one to the other with an intensity that was a little unsettling. "You look really hot together."

"Thanks," said Ben, blushing furiously.

"It's obvious what you've got with each other," the guy said, looking at me. "I can feel it from here. It's like standing by a campfire."

I started to make a lame crack about being flamers— largely out of nervousness—but our admirer had turned his electric gaze back to Ben. "So he's your daddy, huh?"

Ben gave him that patented gap-toothed grin. "Sometimes," he said. "And sometimes I'm his."

The guy nodded. "I hear you."

"Nothing formal," I added. "No leashes or collars."

That got a laugh from him. "Do you guys ever . . . ?" He chose not to finish this question.

"Ever what?" I asked.

"No big deal," he said. "Take it easy, my brothers."

Then he headed off to the bar.

Okay, here's the thing: Ben and I had never had a three-way. Not together, anyway. We'd never made a rule against it or anything; in fact, we'd always considered it a pleasant possibility one of these days, when the circumstances were right. Like, say when we're traveling together and a long way from home and it's someone we're both attracted to who's attracted to both of us and who we're never likely to see ever again.

"Okay," I said as soon as he was gone, "one of us has to say it first."

"He's fucking hot," said Ben.

"Thank you," I said.

"Was he hitting on us," Ben asked, "or just admiring our marriage?"

"I have no idea."

"Maybe he's just the Welcome Wagon here."

"Maybe. My wagon sure feels welcomed."

Ben laughed. "I think he might wanna play."

"Yeah . . . with *you*."

"C'mon. You heard all that daddy talk."

"He was getting off on the idea of *you* with a daddy."

"He was practically slobbering on you, sweetie."

"Really?" I squeaked, sounding decidedly undaddy-like.

153

"Yes."

"Well, what should we do?"

Ben shrugged. "Are you sure you want to?"

"I guess so," I said. "If you do."

"He's awfully nice," said Ben. "I mean, he seems like a decent guy."

"He does, doesn't he?"

Ben chuckled. "Listen to us."

"Shall we go ask him?"

"Now, you mean?" He glanced across the room to the far end of the bar, where the object of our lust was standing alone in a pool of blue light.

"Sure," I said. "Why not?"

"Well . . . as long as it's okay with you. I don't wanna fuck things up between you and me."

"That's why it's okay," I told him, cupping my hand against his cheek.

So, with eyes on the prize and hearts pounding in unison, we made our way across the room, only to be thwarted by the pot-smoking Jesus queens from Winter Garden. "Hi, guys!" the short one yelled, grabbing Ben's arm.

"Oh . . . hi," said Ben with a noticeable lack of enthusiasm.

"Good stuff, right?"

It took me a moment to realize he meant the pot. "Oh . . . yeah . . . thanks, it's great."

"Nice easygoing buzz."

"Yes," I replied vacantly.

"Lonnie's cousin has grow lights in his garage."

I presumed that Lonnie was the taller one, but this was no time to inaugurate introductions. Over at the bar, Mr. Johnson was pulling on a brown leather flight jacket in preparation for takeoff. Ben noticed this, too, and signaled his distress with a not-too-subtle jerk of his head.

"So where are y'all staying?" This was the taller one, gazing pointedly at both us. "With friends or some-thin'?"

"At a motel," Ben said. "His family lives here, but we'd rather ... you know..." He let the thought evaporate, too distracted to continue. Mr. Johnson was zipping up his jacket, slapping down coins for the bartender.

The shorter one was on us now. "We've got plenty of room at the condo." He smiled luridly. "And plenty more weed."

By now Mr. Johnson was headed straight for the door.

"You know what?" Ben said. "I've gotta catch our friend before he gets away." He turned and gazed at me pointedly. "I'll be right back, honey." And he hurried toward the door, throwing me to the Christians.

"Which one is your friend?" asked the tall one.

"Uh . . . just that guy down there."

"The black one?"

"Yeah."

Ben had caught up with Mr. Johnson and they were talking. Or rather Ben was talking while Mr. Johnson listened intently. I tried to focus on the Jesus queens, I really did—since I was about to decline their offer of a bacchanal at the condo—but my mind was full of the gripping silent movie across the way.

"How do you know that guy?" the short one asked.

"Uh . . . what?" *They were leaving now, Ben and Mr. Johnson, heading out the door together.*

"That guy. How do you know him?"

"Oh, just . . . from around. He's an old friend."

"I thought you were from San Fran."

"Well, yeah, but—" I knew that Ben was just presenting our offer in a quieter place. I knew that, and I trusted him. I knew he wouldn't be snogging Mr. Johnson until I was there snogging him, too. And I knew that if Mr. Johnson proposed sex with Ben without the participation of yours truly, Ben would politely decline—and probably never tell me what the deal breaker had been. I knew all of that about my amazingly thoughtful husband, and I was still a wreck.

"So . . . does that sound like a plan?"

The Jesus queens were both blinking at me

156

expectantly, though the question had come from the shorter, brasher one.

"Uh . . . I'm sorry . . . what?"

"Coming to our place for a nightcap."

"The two of you," added the taller one.

This time their meaning was unavoidable. "Oh . . . right . . . thanks but . . . I think we're gonna turn in early tonight. Jet lag." The door was opening again. Ben stepped into a patch of light and beckoned me to join him.

"Sorry," I told the Jesus queens. "I think my honey's ready to split."

"That's too bad," said the taller one.

"Y'all take care, " I said, beating a hasty retreat.

When I reached Ben, he was grinning in sheepish apology. "Sorry," he said, pecking me on the mouth. "I figured we needed to act decisively."

"So what's the deal?" I asked.

"He's meeting us at the B&B."

"Did you tell him I'm positive?"

"Yep."

"And he's cool about . . . both of us?"

"More than cool. Said he wouldn't dream of breaking up the set."

I smiled. "Did you grab his ass?"

Ben turned Huckish on the spot. "Maybe just once."

"Hey . . . go for it."

"I grabbed it for both of us."

"Sure you did."

"I asked him not to come till eleven," Ben added. "So your pill can kick in."

"What a husband." I thought about that for a moment. "Is that what you told him?"

"Of course not."

"I wouldn't mind if you had," I said. "I'm not Viagraphobic."

Ben squinched his eyes at me. "That's not a word, is it?"

"I hope not."

"It might be one back home," Ben said. "We've been gone for almost a week."

"Yeah . . . by now there's probably a *Council* on Viagraphobia."

"Stop." Ben laughed. "You can't dis the city when you're abroad."

"Is that a rule?"

"Yes. It's like talking about her behind her back."

"Are we abroad? Is that where we are?"

"We're certainly not home," said Ben.

No, I thought. *We certainly aren't.*

13

The Chances
of This

For some reason, Ben and I both felt compelled to tidy up for Mr. Johnson. We tore through the place like dervishes, fluffing pillows and flinging socks into suitcases and rearranging toiletries around the sink. We might have been a couple of nervous hotel maids confronted with a surprise inspection from Leona Helmsley.

"You first in the shower," I said as Ben helped me fold the polyester bed cover and stash it in the closet. So he grabbed a razor and the red rubber travel douche from his shaving kit and headed for the stall. He was in there for a while—shaving his balls, I figured—so I made a mental note to do the same. If you're going to barber down there at all, you'd better be faithful about it. A little stubble may be forgivable in a marriage, but it's downright inhospitable when you're—how shall we put this?—receiving guests.

When Ben reemerged, smelling deliciously of blue malva shampoo, he was dressed in gray boxer briefs and a white V-neck T-shirt.

"Is that what you're wearing?" I asked.

He looked affronted. "What's wrong with it?"

"Nothing. Just wondering about the dress code."

Ben fondled my crotch. "Wear your sweatpants. You look hot in those."

"All righty, then." I looked around the room. "Have you seen my cock ring?"

"In the soap dish."

I swear, Mikey, you'd lose your head if it wasn't attached.

This wasn't Ben but my mother, spinning one of her golden oldies just when needed the least. I wondered if her death would finally release me from this telepathic nagging. Or if I was doomed to spend the rest of my life in Norman Bates territory.

"Better get a move on," Ben said. "He'll be here in five minutes."

But half an hour later, after I'd shaved and showered and squeezed into my finest brushed stainless-steel groin jewelry, Ben and I were still perched tentatively on the edge of the bed, awkward as wallflowers at an ROTC ball. The lamp we'd left burning to lend a sultry glow to the room was already—thanks to the Viagra—blazing with a brilliant blue-white intensity. Meanwhile, my growing hard-on was growing superfluous.

"You sure you told him the room number?"

"Absolutely."

"And he seemed . . . amenable?"

Ben was amused by my wording. "Yes, he seemed amenable."

"So . . . what? He got cold feet?"

"Maybe."

"Or maybe he just lost interest. Or got a better offer." Ben shrugged. "Who knows?"

"So what's wrong with *us*? I'd fuck us in a second." He laughed.

"I'm serious. Don't you feel abandoned?"

"It's a three-way, honey. I don't think two people can be abandoned."

"Can't they?"

"He might just be late, you know."

I looked at the clock again. "Twenty-five minutes. Only hustlers can get away with that." I considered that for a moment. "He's not a hustler, is he? You're not withholding something, are you?"

Ben turned and looked at me in amazement. "You think I bought us a hustler and didn't tell you?"

"Well . . ."

"How pathetic do you think I think we are?"

I smiled. "Some people would see that as thoughtful."

He looked at me again. "Why would you think he's a hustler, anyway?"

161

"I don't know. It sorta felt like he'd . . . targeted us. Like he'd been watching for a while before he jumped into the conversation."

"I didn't get that sense," said Ben.

"Maybe I'm wrong, then."

Ben smiled sympathetically. "Poor baby. You're disappointed."

"No," I said. "Just annoyed."

He gazed down at my tented sweatpants, then pulled down the waistband and stooped to give me a friendly lick.

"No," I said. "I don't need a mercy suck."

He looked up, chuckling. *"Mercy suck?"*

"Well . . . whatever . . ."

Undeterred, Ben got down to business.

"Mercy," I said, making him laugh with his mouth full.

And that, of course, was when Mr. Johnson knocked on the door.

I should stop calling him Mr. Johnson, I guess, since you may have figured it out by now. Ben and I certainly hadn't. To us he was still what Quentin Crisp used to call—without reference to race, of course—The Great Dark Man: a mythical (and therefore slightly two-dimensional) object of desire. Which is probably why we jumped to attention like a pair of guilty

162

schoolboys when we heard his sturdy knock at the door.

"Jesus," I murmured, tucking the incriminating evidence under the band of my sweatpants.

"Well . . . better late," said Ben, heading for the door.

"Wait!" I whispered. "Let this go down first."

"Why?"

"I don't know. It seems rude."

Ben widened his eyes at me. "Did you learn that from Miss Manners?" He reached for the doorknob, so I sank to the bed again, hiding myself in the folds of the sweatpants. This probably made me look a little grand, like some pompous old top awaiting service, but that somehow seemed preferable to greeting him upright with flag already flying.

Ben opened the door. The guy was standing there looking mortified, still wearing those camouflage fatigues. "I'm sorry, fellas."

"No sweat," said Ben. "C'mon in."

Our visitor, I noticed, shot a quick glance at Ben's boxer briefs before following him into the room. "Can we get you something to drink?" I asked, remaining graciously seated like a dowager hostess. "There's a soda machine on the landing."

"No thanks," he said.

"Did you have a hard time finding us?" I asked.

The guy just shook his head.

163

"I'm Michael," I said, finally standing at half-mast, "and this is Ben."

He shook our hands sheepishly, seeming, for some reason, far less comfortable than he had in the bar. "I'm Patreese," he said. The name was exotic enough to have rung a bell immediately—or set off a whole carillon of recognition—but it didn't.

Ben moved next to the guy and slipped an arm around his waist, as if to reassure him. I'd worried that the first sight of my sweetie with a stranger might make me squirm, but I found this gesture so gently hospitable, so typically Ben, that it actually put me more at ease. "We're glad you came," Ben said, while his other hand slipped into those high-tech fatigues to work Patreese's nipple. Patreese moaned a little, then kissed Ben voluptuously on the mouth before doing the same to me. "Y'all are sweet," he said.

Ben caught my eye with a private inaugural smile, then dropped to his knees and tugged Patreese's cock out of the fatigues. He began to rearrange the voluminous foreskin with the tip of his tongue, but I caught only the briefest glimpse of this action since Patreese had responded to it by ramming his own tongue into my mouth. It stayed there for quite a while, so warm and invasive that it actually seemed to swell like an erection. When he removed it he said, "I hope it's okay. I'm sort of a kiss pig."

164

"No problem," I said as I caught my breath.

Looking up at us, Ben removed Patreese's cock from his mouth. "No problem here, either," he reported, getting a big laugh from the troops.

Patreese suddenly seemed distracted. "I should tell you something."

I'm used to this moment arising—what gay man isn't?—so I tried to make it easier for him. "We always play safe," I said, "if you mean that you're positive."

He shook his head. "No. It's something else . . ."

We waited for the penny to drop.

". . . I do your mama's hair."

This simply did not compute.

Ben looked up at him, completely openmouthed—well, *almost* as openmouthed as he'd been a moment earlier. "What?" he murmured.

"I do his mama's hair," Patreese repeated. "At the Gospel Palms."

In this moment of raw revelation, my mind raced back to my mother's room at the rest home in Orlovista and the obvious pride she had shown in her smart new pastel do: "Patreese did it . . . my new hairdresser . . . black as the ace of spades but very talented."

Somehow I managed to keep from saying "I thought you were a woman" to a man whose proud sea horse was still prancing in the vicinity of my husband's face.

"How'd you know who we were?" I asked.

165

"Yeah," said Ben, rising to his feet in obvious fascination.

"She's got a picture in her room," Patreese said. "Y'all by a waterfall. She talks about you all the time."

Ben and I swapped dumbfounded glances.

"She said you were coming to visit, and I recognized you in the bar."

"Jesus," said Ben. "What are the chances of *this*?"

Patreese shrugged. "There's not that many bars in Orlando."

I asked the obvious question. "Why didn't you say something earlier?"

"I wanted to suck some dick," he said with a sleepy smile. "That ain't gonna happen with your mama in the conversation. She takes too much explaining."

I liked the way he nailed that down. "That's the truth," I said.

"I felt bad about it later. It wasn't very sociable."

"Oh, I don't know," Ben said.

"I almost didn't come," said Patreese. "That's why I was late. Then I thought, fuck that shit. I need a break from her, and it might as well be y'all."

Ben chuckled. "How often does she get her hair done, anyway?"

"I don't just do her hair. I do her makeup, too."

"Oh," I said. "You cover up the blue."

"It's not that blue," he said. "It's not near as bad as

she thinks it is. Somebody told her she was a blue bloater and . . . she got to worryin' about it."

Lenore, I thought. *It must have been Lenore.*

"She looks really good," I said, since it seemed to matter to him.

He nodded. "I like to work on old ladies. They appreciate it."

That was the worst possible segue for what happened next, but no one objected. Patreese knelt and nuzzled the mound of Ben's briefs, while pulling me closer by the crotch of my sweatpants. Within seconds he had us both in hand, squeezing our dicks together like an eager child introducing her Barbie dolls to each other. Then he went down on both of us, one after the other, never neglecting either for long: a symphonic performance by a true multi-instrumentalist. Ben pulled my face into his and kissed me hungrily.

In a three-way, of course, there's always the danger that someone will feel left out, but Patreese didn't let that happen. I'm pretty sure he saw Ben as the brass ring on this merry-go-round, but I never felt unwelcome on the ride. By the time we were naked on the bed and both of them (at Ben's prompting) were sucking on my chest, I was feeling so generous that, once I'd shot my load, I grabbed a condom off the bedside table and rolled it onto Patreese's cock. Ben realized this was meant for him, and gazed at me in tender appreciation

167

before grabbing a bottle of lube and going to work. He came on all fours, the little spunk bucket, never even touching himself, while Patreese was fucking him. I know because I was underneath, catching the splash and offering kisses and feeling flat-out wonderful. Patreese more or less fucked him into my arms. Ben stayed there for some time, laughing from the pleasure, his heart beating hard against my chest.

Then my cell phone rang in my suitcase. It's programmed to ring like an old forties telephone—like Barbara Stanwyck's, say, in *Sorry, Wrong, Number*—and that always lends a certain jangly melodrama to the moment.

"Leave it," said Ben from the middle of this panting stack of men.

"Good idea," I said from the bottom.

"Nobody move," said Ben.

There was a brief silence, followed by the little groan Ben makes whenever someone pulls out of him. (Or at least when I do.)

"Sorry," said Patreese.

"That's okay," said Ben.

Patreese rolled off the pile and sat on the edge of the bed, skinning the condom off his cock. Then he took it to the bathroom and flicked it into the toilet.

"What's this?" he called.

"What?" I asked.

168

"In the toilet."

"Oh," said Ben, grinning. His head was on my chest now, while his hand roamed the familiar volcanic slopes of my belly. "That's an orchid."

"I got that much," said Patreese.

"They put one there every day," Ben explained. "Sorta like a mint on the pillow. We flush it every night, but it keeps coming back."

"One of those little extra touches," I added, "that mean so very much at Inn Among the Flowers."

Patreese stared down at this deeply Floridian floral offering. "It don't look right somehow."

"I know," I said. "Especially with a condom on it."

Patreese chortled and flushed the toilet and cleaned up at the sink. When he came back to the bedroom, he started gathering up his clothes.

"Hey," I said. "Hang with us for a while." I wanted him to know he didn't have to fuck and run on our account, that we weren't that kind of couple.

"Busy day tomorrow," he said, pulling on a sock.

"Not with my mother, I hope."

He chuckled. "My other job. A bachelorette party."

Ben sat up on one elbow. "They get their hair done for that?"

"I strip for private parties," Patreese explained. "That's what *this* is for." He was stepping into his

169

fatigues now, stuffing all the goods back in. "Got a cop uniform, too."

"No shit," said Ben, apparently impressed by the rich array of employment opportunities available to a hairdresser here in the sovereign state of Disney.

Patreese grunted. "It ain't worth the bus fare half the time."

"Why not?" asked Ben.

Patreese shrugged. "I don't care *how* big your dick is—if a sister's got a plate of ribs in front of her, there ain't no way you're gonna hold her attention."

Ben and I laughed raucously.

"I'm *serious*," said Patreese, clearly tickled by our response and warming to his material. "I'm up there workin' my ass off . . . just *flangin'* my stuff around. And they're sittin' down there in their nasty-ass press-on nails, pickin' meat outta their teeth."

Ben hooted again. "Tough crowd, eh?"

"Oh, the sisters say they like the mens . . ." Patreese drew out the last word with a histrionic hiss, so we'd know it wasn't his own particular vernacular. "But they don't like the mens near as much as the mens like the mens." He was tying his bootlaces, so he finished with a punctuating yank. "They don't tip as good, either."

He came to the bed fully dressed and wriggled between us until we became his naked bookends. There was something strangely intimate and sweet about

170

holding him in his clothes. He lay there for a while, sighing a little, then kissed us on our foreheads and got up again, heading out. "Be well, my brothers," he said at the door.

"You too," we said in unison.

"Y'all make a nice couple."

"Thanks."

"I'll see you on Thursday," he said. "When we sign that thing for your mama."

It took me a while, but I gaped at him until I got it. "You're the other witness?"

Patreese nodded. "You be nice to her, you hear?"

He opened the door and left, closing it behind him.

Ben turned to me and dropped his jaw dramatically. "Jesus. What are the chances of this?"

I told him he'd said that before.

"Yeah, well . . ."

"Do you think she put him up to it?"

"Who? *Your mother?*"

"I wouldn't put it past her."

"For God's sake, Michael. We were the ones who picked *him* up!"

Were we? I wondered.

Ben rolled over and nuzzled my neck. "You ascribe way too much power to her."

Do I? I thought, staring up at the floral-patterned ceiling.

14

Her Raggedy Soul

The next morning Ben and I wolfed down a huge breakfast at the Denny's across the street. A touch of gluttony seemed a fitting follow-up to our late-night pig-out with Patreese. Besides, I rather liked the idea of ordering the Biscuit and Gravy plate in what remained of my beloved Southern homeland. Until I actually ordered it, that is.

"Will that be the *Senior* Biscuit and Gravy?"

Our waitress, a hefty young gum-chewing black woman, could easily have been one of Patreese's bachelorettes.

"No," I told her with a measured smile. "I don't think I qualify quite yet."

"How old are you?"

I hadn't been asked this in a place of business since I was seventeen, when I tried, unsuccessfully, to buy a fifth of Jack Daniel's at a liquor store across the highway from Mr. Grady's gas station. It was just as unsettling to be carded at the other end of my life, for a fucking biscuit, no less, but I answered as civilly as possible.

"I'm fifty-five."

The waitress nodded triumphantly, scribbling something on her pad, like she'd just guessed my weight at the country fair. "This is your lucky day, peaches."

Then she sashayed off, leaving me in the dust of her righteousness.

Ben picked up the big plastic menu and read the fine print. "She's right," he said. "Fifty-five and older."

I told him that was another reason not to live here.

He smiled crookedly. "I think this applies at *all* Denny's."

I took the menu from him and perused the Senior section: the Senior Omelette, the Senior Scramble, the Senior French Toast Slam. "Are the Senior meals any different from the regular ones?" I asked. "Do they come with a bib or something?"

Ben rolled his eyes at this useless display of gerontophobia. "You know," he said, "if it bothers you that much, you can always pay full price."

"It doesn't bother me," I said, laughing it off, since I was certain it didn't bother *him*. It probably turned him on, in fact, that I'd just been certified an old guy

173

by a leading family restaurant. Such is the nature of my greatest blessing. I know not to mess with it.

I reached across the table and took his hand. "That was so hot last night."

"Oh, man," said Ben, squeezing my hand.

"He was sweet, too."

Ben nodded with a sleepy smile. "Definitely the right choice."

"You'll tell me when I start looking like a silly old fool, won't you?"

"Fuck, no," said Ben.

I grinned feebly. "I didn't mean to say that out loud, actually."

"You looked like a sexy daddy to me."

Two tables away, an obese white woman stopped wiping her obese child's face long enough to stare us down. Ben smiled at her pleasantly, then returned his gaze to me, still holding my hand. "Did you ever check your cell, by the way?"

I flashed on the night before and the phone call that had come just after we had. I fished the cell phone out of my jacket and checked the readout.

"It's from Anna," I said.

"Better check it," he said.

All he meant was that Anna was old enough to require our attentiveness, but I still felt a sudden shiver of anxiety. That's usual for me when I'm away from home for any length of time whatsoever. I expect all hell to break loose.

But Anna's message was soothing: "Oh . . . uh . . . hello, dear, just sending my love. I hope you and Ben are having a lovely time. There's no need to call unless you feel like it. Everything is fine here. Do give my love to your mother. Goodbye, dear."

Sweet. Typically Anna in its gentility and thoughtfulness. Her sign-off had a finality that unsettled me, but I wrote that off to her general inexperience with leaving voice messages. On the other hand, when you're eighty-five years old, maybe you know to treat every goodbye as potentially your last. Maybe you're just more *conscious* by then.

It was too early to return her call, so I waited until mid-morning, when Ben was doing his yoga down in the motel's workout room. She answered on the first ring.

"Madrigal."

"It's me, Anna."

"Oh . . . dear. How lovely."

"It's good to hear you, too."

"I hope I didn't call at an inconvenient time last night."

"Not at all." I smiled to myself when I said that, but I meant it just the same. More than anything, sex with Patreese had been a well-deserved escape from the bullshit of the biologicals, so it struck me as sort of charming, really, that Anna's good wishes had reached us—shall we say?—post-climactically. It was like a transcontinental blessing.

"How is your mother doing?" she asked.

"No better," I told her, "but no worse."

"Ah . . . well."

"She seems to be in a good place, though. The home, I mean. Christian as all hell, but what can you do?"

"What *does* she do?" asked Anna.

"Not much," I said. "There's a man who comes by regularly to do her hair and makeup."

"Well, that's good," said Anna. "I know that's important to her." *How* she knew this, I couldn't tell you, given how little time she'd spent with Mama all those years ago. Maybe she just meant that women in general—and those who've successfully achieved womanhood—often appreciate the value of hair and makeup.

"He's a sweet guy," I said. "And when he's not doing hair, he strips."

Anna hesitated for a moment. "I take it you don't mean floors."

I laughed. "He gets nekkid for the ladies."

"Well, that must be a hit at the home."

I laughed. "It's just how he moonlights . . . far as I know."

"What a pity. How's the rest of the family?"

"Pretty much the same. My brother's still bragging about his boats. My sister-in-law's still heavy into her Jesus puppets."

She uttered a tolerant sigh. "Well, to each his own, dear. Have they been sweet to Ben?"

"Everybody's sweet to Ben."

"I suppose you're right," she said.

"My seven-year-old great-nephew has a huge crush on him."

"Indeed?"

"It's platonic," I told her, "but the kid is *definitely* a nancy boy."

Anna paused for a moment. "Isn't seven a little early to know who you are?"

"It wasn't for me," I said.

She took that in for a moment. "No," she said softly, "not for me, either."

"I'm worried about him," I told her. "I think his grandfather's on to him. He's been making noises about boot camp."

"*Boot camp?* For a seven-year-old?"

"It's something they saw on *Maury*."

"On *what*?"

"A TV show. Never mind. I think my brother was just thumping his chest."

Anna's wheels were already turning. "Get them to send him out here for the summer."

177

I chuckled. "They'd sooner send him to Afghanistan."

"No . . . really, dear . . . we could take him to the new museum. And Crissy Field . . . and the Exploratorium. The redwoods, for heaven's sake."

Anna hadn't had a kid to raise since Shawna (unless you count the thirty years she's been raising me), so it was touching to see how quickly she could still embrace her inner landlady. I loved the thought of nellie little Sumter basking in her all-forgiving aura, but she and I both knew she didn't have the strength for it.

"Have you been keeping busy?" I asked.

"*Keeping* busy? That's a terrible thing to ask someone."

"Sorry."

"Only the bored keep busy. I am busy."

"I have no doubt of that."

"Brian and Shawna took me to see *The Black Rider* the other night."

"What's that?"

"A musical. Sort of. Tom Waits and William Burroughs, if you can imagine. Tuesday is acid night, apparently. The kids get high and take over the first six rows."

"And what decade was this?"

Anna giggled. "I know . . . *plus ça change*, eh?"

I could feel her glow warming me across the miles. It

178

made me get serious for a moment. "You're doin' okay, though, aren't you?"

"Of course, dear."

"We'll be home in a few days. You can take *me* to the museum."

"It's a date," she said. "Then we'll get me a cat."

"Beg pardon, ma'am?"

"I'd like to go to the SPCA and adopt a beat-up old cat."

I smiled. "Very well."

"Someone to sit in the sun with me. Who doesn't want to go anywhere."

I knew this wasn't a veiled plea for sympathy. Anna doesn't veil anything beyond her head and an occasional lampshade. She would have been mortified, in fact, to know she'd come off as anything less than blithely self-contained.

But she did, somehow; somehow she sounded sad.

She had a cat when I met her. An old tiger tabby named Boris that prowled the mossy boardwalks of 28 Barbary Lane, slipping into windows at will. He didn't live with Anna—or anyone else, for that matter—but she considered him her own. She was in her mid-fifties then and already *grandedame*-ing it in kimonos with a houseful of tenants who felt privileged to live under her spell. I was one of them, of course. Another was Anna's biological daughter, the child left behind by—as Anna put it—the "lesser man" she used to be. Mona was restless and loving and funny and utterly impossible sometimes. She moved to England early in the reign of Princess Di and married a queer lord so he could get a green card and wag weenie in San Francisco. Whereupon Mona—well, Lady Mona, technically— began to take in lodgers at the rundown country house left behind by the weenie-wagging lord. The place just climbed into her raggedy soul. At forty she adopted a teenager of Aboriginal descent and decided to stay for good.

Having lost her daughter to another country, Anna resigned herself to a life of vacations. I went over there a few times myself, since Mona and I had always been close. (We had roomed together once, and she had been my first lesbian fag hag.) When I saw her ensconced at Easley House, I realized how perfectly it suited her, and that somehow helped to shrink the planet she had put between us. Back in the city, I could still picture her clomping around in her wellies as she collected rent from the villagers. Or serving tea and shortbread in the Great Hall to goggle-eyed tourists from Texas. She had followed in her father's footsteps, our Mona, becoming a landlady *extraordinaire*.

I should have been better about keeping in touch, but I've never been a regular letter writer. Anna, of course, remained faithful in that regard, filling page after page of flimsy blue stationery with spidery lavender handwriting. When email came along a decade later, I mended my neglectful ways and began regular correspondence with hasbian@ easleyhouse.co.uk, a handle Mona devised to suggest a lesbian who'd lately been straying with men. This was true only in the sense that once on Guy Fawke's Day she'd gotten loaded on Quaaludes (you can still get them in Switzerland—who knew?) and fucked her stonemason, a guy she claimed looked "too much like Brad Pitt to pass up." The hasbian label worked wonders, though. Half the dykes in the Cotswolds, many bearing pies and garden cuttings, showed up on Mona's doorstep in a fevered effort to return her to the labial fold. "Got me laid for weeks," she told me triumphantly.

There were live-in girlfriends from time to time, but none lasted very long. Mona was way too independent, and her life was full. It was Wilfred, Mona's adopted son, who called me with the news. He hated asking this, he said, but it would probably be better if someone told Anna in person. So one warm October afternoon, after brunch in the Castro, I walked her back to the Duboce Triangle and told her that her daughter, my oldest friend, had been undergoing treatment for breast cancer for the past two years but didn't want us to "make a big fuss about it." The late delivery of this bombshell angered Anna as much as it had me, and we agreed that we damn well would make a fuss about it if we wanted. Indignation had been our only shield against the nasty bitch slap of reality.

Anna had about five weeks with Mona; I was allotted the last five days, maybe because she knew me well. When I arrived in England, she was flying on morphine, so it went better than I'd imagined. She told me to fuck myself more than once, and said it with a smile on her face. It was quality time, as they say, which for Mona meant ranting and reminiscing and joking about Bill Clinton's dick. Several years later, when those planes hit the Twin Towers, I remember thinking how shrewdly she had timed her exit. Her big wounded hippie heart would not have prospered in this cold new climate.

She'd been gone for almost eight years, and her surviving parent wanted a cat.

Someone to sit in the sun with me. Who doesn't want to go anywhere.

15

Word One

On Thursday morning Ben holed up at Inn Among the Flowers with his laptop and a backlog of furniture orders, so I could be alone with Mama before signing the papers. When I arrived at the Gospel Palms, she was propped up in bed watching Bill O'Reilly on a TV set bolted to the ceiling. Her makeup seemed fresh, so I figured Patreese had already made his rounds. I wondered if he'd talked about meeting me and Ben, and, if so, how free he'd been with the details. He was a hairdresser, after all.

"Where's your friend?" Mama asked, meaning Ben.

I sat on the edge of the bed and looked at the floor. "He's my husband, Mama."

She scowled at me.

"Irwin told you that, didn't he? That we got married a few years ago."

A long, brooding silence and then: "Don't be like that, Mikey."

All I could do was smile. Mama had been telling me not to be like that as long as I could remember. "All right. I won't be like anything."

She fussed with the tiny blue curls around her temples. "What do you ... ssss ... want with a husband, anyway?"

I laughed.

"They're nothin' but heartache," she added.

I scoured my mother's face for clues to her state of mind. In half a century of knowing this woman I'd never heard her speak a word against my father. I decided to be bold in return. "Why didn't you leave him, Mama?"

She recoiled visibly. "Watch your mouth, son."

"I mean it. Why didn't you?"

She fidgeted with the hem of the sheet. "I was going to, believe me."

"And?"

She shrugged her shoulders. "He died."

I suppressed a smile; then I realized she found this funny herself.

"I reckon he saw it comin'," she added dryly.

Papa had died of colon cancer in 1987—not that long ago in the general scheme of things. "You never considered it before then?" I asked.

184

Her lower lip stiffened. "I did more than . . . ssss . . . consider it."

"You *left* him, you mean?"

She grunted and looked up at the big white face of Bill O'Reilly, hovering above us like a hot-air balloon. I found his aura of white-guy entitlement especially intolerable at that moment, so I reached for Mama's clicker and turned him off.

"I was watchin' that," Mama said.

"When did you leave Papa?" I asked.

She sighed in the same put-upon way she used to sigh when I was twelve and asked her if she'd seen my neckerchief slide or knew where Irwin had left my bike. "Remember the summer . . . ssss . . . we drove you boys up to . . . ssss . . . Camp Hemlock?"

"Yeah."

"I left him on the way home. After we dropped y'all off."

"*How?* How did you leave him?"

"On the side of the road."

"You're shitting me."

Mama, I have to say, looked a wee bit proud of herself. "He stopped to get a Nehi soda . . . ssss . . . and I just drove off and left him."

I was grinning shamelessly. "I take it you went back for him."

"I did not," she said, smoothing the sheets. "I went to

185

the Baptist retreat . . . ssss . . . at Blowing Rock. I didn't get home for ten days."

"Papa never told me this."

She twisted her lips into a small, triumphant smile. "He was a proud man."

"How did he get home?"

She shrugged. "Never told me."

"Did he have to cook for himself?"

"I reckon."

"Musta bought Moon Pies from ol' Drool Rag."

She let that go without a smile. "I needed some private time with the Lord . . . ssss . . . and it never cost Papa a cent."

"How'd you manage that?"

"Green Stamps," she said proudly.

"*Green Stamps?*"

"From the . . . ssss . . . Piggly Wiggly."

Green Stamps were Mama's personal currency back then. She'd sit in front of the TV at night with a wet sponge and fill up whole booklets with them, later redeeming them for toasters and curtains and, once, even an Electrolux vacuum cleaner. They offered her the illusion of wealth, since all she ever *really* bought were groceries.

I still didn't get it. "The Baptist retreat took Green Stamps?"

She shook her head. "I traded 'em in for a kitchenette

186

set . . . ssss . . . and sold it to Mee-Maw." Mee-Maw was my grandmother, my mother's mother, who died in a car wreck in South Carolina a few years before Mama joined the Anita Bryant Crusade.

"So Mee-Maw was in on this?"

"Oh, no . . . ssss . . . I didn't tell a soul."

"Nice work, Mama."

"Don't you tease me. "

"I'm not," I said. "I mean it."

"Turn the TV . . . ssss . . . back on."

"No. I want to talk about the . . . power of attorney . . . thing."

She arranged her hands in front of her, one over the other, the way a cat does. "All right, then . . . ssss . . . talk."

"I'm just . . . I just want to make sure it's what you really want."

"You're hearin' it . . . ssss . . . from the horse's mouth."

"All right, then."

"I wanna go . . .. ssss . . . when the Lord calls me. When he takes . . . ssss . . . my last breath. I don't wanna lie here like a lump on some infernal . . . ssss . . . machine with Lenore praying over me . . . ssss . . . you hear?"

"Yes, ma'am."

"And those puppets better not come around after I've passed."

Smiling, I took her hand in mind. "I'll do my best."

"You don't have to be here," she said. "I . . . ssss . . . didn't mean that."

"I want to, Mama . . . if I can."

She shook her head emphatically, withdrawing her hand. "This is between . . . ssss . . . me and the Lord, Mikey."

She wasn't trying to be brave; she meant it. The Lord was the only man who'd never let her down. He was not her angry, bullying husband or her unrepentant homosexual son or even her good son, the one who worked so hard to be a Christian but was hopelessly indentured to a woman Mama despised. As long ago as Blowing Rock the Lord could be counted upon to be exactly what Mama needed, when Mama needed it.

There was no point in wasting time with the others.

The signing process was surprisingly quick. Ben arrived in a taxi at noon and met the lawyer in the lobby. (Mama had chosen this guy from the Yellow Pages, reasoning that someone named Joel Bernstein wasn't likely to know anyone in Lenore and Irwin's crowd.) When Patreese arrived, resplendent in a crisp pink shirt and gray tie, the three of them joined me in Mama's room. We looked more like a caucus at an ACLU convention than the hastily assembled support group of a dying Christian lady.

188

Patreese pulled me and Ben into a huddle while the lawyer was conferring with Mama. "Y'all doin' all right?" he whispered.

"Pretty good," I said.

"I came in this morning," Patreese said. "She wanted to look pretty for y'all."

"Thanks," I said. "I noticed."

"I told her we bumped into each other."

Ben smirked. "One way of putting it."

Patreese rubbed my back with a big warm palm, while doing the same to Ben. For a moment we were a threesome again, and it was oddly reassuring.

I glanced toward the door. "What if we have visitors?"

Patreese frowned. "You mean the puppet lady?"

Ben stifled a giggle.

"Don't sweat it," said Patreese. "Mohammed's looking out for us."

I almost took this as a declaration of faith, considering Patreese's less-than-predictable profile, but stripper/hairdresser/Muslim seemed like one note too many.

Ben caught my confusion. "Mohammed's the guy at the desk," he said.

When we were done with the signing, Mama dismissed the lawyer, kissed me goodbye with brisk efficiency, and declared her need for a nap, thereby banishing the three of us to the Starbucks across the street. (Mr. Bernstein had to be in court.)

"Are y'all still headin' home tomorrow?" Patreese asked.

"Yeah," I replied, feeling the strangest mixture of relief and guilt. "I really gotta get back to work."

"I'll keep an eye on her for you."

I told him that would be wonderful and wrote down our phone number and email address on a napkin. "Don't get that mixed up," I said, "with all the *other* ones you get."

Patreese lowered his eyelids playfully. "Listen here," he said. "I don't mess around with just any ol' coupla white boys."

I thought that was a charming thing to say. "Hang on to your copy of the document," I told him. "Just in case my sister-in-law gives you any shit."

"Don't you worry about that," said Patreese. "I got the goods on *her*."

This puzzled me. "What do you mean?"

"Just don't you worry."

Ben smiled impishly. "Did you strip for her or something?"

"Oh Lord, honey," Patreese replied. "She wishes."

That evening Lenore fixed dinner for us at the house. Sumter was there as well, still buzzing from a puppet show with his grandmother at a Christian academy in Pine Castle. It was a pleasant enough gathering, since we stayed off the hard stuff—by which I mean politics, religion, and sexuality—and my brother, touchingly, worked hard to support the illusion of a cozy family reunion. While Lenore was stacking the dishes and Sumter was watching *American Idol* with Ben, Irwin pulled me aside with a wink.

"Come sit in the boat with me."

"You're kidding."

"Nah ... c'mon ... it's a nice night. The kids are watching TV."

This was another cradle-robbing crack, but I let it go with a curdled smile.

"C'mon," said Irwin, shoving me toward the latter-day ark parked in his driveway.

We mounted the trailer and sat side by side in the padded seats, staring out at a sprinkling of stars and the brutal halogen streetlight across the cul-de-sac. Irwin looked furtively from side to side, then toward the living room window, before taking a flask from under the seat and holding it out to me. "Not a goddamn word," he said.

"What is it?"

"Glenfiddich."

To me, drinking scotch is reminiscent of sucking on pennies, but Irwin had just risked hellfire two times over—drinking *and* cussing—in the name of brotherly bonding. The least I could do was recognize the gesture, so I took a swig from the flask and made an appreciative hissing noise. Irwin took a bigger swig, then put the flask away.

We sat for a while in silence while a dog barked sporadically in the distance.

"Too bad Papa's not here," said Irwin.

"Is it?"

"C'mon, bro."

I tried to find a way to sound less harsh. Like a lot of straight guys, Irwin had concocted myths of his father's greatness out of pure animal need and one too many viewings of *Field of Dreams*. "I think we experienced him differently," I said.

"Remember when we were little, though? That summer he taught us to do sailor knots?"

"I remember how much he yelled when we got them wrong."

"I know he could be an ornery old cuss."

"Ornery?" I turned to face him. "Walter Brennan was ornery. Papa was flat-out mean. Papa was . . . Dick Fucking Cheney."

Irwin gaped at me. "Who's Walter Brennan?"

"You know . . . on *The Real McCoys* . . . Grandpappy Amos." I sang some of the theme song for him. " 'From West Virginny they came to stay, in sunny Cali-For-Nye-Ay.' "

"Oh, yeah. The old guy with the limp."

"He was probably our age then," I said darkly. "The age we are now."

"Nah." Irwin considered that for a moment. "You think?"

"A few years older maybe. Not much."

"Jesus."

The word hung there between us like a mist. Poor ol' Irwin was probably wondering if he'd blown his monthly allowance of blasphemies.

"I know it couldna been easy for you," he said at last. "With your lifestyle and all. Papa could be hard sometimes."

"He was hard on you, too." I remember well how the old man had screamed and yelled and threatened permanent disownment during Irwin's bad-boy days.

"Maybe a little," said my brother.

"He was even harder on Mama. She tried to leave him twice."

Irwin turned and blinked at me. "*When?*"

"The first time . . . when you and I were at Camp Hemlock. She holed up at the Baptist retreat. And she was on the verge of leaving him just before he died."

Irwin's mouth was hanging wide open. "How do you know this?"

I shrugged. "She told me herself. This morning."

"This is nuts."

193

Another shrug. To me it was the sanest thing Mama had ever done.

"No," said Irwin. "I mean, she woulda said something to Lenore. We were livin' across the road when Papa died. Mama and Lenore were really tight."

That's true, I thought. They were praying for Mama's queer son, who was dying of a biblical plague out there in sunny Cali-For-Nye-Ay.

"I'm just telling you what she said," I murmured.

"Anyway . . . why would she just up and leave him? He had cancer."

"Yeah . . . but he'd had the operation a while back . . . and everybody thought he was getting better. Even Papa said he was back in fighting form."

Irwin frowned. "But why would she . . . ? Do you think something *happened*?"

"A wasted lifetime, I'd say. Taking a rough guess."

Irwin was aghast. "I never heard one word about this."

He looked so rattled that I put my hand on his knee in a way-too-awkward gesture of comfort. "She's ready to go, Irwin. That tends to loosen people's tongues."

He nodded numbly. We just sat there for a while, listening to that barking dog and the distant joyful noise of Ben and Sumter, yelling out their choices for American Idol. The kids were watching TV all right, and the grown-ups were facing the facts.

I took my hand off Irwin's knee. "I guess she just needed to tell us."

"She didn't tell *us*," Irwin said bitterly. "She told *you*."

I could understand how he might be hurt. He and Lenore had spent years caring for Mama, and she'd repaid them by saving her biggest secret for the absentee son from the West. For a moment I considered telling Irwin about Mama's fears of having to live on a respirator—and the obvious wedge that had driven between her and Lenore—but I knew that would open a whole new can of worms. It was best to just leave it alone.

"Mama's no dummy," I said. "I'm sure she knew that I'd tell you."

16

Practical
Considerations

Back in San Francisco, we hit the ground running. Ben joined his boss and two other craftsmen at the Concourse Exhibition Center, where they were setting up for a big furniture show. Meanwhile, Jake and I were up in Pacific Heights at the French Consulate, replacing the dead portions of a boxwood hedge. This was my second job at the consulate, and I loved working there, gardening for the government that had seriously pissed off Bush by declining his war.

Consulates aren't my usual thing. I was referred to the job by someone I've known for years, a socialite named D'orothea (the apostrophe was added during her modeling days) who ran a stylish restaurant here in the late eighties. She and her wife, DeDe, knew someone on a committee at the consulate, so I was called in at the last minute to gussy the place up for a garden party. They must have liked us, because there we were again, leaning on our pickaxes in the foggy sunshine. A nice lady from the staff who looked a little like Leslie Caron (the current version) had just handed us a tray of leftover goodies.

"Mmm," said Jake, lifting an éclair. "Freedom pastries." He's a dry little dude, but every now and then he fires off a good one.

Chuckling, I reached for a *pain au chocolat*. "You should take some back to your beau."

Jake looked at me with a cheek full of pastry. "My *beau*?"

"Fuck off. I've been in the South."

"Orlando's not the South."

"A lot you know."

"And Connor's not my anything. We've only had a couple o' dates."

"Connor, eh?" The new . . . whatever . . . had surfaced while I was away, but this was the first time I'd heard his name. I knew only that Jake had met the guy at Lazy Bear, the big gay shindig up at the river. They had taken a walk in the redwoods and talked about global warming. The second date, presumably, had been back in the city.

"It's no biggie," said Jake. "It won't go anywhere."

"Why not? He's gay, right?"

He nodded.

"Does he know the score about you?"

"Oh, yeah."

"And he's cool about it?"

Another nod. "Maybe a little too."

"What do you mean?"

Jake turned over a bucket and sat on it, his hands dangling disconsolately between his knees. "Ever heard of Buck Angel?"

I thought for a moment. "A country singer, right?"

Jake shook his head. "A transman porn star. An FTM."

It took a while to wrap my head around that. "Okay."

"Connor's totally hot for him."

"Hot for him in real life? Or just hot for his movies?"

"His movies," said Jake, sounding a little testy.

I just didn't get it. If Jake, an FTM himself, had a thing for a guy who liked FTM porn stars, what the hell was the problem? It looked like smooth sailing to me.

"Help me out here," I said.

Jake sighed and looked up from his dangling hands. "He's real proud of his pussy, you know."

"*Connor?*"

"No . . . doofus. Buck Angel."

"Okay . . . thanks . . . keep going."

"He calls himself 'a real man with a real pussy.' It's part of his whole macho image. He flaunts it."

The light began to dawn. I remembered the night

Jake and I hooked up at the Lone Star and how utterly alienated he had seemed from the plumbing he was born with. "Don't worry," he'd said. "I'll keep my pants on. I don't like that thing any more than you do." But Connor, apparently, was attracted to Buck Angel, at least in part, *because* of his vagina and the immense pride he took in it. And there, as they say, was the rub.

"So Connor . . ." I began.

". . . wants to fuck me," said Jake.

"Okay."

"No . . . it's not okay. I don't wanna get fucked." Jake gave me a bleak little smile. "At least not *there*."

"Gotcha."

"What should I do, boss?"

"Have another éclair," I said.

I could hardly wait to get home that night to Google Buck Angel. I found a video clip that featured him in a witty scene at a laundromat. He was buff and tattooed, a completely convincing biker dude with a shaved head and a red mustache, and he was slowly feeding his clothes to a washing machine while a trio of beautiful women ogled him delightedly. When he was totally naked, he sat down to read a newspaper, so the women leaned closer to catch a glimpse of what lay beneath. It was a vagina all right.

I was cruising a gallery of still photos when Ben

ambled into the office with a mug of tea and looked at the screen. "Is that him?" he asked, leaning forward.

"That's him."

"Fuck. Look at his pecs."

"I know. And check out the ass. He's got those little dents like you do."

"Is there a frontal shot?"

"Oh, yeah." I found it for him.

"Jesus."

"Shaved and everything," I said.

"You know what?" said Ben. "That's fucking hot."

I shot him a look.

"I'm serious."

"I can see that."

"It's a little . . . unsettling, but . . . under the right circumstances . . ."

"I swear," I muttered. "You young people today."

I was joking, but not really. The world is changing way too fast for me with its Podcasts and pregnant strippers and macho manginas. No sooner have I mastered one set of directions than another comes along to replace it. It's getting harder and harder to keep up with what's going down. My only solace lies in something Anna once told me:

"You don't have to keep up, dear. You just have to keep open."

* * *

200

I saw Anna two days later, when the weekend rolled around. I picked her up at the apartment and drove her to the SPCA on Sixteenth Street in search of the cat she wanted. The adoption center there is a well-designed modern facility that's considered a model for the rest of the country. It's what they call a "no kill" shelter, where animals are guaranteed a home until they're adopted. The dogs live on "Lassie Lane," each in his own sunny private apartment. They have couches, potted plants, and TVs playing cat videos. The cats have a separate "condo" facility, complete with aquariums and picture windows, so they can stare at the birds outside. I went there once between marriages, five or six years ago, thinking that a pet might make a decent stand-in for a husband. As I wandered the halls, peering through doors at recumbent wretches with longing in their eyes, I might have been back at the Ritch Street Baths, where love (or at least a warm body) was potentially waiting around the corner.

You just had to keep looking.

"Where do these kitties come from?" Anna was standing in one of the cat condos, stroking a handsome longhaired domestic on a perch.

"From Animal Control, I think. They find the ones that are adoptable."

"What about the unadoptable?"

I shrugged. "I guess they don't make it here."

"Where is Animal Control?" she asked.

It was barely a block away, so we were there in a matter of minutes. This was a city-run operation, the front line of animal rescue, and the difference was palpable. The rooms were more like cells than condos, and some of the animals were howling in panic and confusion. "This is more like it," said Anna, surveying the scene.

She found a small black cat she liked: a timid war-torn creature with a notch in its ear. A sturdy lesbian staffer let us into the room, where Anna sat in a folding chair and waited for the cat to approach her. It took a while, but it happened. The cat rubbed against Anna's leg, emitting a feeble throaty noise that was closer to "ack" than "meow." Satisfied, it sprang into her velvet lap and curled up to the size of a dinner plate.

"She fits," said Anna, smiling at the staffer.

"We call her Squeaker," the staffer said. "For obvious reasons."

Anna nodded.

"You could name her what you want, of course."

Anna rubbed the cat's chin with her forefinger.

"She's older than the others," the staffer added. "Will that be a problem?"

"It hasn't been for me," said Anna.

She looked up at me warmly. "Let's take her home."

By the time we'd arrived at Anna's apartment, heavily

laden with pet paraphernalia, she had already named the cat Ninotchka. She'd first seen the film as a gender-confused nineteen-year-old and since then had nursed a serious thing for Garbo. "We can call her Notch for short," she said, "after her most distinctive feature."

We didn't call her *anything* for a while, since she crawled under Anna's ancestral oak armoire and refused to come out. All that remained of her was a tiny disembodied voice going "ack" from time to time, like a cricket stranded in the woodwork.

"She's just getting her bearings," Anna said blithely as she poured me a glass of sherry at the kitchen table. Her hand, I noticed, was shaking a little.

"Can I help with that?" I asked.

"What's the matter? Afraid I'll spill on you?"

I smiled at her as she poured her own drink.

"A toast to Ninotchka," she said, lifting her glass.

I clinked my glass against hers. "Wherever she may be."

"And listen to me, dear: If I die before she does, she's not to go back to the shelter."

I admit I was rattled by that. "Well, " I said, "aren't we melodramatic this afternoon?"

"It's a practical consideration, dear. Don't be silly. You just never know."

No, you don't, do you? I was thinking of dear, departed Harry, the poodle I thought would surely survive me.

Or other positive guys who maxed out their credit cards, counting on death to cut them a deal, but ending up broke and alive. Not to mention the virus-free friends who've recently dropped dead of heart attacks. The end can come—or not come—to anyone at anytime, and no one knew that better than Anna. Her mother had died at ninety-something, still running a brothel in Nevada; her daughter hadn't made it far past fifty. Assumptions of *any* kind are a luxury we can't afford.

"All right," I said. "If that happens . . . we'll take her."

She patted my hand in gratitude.

"You're welcome," I said. "I'm sure we've got *something* she can live under."

Anna glanced toward the armoire. "Careful, dear. She can hear you."

Around twilight Jake showed up, letting himself into Anna's flat with the key she had given him. He'd brought her a bag of persimmons from the Farmers Market and a ridiculously large block of toilet paper from CostCo. He stayed for a few minutes in hopes of meeting Ninotchka, but the cat, not unlike Garbo herself, wanted to be alone.

When Jake headed back to his own flat, Anna turned to me with a gleam in her eye that I'd come to recognize over the years. "He's seeing someone, you know."

"I know," I said evenly.

"What's the matter?" she asked, reading my expression.

I explained—perhaps a little too delicately, considering the audience—that Jake was not as comfortable with his "birth genitals" as his boyfriend wanted him to be.

"I thought his boyfriend was gay," said Anna.

"He is. And he relates to Jake as a guy. He just likes the idea of . . ."

"A vagina," said Anna. "You can say it, dear."

Anna had become too much of a parent for me to discuss this issue with any degree of nonchalance. "Jake says he can't relate to his vagina, that it's basically . . . a foreign object to him. To use it having sex with his boyfriend would be like . . . denying his essential masculinity. If you follow me." I smiled at her helplessly. "*Are* you following me?"

"I think so, yes."

"Was it like that for you?"

"Like what, dear?"

"Did you feel that way about your penis?"

"Well," said Anna, widening her eyes above the rim of her sherry glass, "let's just say I wasn't especially attached to it."

I smiled, relieved that she'd lightened the moment.

"You know, dear, some kids today are perfectly content to do without the surgery. They figure that gender is mostly in the head anyway, so why tamper with the parts that are specifically designed for pleasure? Why not let your head have the last word and leave your groin to enjoy itself? That way ... if you were born female, say, like Jake ... you don't end up with ... you know ... some unfortunate, unfeeling—"

"Frankenpecker."

Anna blinked at me in mild horror.

"That's Jake's term, not mine."

"The point is, dear ... to me it wasn't about sex or pleasure or any of those lovely things. It was about identity. And completion. I couldn't feel complete with what I'd been given. It just wasn't possible. I imagine Jake feels the same way."

"But Jake doesn't *want* the surgery," I pointed out. "He wants to ignore that part of himself completely. Doesn't that seem like a waste to you?"

She shrugged. "We're not Jake, are we?"

I took a sip of my sherry and stared out at the growing gloom, the darkening green of the sycamore trees. We were so quiet for a while that I could hear Anna's mantel clock ticking in the other room, and, outside, the sound of children laughing in the street. There were more of them than ever in the Castro these days; the landscape was forever reshaping itself.

"So," said Anna, suddenly chipper. "When did gay men start liking vaginas?"

17

The Cave

My buddy Brian at the nursery has such a passion for Native Americana that he's made a ritual of searching for a local landmark called Ishi's Cave. He takes the N Judah streetcar to Cole Valley, stocks up on trail mix at Whole Foods, and climbs the winding streets above the medical center until he comes to the edge of a forest. Strictly speaking, it's not really a forest, just a big grove of eucalyptus trees planted by schoolchildren one Arbor Day in the late nineteenth century. But somewhere on the slopes of this city canyon lies a cave—no bigger than an igloo—that once sheltered the last Stone Age man in America.

Or so Brian believes.

I have my doubts about this, having joined Brian on one of his many futile expeditions. I think the cave is largely his excuse for telling Ishi's story, which is all the more haunting because it's a matter of historical record. Ishi, as you may know, was the last of his tribe. He lost his entire family to bounty hunters, then stumbled out of his remote California valley, sick with loneliness and grief, throwing himself on the mercy of the white man. This was 1911. There were trains and telephones and automobiles in Ishi's scary new world. He was taken to San Francisco, where a kindly professor made him an exhibit at the anthropology museum. There he became a global celebrity; hoards of sightseers swarmed to the museum every Sunday to watch "the wild man" carve arrowheads and string bows. Ishi, obligingly, would sweep the floor afterward, and generally tidy up the place, then sleep in a small storeroom on the premises, not far from the reassembled bones of his ancestors. When the crowds got too much for him, he took to climbing the hill above the museum and sitting alone in a cave—*that* cave—as if to connect with the world he had lost forever.

The part about the cave is more local legend than established fact—a little too New Age-y romantic to be trusted. But it's comforting to think that Ishi *might* have found such a refuge, however briefly. He died of tuberculosis five years after entering the modern world. The professor had promised his friend not to perform an autopsy (that procedure being contrary to native beliefs), but the professor was in Europe when Ishi died and had apparently neglected to leave instructions. Ishi's brain was removed and shipped away for research. Its whereabouts remained a mystery until the end of the century when it was found floating in formaldehyde at a Smithsonian Institution warehouse in Maryland. After Indian activists lobbied fiercely for the brain's return, it was finally laid to rest in the foothills of Mount Lassen, the homeland of Ishi's people.

The burial spot, understandably, remains a secret.

"Okay," said Brian, apropos of nothing, "this time I got it nailed."

We were at the nursery—a week after I got home from Florida—and he was helping me load an especially weighty laburnum into my truck.

"Are we speaking of a lady?" I asked.

"Nah, man. Ishi's cave."

"That was my second guess."

Brian gave the laburnum a final shove, then collapsed on the tailgate, gasping from the effort. "Seriously. I met this old hippie who says he stayed there overnight at the Winter Solstice."

"No shit?" I sat next to him, brushing the burlap dirt off my hands. "Did he say what he was on?"

"Okay, fuck it. I'll go on my own."

"You're going back *again*?"

209

"I'm telling you, Michael, I know where it is now. I've been looking too low down. It's up near the rim of the canyon. Not that far from the road."

"Where did you meet this guy?"

"He was blogging about it."

Blogging about Ishi.

"He wouldn't get specific with me," Brian added, "but he mentioned enough landmarks that I got a pretty good idea where it is."

There was this goofball quixotic gleam in my old friend's eye that I've always found hard to resist. And given how little time I'd spent with him since meeting Ben, I couldn't see the harm in tromping through that damned forest one more time.

I asked him when he wanted to do it.

"I dunno. Sometime in the next week or so. I wanna show it to Shawna." He smiled sheepishly, rubbing his palm on the back of his neck, like an old lion with a pebble stuck in his paw. "I want her to see her old man's not a total flake."

Shawna had grown up on the Ishi story, but, like me, had grown jaundiced about that cave. I knew she'd be kind, whatever the outcome, but it made me nervous that Brian was banking so much on this Tom Sawyer fantasy of Injun Joe's Cave.

"Maybe we should find it first," I suggested.

He seemed to catch my drift and didn't take

issue with it. "What's a good day for you?" he asked.

"How about Thursday. I've got a client in Parnassus Heights. It's easy to get to the woods from there."

"Cool," said Brian, hopping off the tailgate.

When I was behind the wheel with the engine running, he leaned down for a final word. "Shawna's moving to New York, by the way."

Brian's daughter, as you know, had already shared that information with me, but I thought it better to play dumb. "No kidding?"

"Déjà vu, eh?"

He meant his ex-wife, the one who'd left him—left both of us, really—all those years ago.

"It's not the same thing," I told him.

"No," he said quietly, "you're right." He whacked the side of the truck as if sending a horse on its way. "Give my love to the hubby."

Two days later, when Brian met me at my client's house, he was decked out in cords and a multipocketed canvas jacket that gave him a semi-safari look. He'd brought with him a couple of rustic walking sticks, still golden with shellac, that he and Shawna had bought years earlier in a souvenir shop outside of Yosemite. Seeing me hunkered there in the rose bed, he held the sticks aloft and shook them like spears.

"Cave ho!" he hollered.

211

And I said, "Who you callin' a ho?"

He laughed and turned to my assistant. "How's it goin', Jake?"

"No complaints," said Jake.

"Awriiight," said Brian.

(I can't help but notice that Brian acts a little bit butcher with Jake than he does with me. Outnumbered by women and queers in the family circle, he seems to welcome the chance to engage, unapologetically, in a little masculine folderol.)

I grabbed my knapsack and turned to Jake. "I'll be back in an hour or two. Take your lunch break whenever you want."

"No sweat, boss."

The edge of the forest was four houses away, so we were there almost instantly, peering down into the gloom of the chasm. A week of hot weather had finally summoned the fog from the ocean, turning the ivy-hung eucalypts into a blurry old black-and-white movie. Amazing as it may seem, we weren't far from the geographical center of the city.

I have to admit, those walking sticks proved useful. I'd forgotten how steep the slope was at this entrance of the forest. There was a crude trail, but it was narrow and crumbly, weaving through a nasty barbed-wire tangle of blackberries. Here and there, amid the thorns, late-blooming calla lilies poked toward the sky, but since I was playing Lewis to Brian's Clark, I resisted the urge to do my Katharine Hepburn impersonation.

"It's hard to believe this used to be a sand dune," I said.

"It did?" said Brian.

"All the way to the ocean. Old Man Sutro bought up this half of town with the money he made in the Comstock Lode. He wanted to call this Mount Sutro, but that didn't work too good for a sand dune, so . . . he brought the trees in."

"Well, you're a font of information."

I shrugged. "I'm a Southerner. I like that sorta shit."

It's interesting how I don't mind owning my heritage when I'm in San Francisco; it's only in Florida that it completely sticks in my craw.

"So here's what I'm wondering," I added.

"Yeah?"

"How do you have a cave in a sand dune?"

"O ye of little faith," said Brian.

"Really, though."

"I think it's more like a rock ledge with . . . you know . . . a space under it."

"What did the wise old hippie tell you?"

Brian ignored this gentle poke and kept trudging ahead. The path began to wind upwards again until we reached a paved road running along the edge of the canyon. We took the road up the hill for a while, then

Brian stopped in his tracks and peered down into the abyss with the nervous, beady-eyed gaze of a terrier spotting a rabbit.

"That's it," he said.

"What's it?"

"See that ledge down there? I think it's beneath that."

"And how are we supposed to get there?" It wasn't a sheer drop-off, but the slope was steep and unstable-looking and riddled with briars.

"You don't have to go," Brian said. "I'll scout it out first."

"Sure thing, *kemo sabe.*"

So I watched from the road as Brian made his wobbly way down the slope toward his own private Holy Grail. Each time his stick struck the ground, it set off a little avalanche of pebbles and dirt. "Be careful," I said nervously. "It looks shaky."

No sooner had I spoken than Brian hit a patch of loose ground and landed on his ass, luging his way downhill into a thicket so dense that I lost sight of him completely. It sounds comical—it was, in fact, for a little while—but something told me not to laugh.

"Brian?"

There was no reply—and no sign of movement in the undergrowth.

I scooted down the slope with a growing sense of dread. "Jesus, Brian."

214

Nothing.

I swatted at the briars with my walking stick until I could see him. He was still on his back, his face crisscrossed with fine red lines. He was not moving at all.

"Oh, fuck, Brian . . . oh no, Jesus . . ."

"Get a grip," he said.

I made a peculiar sound that was somewhere between laughter and groaning, then crawled through the hole I'd made with my stick. "Are you all right?"

"Do I look all right?"

"I mean . . . can you move?"

"I think I hit a rock with my foot. It feels like I've been hobbled."

That term meant only one thing to me—Kathy Bates in *Misery*, looming over James Caan with her sledgehammer—so I glanced down at Brian's sneakered feet with considerable trepidation. Neither one, however, seemed to be lying at an unusual angle.

"It's the right one," said Brian.

I squeezed through the briars on my hands and knees to get a closer look. His ankle did seem to be swelling. I tugged his socks down gently.

"Ow! Fuck! Ow!"

"Sorry." It was all too clear that even with my assistance Brian would never make it up to the road, so I took off my backpack and started digging through it.

215

Brian wrinkled his brow at me. "Don't tell me you brought a first-aid kit."

"Even better," I said, holding up my cell phone.

I was about to dial 911 when I remembered that the medical center was only a few hundred yards through the woods, so I called Jake instead and explained the situation, giving him our exact location. I knew he would welcome this manly challenge, and he sprang to action like a commando. "Stay cool," he said. "I got it covered, boss."

"He's running to the emergency room," I explained to Brian afterward.

He was up on his elbows now, already looking embarrassed. "That's not necessary. I'm perfectly—"

"Lie the fuck down," I said. "Stop being such a guy."

Brian obeyed with a grunt. The deep scratches on his face had started to run, forming a road map across his features. I fumbled in my backpack again.

"What's that?" he asked as I started to dab at the blood.

"A Wash 'n Dri."

"Jesus, you're a fag."

"I brought it for lunch. Do you want an Orangina?"

"I can't drink it lying down."

"Sit up, then. But do it slowly."

He sat up and took the bottle from me. "Thanks."

"You're welcome. How bad does it hurt?"

"Bad."

"Do you want a turkey sandwich?"

He shrugged. "What the hell."

We both munched on sandwiches in silence while we waited to be rescued.

Finally, Brian said, "The cave should be right over there."

"Fuck the cave," I told him.

18

Close Enough

So there we were, curtained off from the world, waiting for a doctor. Brian was flat on a gurney, growing maudlin on painkillers; I sat next to him in a white plastic chair, hypnotized by the low hum of fluorescent lights. Our wilderness epic had somehow evolved into a minimalist play, a couple of actors working without props or scenery.

"Look at it this way," I said. "We may not have found the cave, but we're right next door to where the museum used to be."

"What museum?"

"Of anthropology . . . where Ishi lived."

He winced at this reminder of his disgrace and ran his fingers through his hair. The scratches on his face were turning dark and crusty. "You're right," he muttered, his eyes fixed grimly on the ceiling.

"He must have swept the floors on this very block."

I ignored his sarcastic tone. "Which means . . . we're sort of following his footsteps . . . in a way."

Brian grunted. "We never even got to the cave, man."

"Well, how great a cave can it be if it's the size of an igloo? It's not like there was gonna be hieroglyphics. It's probably full of snails and old condoms."

I thought he'd be pissed at me for befouling his shrine, but he just smiled dimly at a private joke. "Doorknobs, actually."

"*Doorknobs?*"

"Ishi's two favorite things about . . . you know . . . so-called civilization were matches and doorknobs. So this guy . . . the old hippie . . . brought him a doorknob."

"And did what with it?"

"Just left it in the cave."

"Well, that's kinda creepy."

"Why?"

"I dunno . . . it's so . . . me big white man, me bring you firewater and doorknob."

"It's a metaphor, dipshit. Or maybe a spiritual statement." Brian rolled on his side and gazed at me in doleful resignation. "Or something."

"You can find it later," I said. "Don't beat yourself up."

He shook his head. "It was gonna be Shawna's going-away surprise."

219

"Yeah, well . . . now she'll have a crutch to sign."

His eyes widened. *"Crutch?"*

"Cast . . . whatever."

"It was her favorite story," he said. "I wanted to give her an ending."

The tears welling in his eyes caught me off guard. Brian may be the last of the sensitive liberals, but weeping doesn't come easily to him—at least not lately. I figured it was mostly the drugs. I stood up and laid my hand gingerly on his messy white mop. "She doesn't need an ending, sport. She's just moving to New York."

"It's not that," he murmured.

"Then what?"

"Just . . . stupid shit."

"Brian . . . I need more."

"Then take your hand off my head."

I should have known better. I have a way of infantilizing Brian whenever he's hurting, and he's never been really comfortable with the comforting. I removed my hand and sat down again, angling the chair so I could see his face. "That better?"

He said nothing for a moment and then: "Do you think I've wasted my life?"

"Brian . . . c'mon . . ."

"I mean it, man. I'm almost sixty-fucking-two. I've got nothing to show for it but that lame-ass fucking nursery . . . and that was yours to begin with."

220

"What about Shawna?"

"What about her? She's a great kid, but . . ."

"But what?"

"Am I a loser for not marrying again?"

I took the shrink's way out. "Is that how you feel?"

"I didn't used to. I didn't even think about it. Shawna was all I needed. The two of us were pretty much . . . home."

"I think that's your answer, then."

"Is it?"

"Besides, you can always get married, if that's what you want. You're still plenty hot enough." I smiled at him. "Just ask my husband."

Brian returned the smile. "Your husband is a twisted little fuck."

"Thank the Lord," I said.

He laughed. "I'm happy for you, man. You deserve it."

"Well, so do you, buttwipe. Get your ass online. The ladies'll be lining up. Whatever happened to that sculptress you met at Burning Man?"

"She was too much of a purple person."

Purple people, in our private lexicon, are old gray lefties of either gender with a fondness for purple clothing, squash-blossom necklaces, and the like. Brian and I are both purplish, philosophically speaking, but we're put off by the predictability of the uniform. To me it's no more radical or original than, say, Arizona retirees in their pastel pantsuits.

Brian seemed lost in thought, and then: "Heard from Mary Ann lately?"

"Nope."

"You talk to her, though."

It was more of a statement than a question, so I set him straight. "No, I don't, Brian. Not for a long time." I'd been caught between the two of them when Mary Ann left him eighteen years earlier, and I had no intention of letting that happen again.

"Sorry," he said meekly. "I thought you did."

"Not since 9/11," I said. "That's been . . . Jesus . . . four years."

Brian whistled, sharing my amazement. "Time flies when you're waging a War on Terror."

On the day that defined the new millennium, Mary Ann had called Mrs. Madrigal from her house in Darien, Connecticut. She wanted to make sure that "everybody" was still there, that no one from the old crowd at Barbary Lane had chosen that week to travel to Manhattan. From Anna's description, the call had been short and businesslike, more of a schoolyard head-count than a serious effort at reestablishing contact. It was touching to know that Mary Ann had worried about us, but the whole country was worrying that day, so I didn't read much into it. Still, I gave her a call, wondering if she might have lost someone herself, but our talk was limited to the surreal events we'd just watched on television. A crisis does draw people together, but rarely for the right reason. The old wounds flare up again soon enough; the bond lasts no longer than the terror.

But every now and then I can't resist the urge to Google Mary Ann. On a recent search I found her name on a press release for a charitable event in Darien—a food fair for the local Explorer Scout troop that, strange as it seems, runs the ambulance service in that wealthy Republican enclave on Long Island Sound. Mary Ann was expressing her pride in her stepson Robbie, a member of the troop, and pledging her support, somewhat inelegantly, to this "very unique institution." She was pictured with Robbie and her husband of several years, a tall, skinny bald guy in a patchwork madras blazer who had recently retired as CEO of a New York brokerage firm. Mary Ann was identified as a "former television personality." It made me think of one of those "As Seen on TV" labels you find on drugstore packaging for vegetable dicers and anti-snoring contraptions.

Mary Ann's neighbors in Darien must have had to do some Googling themselves to determine the exact nature of her fame. A few folks may have remembered her short-lived cable talk show in the early nineties—a pleasant enough diversion involving minor celebrities and their pets—but she was far more likely to be known as the gracious spokesperson for a line of adjustable beds for the elderly. I remember the first time I saw the commercial. Thack had left me several weeks earlier, and I was holed up in bed with late-night TV and a pint of Cherry Garcia, having just whacked off, with scant satisfaction, to a porn video in which all the Texas Rangers had Czechoslovakian accents.

"Are you like I used to be?" Mary Ann was saying, still amazingly pretty in her mid-forties. "Do you wake up feeling more tired than when you went to bed?"

I guffawed and dropped ice cream on the sheets and thought: *Yes, I am, babycakes. I'm* exactly *like you used to be.* It was a strange little moment of communion, as if she were somehow speaking directly to me. I briefly considered tracking her down and having a rueful hoot about the random fucked-upness of life, until I remembered I was helping to raise the daughter she had left behind. Shawna was a teenager by then—and something of a handful—not to mention the fact that I was closer than ever to the guy whose heart Mary Ann had broken. There had been way too much chilly water under the bridge; it was foolish, even dangerous, to pretend otherwise.

So after the brief emotional ceasefire of a terrorist attack, our separate lives—and the silence—continued

224

as if the towers had never fallen. The urge to reconnect didn't arise again until Ben and I were married at City Hall. Maybe my guard was down because my heart was so open, but I wanted to share the good news with Mary Ann. I wanted a fifty-something housewife in Connecticut to be happy for me, her old friend Mouse: the guy who once believed—as she surely had—that he'd never live to see forty.

But I resisted the impulse. I wasn't even sure if I knew her anymore.

"Where the fuck is the doctor?" asked Brian, growing restless on the gurney. "I could be dead by now."

"Relax," I said. "Enjoy your drugs."

He grunted and stared at the wall.

"Do you think she'll look her up?"

"Who?"

"Shawna. When she gets to New York."

I told him that Darien was a far cry from New York.

"That's not the point."

"She doesn't talk about Mary Ann at all. It's not something that concerns her. She's always been more curious about Connie."

"Yeah," he said numbly. "I guess you're right."

Connie Bradshaw, Shawna's birth mother, was a not-that-close friend of Mary Ann during high school days in Ohio. Connie had become a stewardess for United (back when there were still stewardesses) and was Mary Ann's only contact in San Francisco when she defected from Cleveland. She crashed on Connie's sofa bed in the Marina just long enough to get her bearings, and more than long enough to realize that her once envied classmate (a head majorette no less) was not quite as sophisticated as she'd remembered. Connie was a daffy, good-natured sleep-around. (Later, in fact, she would share an awkward one-night stand with Brian, before he finally hooked up with Mary Ann.) Mary Ann wanted no part of Connie's free-range tackiness—not the Pet Rock or the plush python or the Aqua Velva she kept in the bathroom cabinet for the guys who slept over. She fled within the week, as impulsively as she had fled Cleveland.

San Francisco, however, is basically a village, so Mary Ann never quite escaped Connie's worshipful attention, especially as Mary Ann's star began to rise. In a weak moment, during a chance meeting at the zoo, Mary Ann told Connie (then pregnant with Shawna by an undetermined father) that Brian wanted a baby but was shooting blanks. Connie never forgot this. Months later, as she lay dying on the delivery table, her blood having failed to clot, she bequeathed her newborn daughter to her famous classmate from Cleveland and a guy she'd mostly remembered as having once been sweet to her.

When Connie's brother delivered Shawna (literally) to the startled couple at 28 Barbary Lane he brought them a trunk of Connie's treasures—her legacy as it were—a sad collection of dried corsages and pep buttons and yearbooks scrawled with smiley faces. Mary Ann waited until Shawna was five to open the trunk, an event that Shawna remembers as both tender and curiously momentous. Not a bad call, given the fact that Mary Ann left for New York only days later. I've often wondered if Mary Ann saw that little ritual as a moment of divestiture, a changing of the guard. *Here's your real mom, darling. She's the one who deserves your love. She's the one that you'll be missing.*

As it happened, Shawna took Mary Ann's departure rather well and began a serious fascination with Connie. Flight Attendant Barbie became the centerpiece of Shawna's toy collection and was often drafted for theatrical extravaganzas requiring a mother figure. Before long I found myself being interrogated about a woman I'd met only once—when Brian brought her to one of Anna's Christmas parties. I'd end up telling Shawna how pretty Connie was, and how nice, and how much genuine cheer she brought into a room. But the kid was no dummy and demanded more as she grew older. She was about twelve when she grilled me one afternoon on Heart's Desire Beach, a tree-lined cove on Tomales Bay, where we'd settled with a picnic lunch. She waited until Brian was dog-paddling offshore before asking me if I'd ever met her "real dad."

I told her—coward that I am—that I'd always thought of Brian as her real dad.

"The other one," she said. "The one that got my real mom pregnant."

What was I supposed to say? "Well, no, honey . . . I never did."

Shawna dug in the sand with her toes, idly making a trench. "Do you know where she met him?"

All I could remember from Mary Ann's account was that Connie had narrowed Shawna's paternity down to two "really nice guys." Only one had come with an actual location, so that's the one I went with. "I think it was the Us Festival."

"The what?"

"It was sort of like Woodstock, I guess, but a lot more calculated and commercial." (A few weeks earlier we had watched the Woodstock documentary on Brian's VCR, so it made for an easy reference point.)

"Was everybody naked?"

I smiled, shaking my head. "This was the eighties. Things had changed by then. Your mom was probably wearing something shiny."

"Did she see him after that?"

"I'm not really sure." I smoothed a patch of sand with my palm, hoping we'd get the hell off this subject. "I just know where she met him."

There was a long uncomfortable silence, so we both gazed out at the water. While Brian splashed in the distance like a drunken seal, the waning sun was copper-plating the surface of the bay. It was easy to forget that this sleepy inlet marked the exact location of the San Andreas Fault. Many eons earlier (as Anna had once explained to me) the earth had ripped open here, leaving only this shimmering, seductive scar.

Shawna turned to me: "So . . . was my real mom a ho or what?"

My jaw must have hit the sand. "Jesus, Shawna, what sort of question is that?"

She shrugged her delicate nut-brown shoulders. "Just a regular one."

I felt like one of those big-bosomed matrons in *The Three Stooges* movies who were always huffing "Well, I never!" so I softened my tone to keep from losing the girl completely. "Let's put it this way," I told her. "If she was a ho, then I was one, too. And so was your dad, for that matter. Back in those days we were all a bit . . ."

"Ho-ish," she said, filling in the silence.

I flicked sand at her blue-jeaned legs. "You just watch it."

"No, you do!" she said, flicking back and giggling.

She could still be a little girl sometimes, and it never failed to melt my heart.

The conversation ended when Brian came in from his swim, swaddling himself in an ancient Grateful Dead beach towel. Shawna offered him a sandwich from the picnic basket, then leaned against him as he ate it, commenting on the gulls that were wheeling above the bay. I envied them both at that moment, but mostly Shawna, for having a father with such a boundless capacity for love. *What must that feel like?* I wondered.

There were footsteps in the hospital corridor, so I wrapped up as succinctly as possible.

"Don't worry about Shawna," I said. "She's yours for life."

"You think so, huh?"

"I know so, Mr. Man."

"Okay, fine, but what if—"

The curtains parted with a sudden swoosh to reveal a young male doctor of South Asian descent. He looked a lot like M. Night Shyamalan, I thought. "Okay," he said as he consulted his clipboard. "What have we here?"

I turned to Brian. "Pay no attention to the man behind the curtain."

Brian chuckled.

The doctor frowned in confusion. "I'm sorry, I—"

"You must be straight," I said, grinning.

The doctor smiled sweetly. "Is that relevant?"

"No, I was just . . . never mind . . . I'm sorry."

The doctor studied Brian's foot for a moment, then asked him how it happened. "He fell into an abyss," I explained.

"Is this your partner?" the doctor asked Brian.

Brian glanced at me and smirked. "Close enough," he said.

19

The Burning
Question

It was almost dark and Ben and I were crammed into our galley kitchen, trying out a new recipe for brussels sprouts that a checkout guy at Trader Joe's had shared with me. Neither one of us is a serious foodie—by anyone's measure—so we tend to approach cooking with the peppy unprofessionalism of fifth-graders assigned a science project.

"I'll fry the pancetta," said Ben, squeezing past me to the stove in a minuet we'd already perfected. "Do you know how to blanch?"

That's a wonderful setup line for a queer of my generation, but I squelched my inner Baby Jane for fear of wearing out her welcome. "It's the same as steaming, right?"

"Yeah . . . I think so."

I grabbed a saucepan and began to fill it under

the tap. "This is gonna be so fucking good."

"I dunno," said Ben, snipping the pancetta with the kitchen shears. "I'm not sure about the maple syrup."

"Why not?"

"With brussels sprouts?"

I've never been a fan of vegetables. To my way of thinking, there are very few of them that would not be hugely improved by the addition of bacon and syrup. Ben, on the other hand, likes his greens unadulterated. He munches them raw like a giraffe.

"Don't you think," he said judiciously, "that the syrup might overwhelm the sprouts?"

"I certainly hope so."

He grinned at me sideways, benignly disapproving, as he dropped the pancetta into a hot skillet. "How long do we bake it then?"

"Ten or fifteen minutes, at least. Long enough for 'em to get all tender and syrupy." I waggled my eyebrows in lascivious appreciation.

That was when my cell phone rang. *Rang off the hook,* as they used to say, back when telephones sounded like my cell phone—noisy and demanding.

I checked the readout and saw my brother's name.

"It's Irwin," I said, looking up at Ben. It was a sobering moment, to say the least, since we both knew that Irwin never calls just to chat.

"Pick up," he said. "I can handle this."

233

I headed for the living room and settled on the sofa, giving a final holler to Ben in the kitchen—"A full half-cup of syrup, please, sir"—before opening the phone and greeting my brother as nonchalantly as possible. "How's it goin', Irwin?"

That seemed to be a tough question.

"Is it Mama?"

"Oh . . . no, she's fine. I mean, not fine but . . . you know . . ."

"Sure." I was growing more and more uncomfortable. I was pretty sure I was about to catch holy hell for the change in the power of attorney.

But Irwin sounded oddly subdued. "Listen, Mikey. I'm headin' out your way in a few days. I thought we could have lunch or something."

"Sure," I said, now completely confused. "What's up?"

"Oh . . . you know . . . just a conference in San Jose."

"What sort of conference?"

"Uh . . . Promise Keepers."

That's the big Christian men's powwow. They gather in stadia and bond over Jesus and promise to love their families and "lead" their wives. Lenore has not been led anywhere for years, but guys like my brother are so starved for male-to-male intimacy that they have to grab it wherever they find it. I could hardly give him shit about it.

234

"Why don't you come for dinner?" I said. "We've got a great new recipe for brussels sprouts."

Ben hooted from the kitchen.

"You know," said Irwin, "I mean no disrespect to Ben, but . . . this is more . . . brother to brother."

What the fuck was he getting at?

"Okay," I said evenly. "We can get a bite somewhere. The two of us."

"Could you come to the hotel?"

"In San Jose?"

"I'll be out at the airport, actually."

"Jesus, Irwin, that's bleak. At least come into town."

There was silence, so I figured I'd upset him with the J-word. "Sorry. I just meant there's better places to eat if—"

"I don't care about the food, Mikey! I just want to get together!"

"Okay. Fine. Whatever." I was surprised by the anguish in his voice. "Can you tell me what this is about?"

"No . . . not on the phone."

"Will Lenore be with you?"

"No."

"Well . . . call me when you get in."

"I will, bro." His tone was softer now. "Thanks for this, you hear?"

* * *

Thanks for *what* was the burning question.

I have a gardener friend up in Sebastopol who likes to tell people that he has a mind like a steel trap—sometimes he has to gnaw his leg off to get away from it.

That's me to a T. Once I start fretting about something, there's no escaping its viselike grip. It pops up on the treadmill at the gym. Or during sex. Or in the middle of a pleasant dinner at home when you should be concentrating on the food.

"They're actually pretty good," said Ben.

I drew a blank. "Uh . . . sorry . . . what?"

"The brussels sprouts."

"Oh . . . yeah . . . it works, doesn't it?"

Ben set his fork down and regarded me with a gentle, knowing smile. "I wouldn't worry about it, babe. Maybe he just wants some time with you."

"He's never wanted time with me."

"What about when you were molesting alligators?"

"That was the last time, believe me. He just needed an accomplice."

Ben took a sip of his wine. "Maybe he wants to come out of the closet."

I rolled my eyes at this deliberate mischief. "How did I know you would say that?"

A wicked chuckle.

"Trust me," I told him. "That ain't it. And if it were,

236

he wouldn't be doing it during a Promise Keepers convention."

"I know."

I smirked at him. "You and your Suit Daddies."

"You think he had a fight with Lenore?"

I shrugged. "It's possible."

"Maybe he just got sick of the puppets."

I smiled.

"*Or* he wants your advice about the gay grandson."

"Right. Like *that* would happen."

"So . . . it has to be about the power of attorney."

"But why wouldn't he say that on the phone?"

Ben shrugged. "Beats me."

"He obviously wants privacy. He's traveling without Lenore and he didn't even want *you* there."

"Maybe he's having an affair."

I considered that for a moment. "And wants to tell his gay brother?"

"Why not? People usually wanna tell *somebody* . . . and he knows you won't haul out the hellfire and brimstone."

"I might."

"No you won't. You're kind. That's why I'm with you, baby . . . and that's why he wants to talk to you, whatever it is."

I wasn't so sure about that.

* * *

237

After dinner we headed for the hot tub. We did our usual thing: taking turns carrying each other, allowing the other to be weightless, like Superman in flight with Lois Lane. (You can do that in a redwood tub, unlike those shallow fiberglass spas that won't let you float.) It was my turn to be Superman, so Ben's head was tucked under my chin as I padded around the tub, setting our course in the darkness. A gauzy fog had stalled on the hillside, making the amber porch lights of the valley as dim and fuzzy as fireflies.

"I wish you'd known Mona," I said.

"I know. I do, too."

I was quiet for a while. "Do I talk about my past too much?"

"No, honey . . . not for me."

"It's just that there's so *much* of it."

He chuckled, then climbed out of my arms and sat on the underwater bench, pulling me next to him. As silly-old-fool as it sounds, I never stop being astounded by the sheer accessibility of that body, that heart, that "mortal, guilty, but—to me—the entirely beautiful" comrade that W. H. Auden—the ultimate silly old fool—taught gay men to dream about. "What made you think of Mona?" he asked.

"Just joy, I guess. You take me back to my best times. I feel connected to them again." (This was true enough, but not the whole truth. I was also dwelling on the pain of impermanence, the way love is always on loan, never the nest egg we want it to be.)

Ben put his hand on my thigh and squeezed.

"Anything specific?"

I grinned. "The Jockey Shorts contest at the Endup."

"When?"

"Late seventies, I guess."

"You went to it?"

"I entered it."

"No way."

"Doesn't sound like me, does it? I wasn't nearly as self-conscious back then. I'd take off my clothes at the drop of a hat. I went to orgies like they were brunches."

Ben chuckled.

"Some of them *were* brunches . . . come to think of it. Anyway . . . I won the fucking thing . . . the dance contest, I mean. They must've given points for boyish panic."

"What does this have to do with Mona?"

"She was *there*. She was cheering me on."

"Ah."

"She just *knew* me, you know? There was no bullshitting that woman. When she gave you hell about something, it felt like the deepest kind of love."

Ben laid his head on my shoulder, saying nothing.

"She used to say she didn't need a lover at all—just five good friends."

239

"You must've been one of them."

"I suppose." I surprised both of us with a long, histrionic sigh. "I really should have gone to England more often."

I wasn't feeling guilty. What I felt was the depletion of my memory bank, a hunger for more memories to hoard. I like remembering Mona at Easley House, the "simple English country dyke" she claimed she'd always wanted to be, but those images are few and far between and have largely been overpowered by the older ones: Mona at the Endup, Mona on the nude beach at Devil's Slide, Mona stashing her Quaaludes in a ceramic figurine of Scarlett O'Hara. The Mona who stays with me is the late-seventies model: loose-limbed and free as a sailor, with coils of lava-red hair radiating from her head. I can even remember the telltale sound of her footsteps (both the manic and depressive varieties) on the boardwalk at Barbary Lane. Mona had a full seven years on me back then, so I'd felt like her little brother. Now that I've passed the age she was when she died it's deeply unnerving to realize that she's becoming my little sister.

The same is true of Jon, my first partner—only more so, of course, since he's now been gone for—Jesus!— almost a quarter of a century. How impossibly young we were then. Jon was a gynecologist (I know, I know) and a lovely guy inside and out, if a little buttoned-down around the edges. Had he not died but simply moved to a distant city, I wonder if we'd recognize each other today were our paths to cross at a B&B in P-town, say, or an RSVP cruise to someplace warm and homophobic. Would there still be something he could love—that *I* could love, for that matter—or would we just swap email addresses and walk away, preferring to remember the old version of ourselves?

The young version, that is.

The only version I have left of him.

And this version of Ben, this gentle otter-sleek creature holding on to me in the amniotic warmth of the hot tub, will one day prove just as ephemeral. If the virus doesn't claim me, then old age will start playing dirty soon enough. And once I've slipped from Ben's Greek ideal of a loving daddy into irreversible granddaddyhood, he will surely require another lover. Not just an occasional sex partner but a lover, someone warm and strong to confide in about the hardships of coping with . . . me. Could I give him my blessing? Could I love him enough to be that big? How much was this going to hurt?

"You could take me there," he said softly.

I was lost in the undergrowth of my dread. "What, sweetie?"

"To England. I'd love to see that house."

I told him that would certainly be possible, that

Mona's son, Wilfred, still lived there and would probably welcome a chance to see us.

"Let's do it, then," he said. "I want to go everywhere you've been."

This was all I needed for my heart to swell: a plan for the future, the promise of new memories, one more shot at the pipe dream of forever.

I sealed the deal with a peck on the side of his head.

"Okay," I said, "and then we'll go somewhere that'll just be ours."

20

Here and Now

The new version of the de Young Museum is where the old one used to be: adjacent to the Japanese tea garden and just across the road from the music concourse. It's a sprawling, low-slung building sheathed in copper panels with perforations that are meant to suggest the dappling effect of sunlight through leaves. That's a bit of a stretch, but I do love the building. Its contorted rectilinear tower—*Road Warrior* by way of the Mayans—rises above the park like a mystery begging to be solved. The whole thing will become even more magical when the copper corrodes and recedes into the greenery.

I parked the Prius in a new underground lot—an odd concept for old-time park-goers like Anna and me—and we made our way across the concourse through a regiment of recently barbered trees. As we approached the museum, I stopped in front of a favorite landmark, a bronze Beaux Arts statue of a loin-clothed hunk straining at a cider press.

"Shall we take a breather?" I asked, conscious of Anna's limited energy.

She gave me a sly-dog look, casting her eyes heavenward at the near-perfect naked haunches flexing above us. "Is *that* what you call it?"

"C'mon," I said. "Lemme get my jollies."

Anna pulled a tissue from her velvet bag and dabbed at her watery eyes. "I should think you'd get enough of those at home."

I smiled at this odd-familiar blend of maternal scolding and man-to-man ribbing. In some ways, I felt more linked to Anna's generation than I did to Ben's, though the gap was considerably wider. Not only had Anna been where I was going, she had seen where I had been. We fit together naturally, like the two Edie Beales, if those old dames had been nice to each other. These days, I realized, Anna and I even shared the watery-eye thing, since the slightest nip in the air can make me leak like a colander. I find myself telling sympathetic strangers that I'm perfectly fine, thank you, and having a lovely day.

"Is there one in there for me?" I asked, nodding toward her bag.

She tugged at the drawstring, her hand fluttering slightly.

244

"I'd carry them myself," I added, "but I'd be blotting all the time. I'd look like Madame Butterfly."

She smiled, handing me a fresh tissue. "Nothing wrong with that."

I gave my eyes a serious blotting. "Easy for you to say, Kimono Girl. I still wanna look like him." I jerked my head toward the sinewy statue.

"Oh dear," said Anna, widening her eyes.

"I know . . . never mind."

"Where is Shawna meeting us?"

"In the café. At three."

"Good. Very clever of you."

"Yeah, at least we'll be sitting if she's not on time."

One of the trademarks of Shawna's young woman-hood is her chronic tardiness. For the mastermind of a budding blog empire she's appallingly disorganized. By my count she's lost three cell phones in the last two years. It must be the artistic thing.

"Meanwhile," said Anna, "you and I will climb the tower."

I took her arm again. "As Jimmy Stewart said to Kim Novak."

It was a nervous response more than anything. Anna had mentioned the tower twice already that day, and it seemed to carry a certain weight for her.

Unless I was imagining things.

* * *

Inside, the museum had a casual meandering quality that defied the dramatically blank exterior. It was tempting to wander, to get a little lost amid the textiles and oceanic art, but I wasn't sure how taxing the climb to the tower would be.

As it happened, there was an elevator. We rode it to a glass-walled observation deck that turned the park into a dark-green comforter flung over the city. We were higher than anything around, yet still low enough to see birds threading through the trees. It was like a fire tower in a well-groomed forest, bordered on every side by bay or sea or city.

"Well," said Anna softly, seeing the view, "this is a new one."

I murmured my agreement. There was a long mutual silence—the silence of churchgoers—as we gazed at the mystic model-train village laid out before us.

"It's good to be a tourist," Anna said at last. "We joke about them, but it's quite a worthwhile thing. To . . . appreciate . . . deliberately."

The way she broke up the words told me we'd moved into another realm.

"I've *tried* to do that," she went on. "To name the things that have brought me joy." She didn't look at me as she took my hand in hers. It was as large as mine but fragile. Cool silk over bones. "You've been good company, Michael. You've been a good son. I want you

246

to know that. Here and now." She was briskly efficient about this, like someone tidying up before a trip. I couldn't handle it; I sabotaged the moment.

"You're not planning to jump, are you?"

She squeezed my hand reprovingly. "I want you to hear this, dear."

"I'm hearing it . . . I hear you."

"Good." She squeezed my hand again, as if to seal the deal.

I should have reciprocated and told her everything she'd meant to me, but I couldn't. It would have felt too official somehow, too final. I told myself there would be other times, better opportunities, that it didn't really have to be here and now.

The café overlooked the sculpture garden. It was a little too big for a café, and a little too austere, despite the gumdrop globes dangling whimsically from the ceiling. We ordered sandwiches made with chunky slabs of bread. Mine was roast beef, Brie, and horseradish mayonnaise. Anna, somewhat to my amusement, chose the peanut butter and strawberry jam. Most of the ingredients were "artisanal," according to our server.

"Such a peculiar word," Anna observed. "Like they hammered it out on an anvil. Or wove it on a loom. Why can't they just say homemade?"

Right on—as we used to say. Sometimes Northern

California just wears me the fuck down, and I get fed up with our precious *patois*, our fetishizing of almost everything. Then I remember the places (some of them not that far away) where no one seems to mind if milkshakes taste like chemicals and tomatoes taste like nothing at all.

Which made me think of Florida. And Irwin.

"My brother called," I began. "He's coming out to visit."

"That's nice."

"It's not exactly to visit. It's just to talk, apparently."

Her brow wrinkled as she munched laboriously on her sandwich.

"It's not about our mother," I said. "At least, I don't think it is."

"Was there . . . friction when you were in Florida?"

"Nothing to speak of. He was sweeter than usual, actually. We got drunk together in his boat."

"That doesn't sound very safe."

I smiled. "It wasn't moving. It was out in his yard. He goes there to get away from his wife."

Anna dabbed demurely at her mouth with a napkin. "I've always wondered why you don't talk about him."

I shrugged. "Nothing to talk about. I'm going to hell and he's not."

"Oh . . . *that*."

"And I think he's pissed at me now, to be honest."

"Why?"

"Because Mama told me something she didn't tell him."

"Oh, my." She widened her eyes melodramatically as if to suggest that this was merely about two grown boys quarreling, a conventional case of sibling rivalry.

"I know it sounds silly," I said, "but he really seemed to be hurt. I felt bad for him. For better or worse, he and Lenore have been tending to Mama ever since Papa died . . . and she ends up confiding in me . . . a virtual stranger in the scheme of things."

"You're hardly that."

"No . . . I am, believe me. She's wanted it that way. She's been terrified of me for years. We're from different planets now."

"So . . . what did she tell you?"

"That she tried to leave my father several times."

Anna set her sandwich down. "For any particular reason?"

"I presume because he was a domineering old bastard."

She nodded thoughtfully. "That's all?"

"Does it take more than that?"

"Well . . . usually."

I smiled at her sardonically. "In the strange twilight world of the heterosexual."

Anna wasn't having it. "In *anybody's* world. When did she last try to leave him?"

"Just before he died. Almost twenty years ago."

"Well, that's even more peculiar."

I shrugged. "It sort of . . . solved the problem, I guess."

"Dear . . . how could it have solved *anything*? There must be huge unresolved feelings. No wonder she wanted to tell you."

"I guess."

"You *know*. It's mostly the *un*spoken things that always cause trouble later. They find their way out of us one way or the other."

I wondered for a moment if that was code of some sort, if she was really referring to my awkward silence in the tower when she called me her son.

But I knew she didn't work that way.

Shawna, amazingly, was on time, striding into the café in a butt-gripping tweed skirt that embraced her calves almost as snugly. She wore big clunky librarian glasses and her hair was more Bettie Page than before, draped on the back of her neck like a sleek black pelt. I thought of Mona, strangely enough, someone Shawna had met only once or twice as a child and did not particularly resemble. There was the same sense of fashion, though—studied and anarchistic all at once—and the

250

same bubbling volcanic spirit. It gave me an un-expected pang. I wondered if Anna ever noticed the similarity.

"You guys," Shawna piped as she approached the table. "I have to show you something really fierce."

"And a good afternoon to you," said Anna.

Shawna kissed Anna on the top of her head by way of a greeting, then twiddled her fingers at me. "You look like you're finished. Is this a bad time?"

"No," said Anna. "It's a wonderful time." She pushed back her chair and attempted to rise, wobbling slightly in the process.

Shawna reached for her instinctively, supporting her under the elbow. "It's not that far, don't worry."

"I'm fine," said Anna.

"We've already been up to the tower," I explained, casting a glance at Shawna. "We're a little pooped."

"No problem," said Shawna, turning back to Anna as she steered her out of the café. "That bag is the bomb, by the way."

"Thank you, dear. It was my mother's."

"No shit? At the whorehouse? How fierce is that?"

Shawna has lately been fascinated by the fact that Anna was raised in a brothel in Nevada. Anna had no shame about this, of course, but she felt the need to clarify things.

"It was actually her *good* bag. She took it into Winnemucca with her. Usually to church."

With her free hand Shawna petted the bag as if it were a small, delicate mammal. "The velvet's held up beautifully."

Anna nodded. "It was much better in those days. The velvet."

"I'm sure."

"I'll put your name on it."

Shawna looked puzzled.

"The bag," Anna explained. "I'll put your name on it."

Shawna shot me a stricken glance, grasping her meaning.

"Say thank you," I told her.

"Oh my God," said Shawna, looking moved and a little bit shaken. "Thank you ... yes ... thank you so much, Anna."

"Where are we going?" asked Anna, all business again.

"Just up one level," Shawna replied. "This thing just blew me away."

The object of her awe was an early-twentieth-century oil by Arthur Bowen Davies called *Pacific Parnassus*. It was basically the ocean side of Mount Tam, Marin's own pinnacle of the gods, made riotous here by swirling fog and golden slopes above a cobalt sea. It was painted in 1905 but it could easily have been

252

yesterday. The things that made it enchanting were still here, still ours. I saw what Shawna meant. Or thought I did.

"This is what I'll miss," she said. "You know?"

"I do," said Anna. I knew she'd be missing Shawna as much as any of us, but her tone was more celebratory than sad.

I told Shawna the painting was captivating, but I'd expected something a little more avant-garde from her.

"The guy was totally avant-garde. He was practically a pagan. He identified with the Ashcan school . . . and he was even a Cubist for a while."

"Still . . . this could be a jigsaw puzzle."

"I'll forget you said that. Look closer."

I leaned into the painting, studying the landscape. "Is there a giant penis in the clouds or something?"

"Close. Check out the mountainside."

It took me a while to find them, since they were almost the color of the fields and barely bigger than a paper clip. "People," I said. "Naked people, in fact."

"You are *correct*, sir," said Shawna, imitating Ed McMahon on the Carson show. She used to do that when she was seven years old, charming the dickens out of grown-ups. She might be young, I thought, but she does remember Johnny and Ed.

"Where are they?" asked Anna, stepping closer to the painting. "I don't see them."

"Here," I said, pointing. "And here . . . and there's a couple down here in the trees."

Without a moment's hesitation, Anna yanked open her bag and removed an enormous magnifying glass with an ornate handle fashioned from junk-shop silverware. I don't know exactly *why* it struck me as hilarious but it did, seeing her there in her sneakers and her turban and Chinese grandma pajamas examining the canvas like Inspector Clouseau on the trail of a murderer. Shawna, I was glad to see, found it humorous, too, so we both dissolved in giggles—to Anna's mounting annoyance.

"Stop it, children. Don't make a scene."

"Are they girls or boys?" Shawna asked, prolonging the mirth.

Anna's eyes were still glued to the glass. "I presume they're gods, if this is Parnassus."

"Maybe they're picnickers from Mill Valley." This was my contribution.

"Really," said Anna, putting the glass away. "How old are you two?"

Shawna looked chastened. "I just figured you'd think it was cool."

"It is, dear. It's extremely cool."

"We weren't laughing at *you*," I put in, taking her arm. "Just that thing."

"It's very handy," said Anna. "You'll see."

254

We spent another half-hour drifting through galleries until Anna discreetly expressed her need for "the ladies room." When we found it, Shawna asked if she needed assistance. Anna shook her head with a smile. "I'm fine, dear," she said, before turning to me halfway through the door. "I'll need to go home, though, after this. Notch will be cross with me."

The door swung shut. Shawna turned to me with a slack expression.

"Who the hell is Notch?"

I grinned at her. "I'd introduce you, but she's still under the armoire."

21

Memory Foam

My husband was doing yoga in the bedroom, attempting the union of body and soul, while I was nattering away. I was pleasantly stoned by then and lobbying for a quiet evening on the sofa with *The French Lieutenant's Woman*. Ben had never seen the film, so I had TiVo'd it in the hope of enlightening him. I was droning on about this wonderful, moody, romantic story and its brilliant author, John Fowles, and the other atmospheric movies—*The Collector* and *The Magus*—made from Fowles' novels.

This is typical of me. Given pot and the nearness of Ben I can be a crashing bore. Ben has a master's degree (and I don't, of course), but I somehow feel compelled to play teacher when we're together, to tell him every little thing he missed by being young. It's tempting to do this because he listens so generously, even with a foot behind his head.

When his cell phone rang, he sighed at this final invasion of his peace.

"Shall I check it?" I asked.

"Please."

I took the phone from the nightstand and looked at the readout. "It's Leo," I said.

Ben untangled his limbs and took the phone from me. I returned to my Morris chair and picked up a magazine, knowing that Ben would not require privacy.

"Say hi for me," I told him.

I've met two of Ben's exes: this one, Leo, the retired Subaru dealer from South Bend, and Paolo, the Italian stockbroker from Sardinia. They are both nice guys, but except for the fact that we're all (I'm told) uncut and pushing sixty from one side or the other, we are wildly unalike. It intrigues me to think that each of us has spent significant time with Ben; each has been his answer to something. But I don't feel especially competitive in their presence; I feel like a clue, a piece of the puzzle. It's much easier not to be threatened by your lover's exes if you don't want to fuck them yourself.

Ben took the call on the bed. This was our new Tempurpedic mattress, designed by Swedes or NASA or somebody to conform to every contour. We ordered it on an impulse at the Denver airport last Christmas when we were visiting Ben's family. Seeing him there on his stomach, pale and glistening in his briefs, I imagined the imprint his package would make on the memory foam, like a nifty Jell-O mold.

"So how's our favorite Wilted Flower?" Ben asked his ex.

Leo and his friend Bill, who worked for Allstate back in South Bend, had recently moved to Fort Lauderdale and bought a little ranch house in Wilton Manors, the gay neighborhood. Most of the homeowners were fairly old and fairly well off, so Wilted Flowers had become the pejorative-of-choice for locals who saw themselves as neither.

Leo's friend Bill is just that, by the way—a friend. The two have never been lovers. They just got tired of selling and wanted to share a place in the sun. As far as I can tell, they've both relinquished romance without a fuss. They garden and play bridge and throw luaus for their neighbors and never have to negotiate the politics of three-ways and afternoons at the baths. They will grow old together, those two, tucked in their separate beds (with their separate collections of porn). There must be a certain comfort in knowing that the guy across the cornflakes in the morning has noticed, just like you, how short the days are getting. At least you're at the finish line together.

There's something to be said for that, no doubt.

But would I trade it for what I have with Ben?

God no. Not in a million years. Not while love is still something I can taste and touch and nurture and pull down the pants of. Not while I still have a shot at this.

I'm the lucky one here, of course. It was Ben who got the short end of the stick. The double whammy of HIV and advancing age makes me a pretty shaky deal in the happily-ever-after department. I can at least *dream* of one day dying in my lover's arms, but he can't do the same with me. He'll have another life entirely, for better or worse.

"Hey," he said, speaking to me but still on the phone. "What's twenty feet long, shaped like a snake, and smells like urine?"

I looked up from my magazine. "Say what?"

"It's a riddle. Leo just told it to me."

"I give up. What's twenty feet long, shaped like a snake, and smells like urine?"

"The conga line at Chardee's!"

I frowned at him. "What the hell is Chardee's?"

"You know. The restaurant in Wilton Manors. The supper club. Where the older guys go to get drunk."

I made a face at him. "Lovely."

Ben laughed. "It was Leo's joke."

"Well, tell him he's a sick fuck. A sick *old* fuck."

Ben obliged. "He says you're a sick old fuck."

I could hear Leo hooting, enjoying the hell out of this.

259

"Ask him," I told Ben, "if he can spell *gerontophobia*."

Ben wouldn't take it that far. It wasn't fair to pick on Leo, however gently. He was too harmless for that. "Cut him some slack," Ben whispered. "It's funny."

"Hilarious," I said, returning to my magazine. "Old people pissing themselves."

Ben ignored me and spoke to the phone again. "Yeah, sure . . . he loved it . . . he always loves your jokes."

It must have been the Florida connection that got me thinking about my brother's impending visit. That steel-trap mind of mine had me gnawing off my leg again. As we lay on the sofa after the movie, Ben noticed the distraction in my eyes.

"What's up, babe?"

"Oh, just . . . the Irwin thing. He sounded so stricken when we talked."

Ben nodded slowly, his intuition confirmed. "Bring him to the house, then. I'll still be at work. You guys can talk all you want."

"He didn't seem to want that. And how can I tell *where* we should talk, if I don't know what he wants to talk about?"

Ben shrugged. "Give Patreese a call. If it's anything at all to do with your mom, he might have some idea."

I thought that was brilliant and told him so.

"I try," said Ben.

I found Patreese's cell-phone number on my copy of the power of attorney. He had scribbled it on the bottom at the very last minute, in case we needed him.

"It's almost midnight there," I pointed out.

"He'll be up. And if he's not, he doesn't have to answer."

He answered, as it happened, on the fifth ring. There was noise in the background: screaming, drunken female voices. "Yeah?" he said, shouting above the din.

"It's Michael Tolliver."

"Who?"

"Alice's son. From San Francisco."

"Oh, Lord, honey. How are you doin'?"

"Great," I said, relieved by his cheerful acknowledgment. "I'm here with Ben." I swapped a private smile with my husband. "Is this a bad time?"

"Nah. These crazy bitches can just cool their engines. Hang on, my brother." He was gone for a matter of seconds while he must have closed a door somewhere, since the din was largely gone when he returned. "That better?" he asked.

"Much. You workin' a gig or something?"

"Yeah. Fuckin' bachelorettes. I'm changin' into my sailor outfit."

I bugged my eyes for Ben. "He's changing into his sailor outfit."

Ben laughed.

"Listen," I said to Patreese. "I won't keep you but . . . my brother's coming out to see me tomorrow, and he's been acting really peculiar since we got home."

"Uh-huh." This was noncommittal at best.

"Has something . . . happened around there?"

"Around where?"

"The Gospel Palms."

A long silence and then: "Well . . . your mama had a fight with ol' whatshername . . . Lenore. I reckon that must be it."

"A fight?"

"Yeah. Knock-down-drag-out. She don't want her comin' around anymore."

"Was this about the power-of-attorney thing?"

Another puzzling silence. "I don't really know for sure."

"Yes you do, Patreese. She tells you everything."

Patreese cleared his throat uncomfortably. "Sorry, Michael . . . I can't do this. You just wait and talk to your brother. You'll be fine. I don't feel right about gettin' all tangled up in family matters. It wouldn't be fair to you, either."

"Okay," I said evenly.

"A lotta shit shakes loose when folks are dying. You don't need to hear it from the hairdresser."

What on earth? I thought.

"You're not pissed at me, are you?"

"No . . . of course not."

"I saw your mama day before yesterday. She's no better . . . but she looked a lot more at peace, you know? Now that she's spoken her peace."

Someone must have opened the door, because that mindless estrogen roar was drowning us out again. "I gotta go," said Patreese. "Say hey to that sweet thing o' yours. I'll call if there's any change with your mama. Don't you worry."

Before I could thank him he was gone. I closed the phone and turned to Ben.

"Now I'm really freaked," I said.

263

22

Keep Me
Company

The restaurant at the Airport Marriott was called JW's
Steakhouse, presumably after old Mr. Marriott himself,
the archconservative Mormon billionaire. It made sense
that my brother had picked it. This was a piece of *his*
America, clean and predictable, a safe refuge at the gates
of Sodom. Whatever his mission today, Irwin would
feel better here, buffered by families and beef-eating
businessmen. These were his peeps.

Me . . . I'd never felt so out of town this close to the
city.

Irwin had chosen a quiet corner of the restaurant. He
stood up when he saw me, fussing reflexively—and rather
touchingly, I felt—with his comb-over. When we were
face-to-face, he thrust out his arm and grabbed my elbow
with the other. He'd learned this trick from our father, an
acknowledged master at keeping love at arm's length.

"Hey, bro," he said. "Thanks for coming."

"No problem . . . I was already in the neighborhood, so . . ."

"Sit down, sit down." He was too distracted to joke. "You ordered yet?"

"Irwin . . . I just got here."

He looked mortified. "I meant . . . you know . . . would you like to?" He handed me the menu. "These places are pretty dependable. I've been to the one in Anaheim and the one in Philly. Fine cuisine every time. The Cowboy Steak can't be beat."

At eighteen ounces the Cowboy Steak would have choked a coyote, so when the waitress arrived, I ordered the seared tuna. "That'll be good, too," Irwin offered gamely. "It's all good here." Then, without a word to me, he ordered double scotches for both of us.

"Hey," I said. "I've got clients this afternoon."

"Just bring 'em," Irwin told the waitress.

When she was gone, there was a lead-footed silence, so I jumped into the breach and asked him, as tactfully as possible, what the hell was going on.

"First off," he replied, "it's not about you havin' the power of attorney. I know about that and I don't care. Mama can die whenever she pleases. She'll get no trouble from me. I want to make her as comfortable as possible. She knows that, too."

I nodded, wondering how he'd found out. "Does Lenore feel that way?"

His expression grew stony. "She's got nothin' to do with this. You and me are the next of kin, and that's that. Whatever we say goes."

"Maybe so, but Mama seems to think that Lenore—"

"Fuck Lenore!"

Under other circumstances, I might have teased him about the language, but there was real anguish in his eyes. He ran his palm along the tabletop, smoothing out his thoughts. "Lenore moved out last week. She's living with Mel Brook."

He said Brook, of course, not Brooks—I heard that clearly—but I got the visual, anyway: Lenore humping away on the beloved entertainer. There had to be a joke in there somewhere—maybe about Christians needing Jews for the rapture, or Lenore confusing Mel Brooks with Mel Gibson—but I managed to restrain myself.

"Is Mel Brook . . . someone I should know?"

He shook his head. His right eye flinched convulsively a couple of times—a tic I hadn't seen before. "Just this gal she knows from Sunday school."

Now I had a new image of Mel: a Bible-toting dyke in a gray mullet and a polyester pantsuit. I couldn't help myself: "She left you for a woman?"

"No! . . . Hell, no!" He looked like I'd smacked him

in the face with a dead flounder. "She didn't leave me for anybody. I . . . banished her."

"*Banished* her? . . . Jesus, Irwin."

"Could we leave His name out of this?"

"Then don't talk like a biblical patriarch. Who the hell says 'banished'?"

"I asked her to leave. I told her to leave. Stop messing with me, Mikey. This is tough enough as it is."

I offered him penitent silence, then spoke in a more reasonable tone. "What happened? Y'all always seemed pretty content to me."

That was not the right word, of course. *Complacent* would have been closer to the truth. Irwin and Lenore weren't as lovey-dovey as they once were, but they seemed resigned to each other for the rest of their days. They had their McMansion and their grandkid and their Personal Savior, and that had seemed a gracious plenty.

Lenore, you should know, wasn't always such a tight-ass. When Irwin was courting her back in the seventies, she was still the social director at a convention hotel in Tallahassee and something of a firecracker. She was Christian, but she didn't make a fuss about it. She was pretty and perky and sometimes very funny, and my folks were openly amazed that their crazy-ass delinquent son had landed someone so presentable.

This was roughly the time they learned of my

"lifestyle," so they were thrilled to have a shot at breeding grandchildren. Irwin bought a split-level house just down Abbott Springs Road, and the four of them—Mama and Papa and Irwin and Lenore—became a functioning unit. Mama would write me effusively about their long road trips in Irwin's Buick: one to Colorado, as I recall, and another to New York to see *Cats* on Broadway. For almost a decade they were Lucy & Ricky & Fred & Ethel, and it got to me more than I would ever have imagined. I would not have traveled with them for anything in the world, but I felt a little jealous sometimes. More of an outsider than ever.

Then Papa died and I announced my antibody status and Mama dug deeper into Jesus, taking Lenore with her. The reason seemed clear at the time: they had already lost one Tolliver man and were almost certain to lose another. Whatever their petty rivalries over the years, grief had made them sisters in salvation. Or so I believed. Irwin did, too, poor bastard, so he began strangling his cuss words and praising the Lord to placate the women he loved. Like me, a fellow male, he was oblivious to the *real* bond between Mama and Lenore, the secret they had planned on taking to their graves.

But I'm getting ahead of myself.

Irwin's eye was flinching again.

"Do you remember," he said slowly, "what you told

268

me out in the boat?"

It took me a moment. "About Mama wanting to leave Papa?"

He nodded darkly.

I still wasn't getting it.

"It's the same reason, Mikey."

"The same reason as *what*?"

Right about then our drinks arrived, though I have no memory whatsoever of interacting with the waitress. The glasses just materialized and remained there undisturbed, while my eyes stayed glued on my brother's flinching eye.

"The same reason as what?" I repeated.

"The same reason I threw Lenore out. Her and Papa . . . they were having a . . . I mean, you know, they'd been . . ." He lifted his palms from the table and tilted them to parenthesize the unspeakable. The gesture wasn't graphic but it screamed its meaning.

I gaped at him. "How do you know this?"

"Mama told me last week. Right after you left."

"Papa and *Lenore*?"

"Don't make me say it again." He reached for his scotch and drank half of it, then pushed the other glass toward me. "Keep me company."

I picked up the glass, took a swig, and set it down again.

269

"Jesus," I murmured.

"Mikey—"

"Sorry." I hardly knew where to start. "When did this happen?"

"Just before Papa died. Mama drove up to Deltona to spend the day at that big outlet store, but it was closed for some holiday . . . Martin Luther King or something . . . so she came back. She couldn't find Papa at the house, so she went down to our place. They didn't even lock the door. She found 'em in the family room."

"*In flagrante?*"

Irwin flinched violently. "I don't know *how* they were doing it."

I did my best not to smile. "I mean . . . they were actually in the midst of . . . ?"

"Yes sir. Yes they were." Irwin just rocked for a while, his hands between his knees, like one of those plastic birds bobbing into a glass of water.

"All righty," I said, always ready with the brotherly wisdom.

"Mama said they were buck naked."

I wanted to be the unhysterical one. I wanted to guide my brother rationally through the labyrinth of sex like enlightened queers are supposed to do. But I screwed up my face as if I'd just caught a whiff of a flaming cow pie.

"Papa just hit the ceiling," Irwin went on. "Throwin'

stuff all over the place. Like Mama was the one who'd done something wrong."

Wouldn't he just? I thought.

Irwin polished off the rest of his scotch. "And then he died."

"*What?*"

"He had a heart attack. Right there in front of them."

"But he died of cancer."

"Cancer can cause heart attacks. The coroner just considered it . . . a complication."

"I'll say. Was Papa still naked when the coroner arrived?"

Irwin shook his head. "They got his clothes back on and put him on the sofa with the clicker."

"The clicker?"

"Like he was watching TV when it happened."

"Jesus . . . sorry, sorry!"

Irwin offered me a weary smile. "You're entitled."

"In that case, Jesus H. Christ! How the hell did Mama make it through the funeral? She looked so . . . composed."

"I guess she was kinda in shock. She said she prayed a lot."

"Did that help?"

Irwin scowled at my sacrilege.

"It's people who have to be good to us, Irwin. Not God."

"You think I don't know that?"

I apologized for the preachiness—the last thing he needed right now. Still, I couldn't help thinking how *biblical* the whole thing sounded. All that begetting and begatting among kinfolk. Not to mention those wailing women dressing the dead patriarch.

"Where were you?" I asked.

"Out showin' a house. By the time I got home, Papa was already at the funeral parlor."

"And Mama and Lenore had worked out their story."

"Yep."

We just sat there for a moment, silent as men, working out our own story, each in his own way. "It's just so . . . pathetic," I said finally.

"What?"

"That Mama just buried it all these years. She never had closure of any kind."

"She didn't want folks to know. She didn't want *me* to know. And Lenore sure as hell didn't want me to know. Mama was pretty much stuck, I reckon. So they drove up to Georgia after the funeral and got born again where nobody would know 'em."

"I'm sorry . . . *who* did?"

"Mama and Lenore. The preacher baptized 'em both. One after the other. Little church on the highway. One o' those aboveground pools."

"Did you know about this at the time?"

"Sure."

"And that didn't strike you as strange?"

Irwin shrugged. "Mama said the womenfolk had to grieve on their own. And Lenore was a Presbyterian, so she'd never been born again. I just reckoned Mama was killin' two birds with one stone. So I stayed home and took Kimberly to Disney World."

Poor Mama, I thought, living with this gothic shit for almost twenty years, protecting Irwin's heart at any cost, while Papa got off scot-free and Lenore grew more and more sanctimonious with guilt. No wonder Lenore had been so solicitous of Mama. And no wonder my unapologetic homosexuality became their mutual obsession; it was something they could fix together, a sin that, unlike Papa's, could still be eradicated.

"So why did she change her mind?"

"Who?"

"Mama. Why did she spill the beans now?"

"Her and Lenore were at each other's throats all week, so I went out to the Gospel Palms and told Mama she owed Lenore some respect since Lenore only wanted the best for her. And Mama went ballistic, said she didn't wanna die lookin' at that evil woman's face, and I asked her why on earth she would say such a thing, and . . . she told me."

"In front of Lenore?"

"No. I went to Lenore myself. She was doin' a puppet show up in Eustis."

I could almost see the felt flying. "What did she say?"

"She said it happened only once or twice, and she did it to keep peace in the family."

"*What?*"

"Papa had been at her for years, she said. She just wanted to put it to rest."

"Do you believe her?"

"I don't know what I believe," said Irwin.

23

Terms of
Abasement

My brother's second drink arrived with the food. He polished it off before the waitress left and ordered another.

"You sure?" I asked.

"I'm sure," he said, sawing ferociously into his steak.

I felt awful for him. As Papa's innately unacceptable son, I'd known the sting of the old man's narcissism for decades, but Irwin had been blindsided in the worst possible way. "He didn't do it to hurt you," I told him. "He did it because he could—because everything revolved around him. He didn't think about anyone else. He took what he wanted."

He grunted as he chewed on a mouthful of steak.

"I'm really sorry, Irwin."

Another grunt.

"At least you'll have the Promise Keepers."

"Say what?"

"The convention in San Jose. That should be a good boost for your spirits. The fellowship and all."

Silence.

"What's the matter?"

"There's no convention," he said. "I just said that because . . . I didn't want you to think I was comin' out just to see you."

"Why not?"

He shrugged. "Too much pressure, I guess."

"Pressure? On *who*?"

"I dunno—"

"I *like* the pressure, Irwin. I like that you thought of me."

He stared bleakly at the tabletop. "Who else am I'm gonna think of?"

It wasn't the declaration one might have hoped for, but it almost warmed my heart. Unless that was the scotch. Whatever the reason, I was grinning over a brand-new irony.

"You *lied* about the Promise Keepers?"

We circled the grotesquerie again and again, making less and less sense of it. When Irwin was done with his third drink, I decided to cut to the chase.

"So what are you gonna do now?"

"What do you mean?"

"Are you gonna . . . lift the banishment?"

He made a nervous circle on the table with his glass. "How can I live with her now, knowing what happened?"

I shrugged. "How can you not?"

"I could do it . . . believe you me."

"Irwin, you can't make scrambled eggs."

"Well, that's not—"

"Has she asked for forgiveness?"

"She said she asks the Lord every day."

"Has she asked *you*?"

"I s'pose . . . I was yellin' a lot."

"Understandably."

A long silence.

"Do you still love her?"

"Mikey . . . she did this in our house! Her and Papa were—"

"I've got the picture, Irwin. But it was eighteen years ago, and you've got a nice new house and a sweet grandkid, and you and Lenore are each other's person in the world. The only way to take your life back is to forgive her. It's obvious she's tried to atone for this. She's been atoning us to death for years. Forgive her and stop the damn puppets."

I caught him suppressing a smile.

"You must love her," I added. "You bought her a Thomas Kinkade." (I couldn't believe I was citing that god-awful "chapel in the dell" as proof of anything, but a desperate situation called for desperate measures.)

"It's not as simple as that," said Irwin. "Mama never wants to see her again."

"Then see that she doesn't. Tell Lenore to stay away from the Gospel Palms. That shouldn't be hard. Just be the man—tell her what you want and what Mama wants. Isn't that what the Promise Keepers would tell you?"

I thought I'd gone too far, but he was still listening.

"And cut yourself some slack. None of this shit is your fault. It's okay to enjoy yourself, Irwin. Especially right now." I widened my eyes suggestively. "If you ask me, the Lord owes you one."

Irwin gazed at me morosely. "What do you mean?"

I picked up the bill holder and slipped my credit card into the slot. Irwin mumbled in protest, but I shooed him away. "You can pay for dinner tonight."

"I have to get back to work," he said nonsensically.

"You have to sober up," I told him. "You have to go back to your room and have a nice hot shower and a nap. I'll pick you up at seven."

"Where are we going?" he asked.

"To town," I replied.

I called Shawna as soon as I'd pulled off 101 onto Cesar Chavez.

"Hey, babycakes."

"Oh . . . hi, Mouse."

"Listen, sweetie . . . I need to talk to you about something."

This must have sounded ominous to her. "Oh, shit, it's not Dad, is it?"

"No, no. He's fine. I mean . . . other than the foot. My brother's in town, and he's really depressed, and . . . I thought I might take him out tonight. I was wondering if you could recommend somebody nice at the Lusty Lady."

"You're kidding?"

"No . . . I'm not."

"Your born-again brother from Orlando?"

"It's complicated. He's had a blow to his self-esteem, and I just wanna make him feel better for a while. Help him let off some steam, you know."

"What does he want?"

"What do you mean?"

"In a *woman*, Mouse."

"He doesn't know about this, actually."

"Okaay."

"I just thought if there was someone . . . you know, really easygoing . . . that he could talk to . . . and mess around with maybe . . . it might make him feel better."

"And he won't consider this a sin?"

"Is it a sin if it happens behind Plexiglas?"

279

Shawna laughed. "Fuck if I know."

"He can always say no, if he doesn't want to. I just thought I'd pave the way for him. Make sure he got the right one."

"What would be the wrong one?"

"Well, Pacifica the Pregnant Lady for one. And you for another."

"I'm way past that story, Mouse. And Pacifica has a beautiful baby boy."

"I'm thrilled for you both."

"I take it you haven't been reading my blog."

"Maybe not lately."

"You should. You're in it."

"Doing what?"

"Coming to the Lusty Lady. Well, maybe not *coming*, but—"

"Jesus, Shawna—"

"Okay . . . my bad. I promise you'll like it, though. I call you my green-collar gay uncle. I didn't mention your name, if you're worried about losing your queer clients."

"Gimme a break."

"You might wanna think about Lorelei."

"What?"

"For your brother. She's blond and hella sweet, and she's famous for her feet."

"Her feet?"

"You should see them. They're perfect."

"What can you do with feet behind Plexiglas?"

"What can you do with anything behind Plexiglas? Oh, wait . . . Cressida . . . that's the one. She really digs older guys."

"Do older guys dig her?"

"Oh, yeah."

"Cressida as in *Troilus and Cressida*?"

"She used to work down at Shakespeare Santa Cruz. She listens well, and she, you know . . . talks them through it."

"So how do we do this?"

"I'll just call ahead and tell 'em he's coming. What's his name again?"

"Irwin."

"Will you be with him?"

"Hell, no."

"You big pussy."

"Don't be disrespectful."

She giggled.

"And don't put it in your blog, either. This is strictly private therapy. It can't get back to Florida."

"You have my word on it, as a pimp."

"Thank you."

"I think it's sweet, actually. What you're doing. I'll leave a message for Cressida. Make sure he brings some cash for the slot."

* * *

That evening I took Irwin to Joe DiMaggio's Chophouse on Washington Square. Back when I was still living on Russian Hill, this corner was occupied by the Fior d'Italia, the city's oldest Italian restaurant and the birthplace of chicken tetrazzini, a spaghetti dish concocted in 1908 in honor of a visiting opera singer. (Mama used to make a version of this herself, using Velveeta cheese and Campbell's Cream of Chicken soup.) I hadn't been to the new restaurant, but I figured its blend of baseball memorabilia and oversized Marilyn photographs would keep both of us sufficiently amused.

While Irwin was working on his first scotch, a pianist was tinkling out a dreamy rendition of "I Wanna Be Loved by You."

"Clever," I said, smiling. (I wasn't drinking tonight, but I had vaporized before leaving the house.)

"What?"

"That was Marilyn Monroe's big number from *Some Like It Hot*."

"Don't think I remember that one."

"Sure you do . . . blond. Big boobs."

Irwin shot daggers at me. "The movie, dickwad."

It felt good to be called that again. It reminded me of the old days—the days of the unsaved Irwin—when his terms of abasement were almost a form of intimacy. We might have been back in that dinghy at Lake Tibet looking for alligators in the dark.

I smiled at him. "They had their wedding photos taken just across the square here."

"Who?"

"Marilyn and Joe. At Saints Peter and Paul."

"Oh."

"They weren't actually *married* there. They were married at City Hall."

Irwin nodded slowly. "Like you and Ben."

I grinned at him. "That wasn't my point, but . . . yes . . . come to think of it. That's pretty cool, actually." I was touched that he'd made the connection.

"You're too old to be saying 'cool,' bro."

"You're right. And fuck you."

He took another slug of his drink. "It don't mean shit, anyway."

"What?"

"Marriage. You give it all you got, and it blows up in your face. It's nothing but heartache in the end."

Mama had said the very same thing when I'd told her about marrying Ben. She and Irwin had come to the same conclusion about the same moment of betrayal by the same two people. It made sense, in a way. Southern families are nothing if not close.

"I can't forgive her, Mikey. I can't do it. I wouldn't know how to start."

I shrugged. "Maybe you could forgive each other."

He frowned. "What have *I* got to be forgiven for?"

Recognizing my cue, I reached into the pocket of my sports coat and removed the envelope I'd brought with me. I handed it to Irwin without a word. He hesitated a moment, then opened the envelope and removed the hand-tinted Victorian postcard I'd found in a Noe Valley shop earlier that afternoon. It depicted a naughty lady in a corset vamping on a saloon piano. On the back I'd written: "GOOD FOR ONE NIGHT OF FUN IN OLD FRISCO. Kearny and Broadway. Cressida."

"Cressida?" said Irwin. "What do I need with a car?"

24

What Husbands Do

I've always had a thing for guys who work with wood: carpenters, lumberjacks, driftwood artists—you name it. It's their hands, more than anything, rough and graceful all at once. I remember a counselor in the crafts hut at Camp Hemlock who could make my pubescent heart turn somersaults just by dragging a plane across a plank. And later, in the seventies (or was it the eighties?), there was that woodworker on Public TV. Remember him? The dude in suspendered jeans and Harry Reems mustache who seemed to be broadcasting from a log cabin in the wilderness? That was some fine craftsmanship.

No wonder I like meeting Ben at work. His studios down on Norfolk Street are part office/part workshop, and more often than not he'll be hunched over his computer. Sometimes, though, when the planets are properly aligned, I'll find him in the shop, lit by the pearly light of the translucent fiberglass roof. He'll be working shirtless in his leather apron, lightly sugared with maple dust, humming as he guides a hand-hewn tenon into a tight mortise.

Anyway, that's how it was on this particular day. Irwin had been back in Florida for almost a month, and the first signs of winter had arrived. Rain was coursing down the corrugation of the roof, and the shop was piquant with ozone and linseed oil.

Ben looked up and smiled when he saw me.

"Hey, husband."

"Hey, baby." I kissed him on the mouth. "That is fucking gorgeous." He was working on a sideboard—a long, narrow one, slightly Asian-looking.

"Thanks." He stroked the maple as if it were the flank of a beloved horse.

"I heard from Irwin today."

"Oh, yeah? How are things with Lenore?"

"Not bad, considering . . . they're going to Cancún for Christmas. He arranged it himself."

"No shit."

"I don't know what he said to her. Or what she said to him. But . . . it's like it never happened."

"Maybe she told him your dad was a bum fuck."

"Eeeeyew."

"Sorry."

286

"I think Irwin needed a secret. And a guy he could share it with . . . even if it had to be me. Mama and Lenore had their own secret for eighteen years. He just needed to level the playing field."

"Tit for tat," said Ben, smiling.

"Or pussy for tat, as the case may be."

It was a lame joke, but I was trying to stay light-hearted for what had to come next: "Listen, sweetie. It's time for me to go back. Mama's close to checkin' out."

Ben absorbed my euphemism, then stroked my arm. "You okay?"

I nodded. "I called Patreese to see what he thought. He said she's got a few days at the most. She seems to know it, too. She asked him to make her look pretty."

Ben's Adam's apple bobbed. For a moment I thought he was going to cry, but he just charged toward his office. "I'll book the tickets, then."

"No." I caught him by the arm. "You don't have to, sweetie."

"Those flights fill up fast."

"I mean, you don't have to go. I can do this myself. You've got work to do, and you've put up with enough already."

"You don't want me to?" He looked almost hurt.

"No . . . of course not. I just didn't want to make you—"

"Don't be ridiculous. This is what husbands do." He

started heading for the office again. "We don't have to stay with Irwin and Lenore, do we?"

"God, no."

"I'll find us someplace nice. Does it have to be gay?"

"I don't care. Just no orchids in the toilet."

The rain lingered as the day wore on, so I called Jake from home and told him I wouldn't need him for a job in the Marina that afternoon. "Anyway," I added, "I've got some loose ends I need to tie up in the office today. My mother's pretty close to the end, so Ben and I are leaving on the red-eye tonight."

"Shit . . . I'm sorry, boss."

"You think you could hold down the fort for a few days?"

"Sure. No problem."

"There shouldn't be much to do, with all this rain. Mrs. Langston wants her hedges trimmed, and you know how she gets, so . . . if there's a break in the weather today—"

"I'm on the case, boss. Don't even think about it."

"Good man."

"Will you be on your cell?"

"Yeah . . . and the house'll be empty, so . . . if you and Connor, or whoever . . . wanna come hang out and use the hot tub . . . consider it your spa."

"You serious?"

"You bet. It'll be nice to think of life going on back here. You know where the key is, and there's some extra towels under the bathroom sink. Just turn off the hot tub when you leave. And don't forget to cover it or the raccoons will have a field day."

"No sweat," said Jake. "I'll tell the roomies." His failure to mention Connor made me wonder if that romance had faded because of the aforementioned plumbing issues, or if Jake was just being his usual private self. "We've got our poker game tonight," he added. "We're cooking paella. Anna's coming up for it."

"Since when does Anna play poker?"

Jake chuckled. "Since a few weeks ago. Marguerite and Selina taught her." (Those were his roommates, the teacher and the investment counselor, both trannies in their thirties.)

"Damn," I said. "She never fails to amaze me."

"She said her mom used to play it in Winnemucca."

I could picture little Anna—or Andy, as she was back then—watching her mother deal cards to her "girls" at the Blue Moon Lodge during the flapper era. Mona, lucky devil, actually got to see that ancient brothel (and live there briefly) before her grandmother—widely known in those parts as Mother Mucca—passed away in the early eighties. The place was deserted for years, then finally torn down to make room for a casino/hotel complex, though some clever soul with a sense of history saw fit to preserve the name. Grasping for atmosphere where I'm sure there's none to be found, the placemats at the Blue Moon Bar and Grill make coy reference to the "colorful house of ill repute" that once stood on that spot.

Anna learned all this from Bobbi, the youngest of Mother Mucca's brood, when Bobbi came through San Francisco toward the end of the millennium. Anna remarked at the time that her mother would have pitched a fit at the notion of her house being one of "ill repute," almost as much as she would have denounced the clinical sound of "sex worker," the newest politically correct euphemism for hookers. Mother Mucca was an old-fashioned gal.

Bobbi was in her forties by then and no longer a hooker. She was married and living in Houston, finally making an honest living. She worked as a receptionist at Enron.

I called Brian at the nursery to tell him about Mama— not for comfort, really, just to keep him in the loop. I was already feeling guilty about not having shared Irwin's crisis with Brian, since I know he would have gotten a kick out of the whole gruesome mess. But telling that story—and the solution I'd offered—would have brought Shawna into the picture, and that would not have amused her father nearly as much. Besides, my gift to Irwin had been a secret of his own, so my obligation—I told myself—was to keep it that way.

Secrets and lies, I thought as I hung up the phone. *After thirty years of insisting on the truth, I'm still my mother's son. The orange doesn't fall very far from the tree.*

I spent the rest of the afternoon doing laundry and online banking. My business account was disastrously low—given that I was leaving town—so I rounded up some stray checks from clients and made a mental note to deposit them at the airport. I hate the grim little dance of finance and always have; it's so lifeless and unyielding, the antithesis of planting a garden. Money, if you ask me, has no right at all to be green.

Ben wouldn't be home before dark—there was still that sideboard to finish—so I began to pack for both of us. I started with my compartmentalized pill box, filling it with a week's worth of meds—just in case. Then I chose a suit bag for both our dark suits: Ben's nice new navy-blue one from Nordstrom and the ancient black crepe one I finally bought in the late eighties when funerals were proving more commonplace than theme parties. (I'd let out the waist a few times, but it was still holding up all right.)

I figured that the rest of our clothes could be casual, so I filled a duffel bag with jeans and socks and T-shirts, leaving room for our shaving kits and a zippered bag we take on the road for condoms, lubricants, and the like. It felt odd to be preparing for sex in the midst of death, but utterly necessary. I drew the line at packing our latest toy: a glass-and-rubber penis pump we had ordered online. It had given us both a rollicking good time (somewhat to our surprise) but it looked like something out of a fifties mad-scientist movie and would almost certainly read as a terrorist device on an airport X-ray machine.

Ben still smelled sweetly of his workshop when he got home. He smooched me at the door without ceremony and headed straight for the shower. When he joined me in the bedroom, he kissed me again and put on a T-shirt and sweatpants.

"Is that what you're wearing on the plane?"

"It's a red-eye," he said with a shrug.

"You're right." I pulled off my jeans and grabbed sweatpants from the closet.

"We should pack the Ambien."

I patted my carry-on bag. "Gotcha."

"Will this be open-casket?" Ben asked.

"What?"

"Don't Southerners generally prefer open-casket funerals?"

"Not this one," I said with a wince, but it did make me think. "Of course. You're right. That's why she asked Patreese to 'pretty her up.' Not before but *after*."

My father's funeral had been closed-casket, to the

obvious disappointment of some of the mourners, but now I could understand why Mama hadn't wanted one last chance to gaze at her husband's face—prettied up or not. The loudest objection to Papa's closed casket had come from an aunt in Pensacola who'd sent the biggest wreath at the funeral. I still recall that monstrosity more vividly than anything else that day: a mass of white carnations surrounding a child's toy telephone. A glittered ribbon at the top said: JESUS CALLED. The one at the bottom said: AND HERB ANSWERED.

Herb, of course, had answered for nothing, but Mama had finally told the truth, and that made an open casket strangely appropriate. She could face the world without shame.

"Should we try to call her before we leave?" Ben asked as he packed his dressy black shoes.

I shook my head. "Irwin says she's really out of it—sleeping most of the time. They've got her on morphine. She's still adamant about staying off the respirator."

"She knows we're coming, though?"

"Oh, yeah."

Ben left the suitcase and pressed against my back, wrapping his arms around me.

"Are you okay?"

"Yeah, sweetie, I'm fine. Why do you keep asking that?"

293

His cheek was against my shoulder blade. "Because you're not crying."

Ben knew better than anyone that I can cry at the drop of a hat. I had cried the night before when we were watching *Victor/Victoria* on Logo, the new queer channel. The movie came out the year Jon died, and I bought the album (remember albums?) just weeks after we buried his ashes at 28 Barbary Lane. I loved the song "You and Me," the sweet little soft-shoe number performed by Julie Andrews and Robert Preston. Those two are, in effect, playing a gay male couple, so the lyrics hit my heart dead center: *"We don't care that tomorrow comes with no guarantee, we've each other for company."* Since then, of course, there have been thousands of tomorrows with no guarantees. Only now I saw Robert and Julie in a different light—as an *intergenerational* gay couple. I was no longer Victor, the *ingénue*; I was Toddy, the fussy "old queen with a head cold," who knows, in spite of everything, that he is loved.

"I'm not gonna cry about Mama," I said.

Ben tightened his grip on me.

"Does that sound awful?"

"No."

"I'm sure she wants to go . . . but . . . that's not the point. It's just not in me anymore."

"Some things are just too big, I guess."

"Or too late," I said.

25

Red-Eye

We took a cab to the airport to avoid a decision about parking—short-term or long-term?—and the implications of that. The security line was relatively hassle-free that late at night, so we made it to the gate without difficulty. But thanks to the annual cataclysm of our first rainfall, our flight was delayed for another hour and a half. The latest update from Orlovista suggested that time was of the essence, so I could feel my gut tightening on the spot. I called Irwin's voice-mail and told him about the delay, assuring him that we were still on the way. Then we dragged our carry-ons to the newsstand and sought diversion.

The magazines we bought spoke volumes about both of us. I bought *People* (because I let myself do that in airports) and *Coastal Living* (because lately I've entertained fantasies about a place on the water—though I have no idea where the place, or even the water, would be). Ben bought *National Geographic* and *Yoga Journal* (because he has no idea how unwholesome his wholesomeness makes me feel). We buried ourselves in words and pictures for over an hour, remaining largely silent, both of us conscious of preserving our energy.

Ten minutes before boarding time I made a run to the bathroom. On my return Ben told me that my cell phone had rung. I dug it out of my bag. There was a brief message from Jake: "Hi, boss. I know you're in the air right now, but . . . gimme a call when you get this."

It was almost two a.m. but I called him back—certain I knew what he wanted.

He sounded tentative when he answered. "Hello?"

"They're in the red box by the front door," I told him.

"What?"

"The keys to the truck, right? I should've told you . . . I'm sorry."

He seemed to be gasping for air. It took me a moment to realize he was crying.

"Jake . . . what is it?"

"Anna," he said, strangling his sobs, "had a heart attack."

I was looking directly at Ben now, who was obviously hearing everything. I knew what I had to ask Jake, but I found it impossible to speak.

"I guess you haven't taken off," Jake said.

"No . . . there was a . . . do you mean she's—"

"She's still alive, but she's . . . not awake. Damn, boss. I figured you be long gone. I hate to lay this on you when—"

"Where are you?"

"St. Sebastian's. Room 5ll."

"We'll be there."

"But won't that make you—"

"I'm glad you called, Jake . . . really."

I closed the cell phone and looked at Ben. He was already gathering our stuff.

"Are you sure about this?" he asked.

"Yes."

But my legs wobbled pathetically as I tried to stand, so Ben grabbed my arm to keep me from toppling. Somehow he got me from there to the corner of a sports bar, where, for at least five minutes, in full view of the sports fans, I did the unimaginable and cried for my mother.

It was raining like all get-out by the time we reached St. Sebastian's Hospital. The whole place was in sleep mode, and the hallways were all but deserted until we reached the one outside Anna's room. Jake had thought to notify Brian, so he and Shawna were there—noticeably distraught—as well as Marguerite and Selina, the flatmates. Jake was at the end of the hallway, deep in

297

conversation with a doctor. Marguerite was the first to spot us.

"Hi, guys." She stood up and hurried over to embrace us, one at a time, briskly and equally, like the elementary schoolteacher she was. Short and partridge plump, she even *looked* like a schoolteacher that night. Or at least a stereotypical one. Her brown hair was wrapped tight in a bun, and there was a cameo at the throat of her high-collared blouse.

"She's stabilized," she said quietly. "She's in a coma . . . but she can still pull through, the doctor says, if she makes it through the next couple of days."

I finally managed to speak. "When did it happen?"

"We're not sure. She didn't show up for poker, so Jake went down to check on her. She was already unconscious by then. Notch was lying by her side."

Someone to sit in the sun with me. Who doesn't want to go anywhere.

Marguerite leaned closer and spoke in a whisper. "Jake is kind of . . . punishing himself. He thinks he should've checked on her earlier. I guess he was working late."

Mrs. Langston, I thought. *Mrs. Langston and her fucking hedges.*

"I'll speak to him," I said.

Brian and Shawna joined us. We didn't hug—somehow it wasn't the right thing.

"I'm glad you're here," I told them.

Brian nodded. "You too."

"Are we allowed to go in?" Ben asked.

"Sure," said Shawna. "It just got kinda crowded in there."

I nodded a greeting to Selina (Jake's other flatmate, the investment counselor, a Korean-Canadian) as Ben and I entered the room. Selina returned the nod. I'd met her maybe three times at the most, but her total devotion to Anna was painfully apparent.

Anna was lying flat on the bed with her eyes closed, robbed of her usual color by a hospital gown and a respirator. I know you're supposed to talk to people in comas, but I couldn't, I just couldn't. It wasn't like Anna at all. There was nothing to connect with but the wheezing of the machinery and the grim drizzle of the rain against the window.

Don't blame the rain, I told myself. *Without it you wouldn't even be here.*

Back in the corridor, I had a few moments alone with Jake.

"How long have you been here?" I asked.

"A few hours. I dunno."

"You looked exhausted. Why don't you go home?"

"I can't, boss."

299

"Yes, you can. We've got cell phones. I can take it from here."

"What am I gonna do at home?" (That pretty much answered my question about Connor.)

"The three of you should go," I told him. "Selina and Marguerite both look beat . . . and we're gonna have to do this in shifts. Get some rest and come relieve me later."

"But, what if—?"

"You've done everything right, Jake." I laid my arm across his shoulders. I knew he wouldn't start crying again. He was being a man about it.

"I was responsible for her," he said quietly.

"No, you weren't. She was. And that's the way she wanted it . . . *wants* it. There was no way in the world to know this would happen."

He seemed to get that I meant this.

"Ben and I were ready for a red-eye," I added, "so now we're just doing it somewhere else. Besides, somebody's gotta check on Notch."

This hadn't occurred to him. "Fuck," he said softly.

"There . . . you see?" I cajoled him with a look. "C'mon, sport. I just blew off my mother's death. Help me make it mean something."

He put his hand on my knee and shook it. "I'll check with the gals. Marguerite's got a class in the morning.

She could use the sleep." He rose to his feet in full bear-cub mode.

"How were Mrs. Langston and her hedges?" I asked.

"A bitch," he replied.

I chuckled. "Same as it ever was."

"Hey . . . it's the job."

I was touched by the pride in his voice. He reminded me of me in my early days at the nursery.

Jake added, as an afterthought, "I bet even ol' Capability had to deal with some crabby old Lady Somebody-or-Other."

I'd recently told Jake about Capability Brown, the eighteenth-century landscape designer who persuaded the British aristocracy to tear out their formal gardens in favor of clumps of trees and free-form lakes. Jake, to my professorial delight, had adopted him as a hero.

"Yeah," I said, smiling. "He probably did."

He gave me a little salute.

"I'll call you," I said. "If there's any change at all."

An hour later, nothing had changed. Brian and Ben went out to scout for food, leaving Shawna and me alone. She was dressed in jeans and a T-shirt—and without her usual makeup—so she looked eerily young. I could still see the girl on Heart's Desire Beach.

"Do you think she *knew*, Mouse?"

"What?"

"That this was gonna happen. Giving me her purse and all."

I told her what Anna had said to me at the top of the de Young tower, explaining that I'd taken it largely as a sign of her general preparedness. "But she's very intuitive, as you know. She knew the very moment her mother died—in Nevada."

"Really?"

"And Edgar Halcyon, too."

"Her big romance, you mean?"

I nodded. "We were all at her Christmas party on Barbary Lane . . . and she was out in the courtyard at one point . . . and she sort of . . . felt him leave."

"She told you this?"

"Yeah. Not until much later, but . . . yeah."

"That sounds more psychic than intuitive."

"She wouldn't call it that. It's more like . . . a connectedness. She doesn't talk to the dead or anything like that. She just feels it when . . . life ends."

I'd struck a more somber note than I'd intended, and a shadow fell across Shawna's face. I made a clumsy effort at changing the subject.

"When's your book coming out? Have you heard from your publishers?"

She rolled her eyes. "The ass monkeys want me to change the ending."

"Oh?"

"Can you believe that? I ended with a chapter on paraplegic sex . . . and they thought that was—get this—too downbeat."

I told her, tactfully, I could sort of see their point.

"C'mon, Mouse . . . it's totally hopeful in a book about sex. It means we all get a shot at getting laid. It's about as upbeat as you can get."

Her eyes were so dark and soulful without the distraction of makeup. Like Natalie Wood's eyes (or Natalie Portman's, if you must). I suddenly felt so blessed to have known her all these years. She was leaving me, too, I realized, and that would sting a little.

"So," I told her, smiling, "tell the ass monkeys how you feel about it."

"I have. Believe me."

"What is it they say? The only difference between comedy and tragedy is where you end the story?"

"Who always says that?"

"I dunno. Somebody." My heart grew leaden again. I sighed and gazed down the empty hallway toward the elevator. "Where will they find food this time of night?"

"Safeway, I think."

"Ah." I smiled at her rather pathetically. "You won't have that problem in New York."

"No . . . I guess not."

A long silence.

"Should I be leaving?" she asked.

303

I took her hand. "It's your dream, babycakes."

"Yeah . . . but . . . I can write anywhere, and . . . Dad's just . . . coming apart at the seams."

"That's not your problem. It's not even about you."

She blinked at me for a moment, apparently understanding, then turned her gaze back toward Anna's room. Even from here you could hear the sighing of the respirator.

"This sucks so bad," she said.

The guys brought us pizza—lukewarm and oily and curiously satisfying. The four of us consumed it tribally in a nook next to the nurses' station.

Then Brian asked me: "Is this déjà vu for you?"

"Yeah," I replied. "A little."

"Why?" asked Ben.

"This is where Michael was laid up back in . . . '77, was it?"

"It was one floor up, actually, but the view was the same."

Shawna wiped her mouth, remembering the story. "The thing with the snooty-sounding name."

"Guillain-Barré," I said, smiling. I had come down with this esoteric syndrome literally overnight and had recovered in a matter of months. In between I was almost totally paralyzed. Jon—my lover, the gynecologist—was working at St. Sebastian's at the time and would stop by on his rounds, bringing his Norse god face into my limited line of vision. Five years later AIDS would turn the tables. Jon died here in 1982, blind and terrified.

I knew not to go there now.

Ben's face lit up. "Then this was where you came out!" (It's amazing, really, how well Ben remembers my stories. I'm not nearly as good about remembering his.)

"What do you mean?" asked Shawna.

"He wrote his parents from here," said Brian. "Told 'em he was gay."

Shawna turned to me. "But you were paralyzed."

"I dictated it."

Brian laughed. We all did, in fact. But back then I'd thought I was going to die in this place. I thought the paralysis would reach my lungs and that would be it; there'd be no other chance to say who I was. I remember the butterfly kite that Anna hung on the wall across from my bed. And I remember the people around the bed the day I wrote the letter—Anna and Mona and Brian and Mary Ann—my "logical" family at 28 Barbary Lane.

"It was a fucking *long* letter, too," I said, grinning. "Thank God Mary Ann knew shorthand."

Her name hung in the air like an unanswered question.

Shawna avoided eye contact with her father by

305

staring down at the pizza box. Ben shot a glance at me, then gazed into the distance. Brian cleared his throat and stood up.

"Too many sodas," he said, heading off to the bathroom.

Once he was out of earshot, Shawna murmured, "Shit," beneath her breath.

"Sorry," I said.

"Nothing to be sorry for," said Ben.

Brian was gone for at least ten minutes. When he returned his face looked ravaged from crying. Standing, he addressed the three of us as a body.

"Sorry, guys."

"No problem," said Ben.

"We have to call her," said Brian. "We can't let this happen without her."

26

Remembered
Perfume

You try it sometime. You try finding a fifty-five-year-old housewife from Darien, Connecticut, whom you haven't talked to for years. That place is a hotbed of cautious white people. It's where they shot *The Stepford Wives*, you know. Both versions of it.

Mary Ann had given me her number on 9/11, but it hadn't worked since the invasion of Iraq. Shawna had a more recent number, but, typically, she'd mislaid it. My only option was to sweet-talk the nurse (he didn't require much) into letting me use his computer.

I tried Googling Mary Ann's husband to no avail. There was plenty of stuff about his former business—and even a mention of his wife—but no phone numbers, of course.

Then I remembered Mary Ann's stepson, the Explorer Scout whose troop ran Darien's ambulance service.

Their website provided a phone number, so I called and got a recording: a croaky-voiced kid telling you to call 911 and not the Explorer post if this is "an actual emergency." I just wanted the Explorer post, so I left a message: "If anyone in the post knows Robbie Caruthers, please tell him to tell his stepmom that Anna Madrigal is . . . very ill. This is extremely important. Thank you very much. The number she should call is . . ."

The pizza made us sleepy, so we slept intermittently, slumped against one another outside Anna's room. In the pearly-gray hour before dawn I took my cell phone to another wing of the hospital and called Irwin at home in Orlando.

"Hey, bro," he said.

"Hope I'm not too early."

"Nah. Lenore's up and fixin' biscuits. You on the ground?"

"No . . . well, yeah, but . . . I'm still in San Francisco . . ."

. . . *three* . . . *two* . . . *one* . . .

". . . I won't be coming back, Irwin. My friend Anna has had a heart attack, and . . . I have to be with her. I'm sorry."

A long silence, and then: "Mama's got two days at the most, Mikey."

"I know that, Irwin."

"I don't understand."

"Yes, you do, Irwin. Anna is family to me."

"More than your mama?"

I took a breath and said it: "If I have to choose . . . yes."

Irwin sighed audibly. "Your old landlady, right? The one with the—"

"Can she talk on the phone?"

"Who? Mama?"

"Yes."

"No way."

"Then I need you to help me, Irwin. I need you to tell Mama that I love her and I wish I could be there and . . . whatever she needs to hear . . . and I want you to tell her, if you haven't already, that I'm glad she blabbed about Papa. Tell her: 'Good for you, Mama.' Tell her I'm proud of her. Tell her I'm glad she came out."

"Okay. That's awful long but—"

"How is Sumter doing around all this?"

"He's holdin' up. He's a tough little soldier underneath."

"I know," I said, bristling at his implication. "He's also a sweet gay kid who needs your support."

"That's not funny, Mikey."

"I'm not trying—"

"How could you possibly know that, anyway?"

309

"How could you possibly *not* know it?"

Silence.

"No boot camps, Irwin. And no more snide remarks. That's all I'm saying. Let him be who he is. Don't deal with this the way Papa did."

The invocation of our father brought even more silence, but I think I got through to him. I was holding the cards now; Irwin had no choice but to listen.

"Will you at least come for the funeral?" he asked.

"Depends on how soon it happens, I guess."

"It won't look right if you don't."

"I don't care how it looks."

"Right."

"I'll try to be there, though. I really will."

I could picture myself at a funeral ceremony—two, three, maybe four days hence—but it wasn't being held at a memorial park in Orlando. I was climbing the wooden stairway at the entrance to Barbary Lane, holding tight to Anna's favorite vase (the Chinese ginger jar she kept on her dresser). There were at least a half-dozen people with me, so we would have to make it simple and quick. The house had been severely remodeled and was a single-family dwelling these days—a young developer and his PR woman wife, both chums of Governor Schwarzenegger. I knew they wouldn't cotton to the notion of a foreign substance being sprinkled in their garden.

"I hope we'll see you," said Irwin.

"I hope so, too," I replied.

Shortly after ten that morning, Jake and Selina showed up to relieve the watch. Brian and Shawna headed off in their separate directions, and Ben and I went home. Anna's condition had remained unchanged, and I was grateful, frankly, to get the smell of the hospital out of my head. I was beginning to feel a familiar tightening in my chest—a function of my meds, probably, or anxiety, or a combination of the two. It happens some-times, I don't know why. I was ready to breathe some clean morning air and take a shower and stretch out on the bed for a few hours. Ben was, too.

It felt odd hauling our luggage back into the house. It seemed like a lifetime had passed since we'd packed those bags. After showering, we unpacked just enough to brush our teeth, then crawled under clean sheets together.

"What would I do if you weren't here?"

"You'd manage," Ben said, smiling. He was straddling my leg like a koala climbing a tree. He's only an inch shorter than me but he feels much smaller in bed. The weight difference has something to do with that (I'm not in denial here), but it's also about the sense of purpose I feel when we're together. I feel like his protector.

"My daddy," he said with a sigh. "My man." (He often adds the man part to the daddy part, for fear, I guess, that I'll find him too hung up on roles. He needn't worry. I love being his daddy—it seems to be the role I was born for.)

"You've been so patient," I told him.

"About what?"

"All this death and dying shit. You didn't sign on for that."

"I didn't sign on at all. I was drafted. And she made you do it, thank God."

He meant Anna, of course—the way she'd brought us together at the Caffe Sport.

I smiled. "We owe her one, don't we?"

"More than one, I'd say."

We lay quiet for a while. A light drizzle was shellacking the leaves in the garden. I felt the warm rise and fall of Ben's chest against my side.

This is my harbor, I thought. *This is where I've been heading all along.*

He stroked my arm deliberately, as if about to say something, but changed his mind.

"What, sweetie?"

"I was just wondering . . . say, assuming she doesn't come out of the coma . . ."

"I don't know," I said. "I don't know what we'd do."

"Do you know what she'd want?"

I swallowed hard. "Probably . . . yes."

"Same as your mother?"

I couldn't answer that directly. "The doctor said it sometimes takes three or four days for them to come out of it."

"Sure." He patted my stomach as if to say that he'd leave that alone for now. "Let's get some sleep."

I slept solidly for a little over four hours. I was awakened by my cell phone—an unidentified caller.

"Hello." My voice was still froggy with sleep.

"I'm sorry," said the caller. "I'm not sure who I am calling. This is Mary Ann Caruthers from Darien, Connecticut."

I noticed, perversely, that she pronounced the town's name the way I've been told the locals do: Dairy Ann. Mary Ann from Dairy Ann. Singleton no more.

"Hey," I said evenly. "It's Michael."

"Oh . . . Michael . . . hi."

"Hi."

Pleasant but stiff, both of us. Like the day we'd met back in 1976. She'd just found the man of her dreams at the Marina Safeway only to discover that he was there with the man of *his* dreams—me. What else could we be but pleasant and stiff?

"One of the posties just called me at Pilates."

"I'm sorry . . . What?"

"The Explorer Post. The place you called?"

"Right. Of course."

"She dates my stepson, Robbie, so . . ." She caught her breath, stopped herself. "It was something about Mrs. Madrigal?"

She sounded so young at that moment, framing the difficult as a hopeful question. Those of us who'd grown old with Anna had dropped the "Mrs." years ago. Mary Ann had to summon a younger version of herself to function in this moment.

"She had a heart attack," I said. "She's in a coma."

"Fuck." She spoke the word softly, like an Episcopal prayer.

"We couldn't *not* tell you."

"No . . . thank you. Thank you for that."

"Brian asked me to call you. Brian and Shawna." (I wanted her to know this; she had to be wondering.)

"Is she likely to . . ."

"We don't know. She's just . . . you know, sleeping."

A long silence, and then: "She didn't ask for me, did she?"

"No . . . it happened pretty quick." I had a terrible sinking feeling. Why had I even bothered with this? "You don't have to be here or anything . . . we just wanted you to know."

"I appreciate the effort, Michael."

"Hey," I said, a little too brightly. "Thank the Explorers."

314

"I'll be at the Four Seasons. I'll call you when I get in."

I really didn't get what she meant. "The Four Seasons where?"

"The Four Seasons there."

"You were already planning to come?"

"No," she replied, "but . . . my husband has a plane."

That slight hesitation redeemed her; she had the good taste to be embarrassed.

Ben and I were slated for the night watch at the hospital, so we decided to take a walk down at Crissy Field. The rain had stopped by early afternoon, but there were a few sodden clouds loitering above the bay. We followed the path through the marshes and inlets that had been—not that long ago—a derelict military airstrip. Now there were herons and sandy beaches and children romping at the water's edge. A new ecosystem was forming where once there had only been asphalt.

We sat on a bench, holding hands, gazing out at the kindly blue of the bay. There were sailboats even today, a rainbow of sails catching the fickle wind. I remembered what Anna had said about bringing Sumter here and realized how right she had been. *I will do that*, I promised her, *no matter what happens. I will sit here and show him this miracle and tell him he's loved for exactly the boy he's becoming.*

The wind shifted and blew toward us, sweet with rain and the sagey smell of the wetlands. It seemed to blow *through* me, in fact, soothing every cell in my body. It was like that moment in *Poltergeist* when JoBeth Williams feels the spirit of her daughter passing through her. "I can smell her," she says, laughing with relief, and that's just how it was with me. Not a remembered perfume or even the scent of her skin, but her essence, a condensation of her spirit. She was passing through me like sunlight through water, on her way to somewhere else. I looked at my watch.

"Should we be going?" asked Ben.

"I think so," I told him.

Ben was driving the Prius up Noe Hill when the call came. I remember looking at Carlotta's navigational map and seeing the Home icon appear on the screen. *Perfect*, I thought. *Perfect*.

And the perfect messenger was bringing the news.

"Patreese," I said quietly.

"Wassup, my brother?" (Shawna says that, too, sometimes, but I've never gotten used to it. A greeting offered as a question seems to lay the burden on the person being called, when the caller, by all rights, should be telling you what's up.)

"Hangin' in there," I said.

"Listen, Michael—"

"It's Mama, right?"

"Yeah. She passed about twenty minutes ago. I was talkin' to Mohammed and saw your folks come in. I hope you don't mind hearin' it from me first."

"I'd rather it be you," I told him.

Ben looked over at me and laid his hand on my leg.

"She went peaceful," said Patreese. "I was workin' on her this morning, and she was . . . you know . . . fixin' to leave already."

"I'm sure," I said.

"She wanted you to have something. You at your computer?"

"I will be in a little while."

"Check your email, my man."

Ten minutes later I did that. It was a photograph of Mama and Patreese, both grinning like kids at a prom as they posed for the camera. Patreese was sitting on her bed in a red T-shirt, his big mahogany arm lying gently on her frail shoulders.

Mama was holding the photograph of me and Ben at Big Sur.

27

Gibberish

Mary Ann hadn't changed dramatically since the days of her adjustable-bed commercials. You could still see that person, at any rate. She was just as slim, just as naturally elegant as the mid-forties version of herself. Her hair was the big difference; short and silvery and feathered against her well-shaped head in Judi Dench fashion. As she sat on my sofa that morning, looking pretty in slacks and a sea-foam silk blouse, I wondered if the new hairdo had been the result of boredom or chemotherapy. That's just how I think these days. Catastrophes are to be expected.

She seemed to read my mind. "Was it a mistake?" she asked, touching the side of her head. "It's fairly new."

"I like it," I said.

"I'm not so sure." She rolled her eyes in self-punishment. "Why am I talking about my hair?"

"Nerves," I said, smiling. "In a minute I'll be talking about mine."

She smiled back. "You really do look good, Michael."

"Thanks," I said, shifting my extra weight in my Morris chair. She didn't call me Mouse, I noticed. The name was an artifact now, part of who we used to be.

"Where are Brian and Shawna?" she asked.

"They're already at Anna's. I told them we'd meet them there."

"Great . . . she's home now, then?"

"Oh . . . no . . . I meant the hospital, actually." I paused for a moment, choosing my words. "You should know . . . she's still not awake. She may never be."

Mary Ann nodded. "I understand."

I had just begun to face this myself, but I'd already resolved, after lengthy discussions with Brian and Marguerite, to help create the sort of send-off that Anna would want: one without panic or regret or excessive sadness on the part of the survivors. We had that opportunity, after all. We had to make the most of it.

"I hope I didn't put you on the spot," I told Mary Ann. "Brian asked me to call you, but, frankly, I wasn't sure if I even had the right to—"

"No. He was absolutely right. I'm glad you called." She looked around the living room, taking it in. "This place just gets cozier and cozier."

"Thanks. Eighteen years will do that."

"And Thack's . . . not around anymore?"

I shook my head. "He took off ten years ago."

"Oh . . . I'm sorry."

"I'm not. I mean . . . it was awful at the time, but it brought me to where I am now. If you know what I mean,"

"I do . . . actually." As she fiddled with the piping on the slipcover I could see that her hands were the only place where her age was evident. I've noticed this about myself as well. We can fool ourselves about our changing faces, but our hands creep up on us. One day we look down at them and realize they belong to our grandparents.

"Still," she said, "you guys seemed happy. I was a little bit envious, to tell you the truth."

"It *was* good," I told her. "For a few years, at any rate. He just got more and more angry."

"At you, you mean?"

"At the world mostly . . . but I was there. I had to live with it. You remember how he was sometimes. It just got worse."

Mary Ann smiled in remembrance. "You called him your little Shiite."

"Well, that's what you do, don't you? Put a cute name on the shit that really bothers you . . . so it looks like you knew what you were getting."

"You're right," she said ruefully. I wondered if she

320

was thinking of Brian (hadn't she called him Mr. Mellow?) or the current husband, the retired CEO who flies his own jet and wears patchwork madras. She was clearly thinking of *someone*.

"The thing is," I said, "Thack did me a favor by leaving. I might never have noticed how little I was getting if he hadn't taken it away."

She nodded slowly, arranging her hands carefully in her lap. "So . . . you're single these days?"

I did something I've never done with another living soul: I held up my left hand and wiggled my wedding band at her. The gesture was straight out of Cleveland, tailor-made for Mary Ann. Or at least the Mary Ann I used to know.

She cooed appreciatively. "You went the whole route, eh?"

I nodded. "Down at City Hall."

She smiled. "I thought about you when that happened."

"Same here. I wanted you to meet him."

"Really?" She widened her eyes. "So where is he?"

"Down at the hospital with the others."

"How sweet that he cares about her so much."

I went to the mantel and grabbed the Big Sur photo—the same shot I'd sent to my mother. "His name is Benjamin McKenna."

"Well," she said, perusing the photo, "he's adorable."

"Yeah."

"And young."

I nodded solemnly. "He was in the Explorers with your stepson. That's how I found you."

Her mouth went completely oval—like little Shirley Temple.

"Kidding," I assured her.

"Oh, God . . . Mouse." She giggled like the girl I used to know. "Why do you do that to me?"

"I dunno," I said. "You've just always been so . . . easy. Where's yours, by the way?"

"Where's my what?"

"Husband."

"Oh . . . back in the hotel. He's having a gym day."

"Well, that's good . . . I mean, a good thing to do."

"He's kind of a . . . you know . . . straight-ahead guy, but . . . I'm really happy with him, Mouse."

I nodded. "You seem to be."

"And guess what . . . we were married the same week you were."

Now I was the one playing Shirley Temple. "How did you know when Ben and I were . . . ? Oh, right . . . the news."

"Isn't that amazing? It's not like we could have planned it."

"No . . . you're right. We couldn't have."

There was a melancholy note in my reply, but she

didn't seem to notice. She just kept chattering away cheerfully—almost hysterically.

"And Robbie is the sweetest kid. He's already certified as an EMT, and he'll be driving the ambulance next year. And I like being a mom, you know . . . even at this advanced age. There's something wonderful about passing on what you know to someone younger . . . even if it's dumb stuff they have no use for whatsoever."

As you might imagine, I was thinking of Ben now, but Mary Ann was already in the process of shifting gears. "I know you all hated me after I left . . . and you had every right to, Mouse, but I just couldn't keep—"

"Look, Mary Ann, there's no point in—"

"Yes there is. There *is* a point. Brian and I weren't right for each other, and both of us knew it, and . . . I couldn't keep pretending that everything was fine. I made it about my career . . . and to some extent it was . . . but I just couldn't do it anymore. And I knew he'd always have Shawna. I knew he wouldn't be alone."

"He hasn't been," I said quietly.

"And there was something else I couldn't admit . . . even to myself: you were gonna die, Mouse, and I couldn't . . . this is so awful . . . ." She was pressing her fingertips under her eyes, the way well-bred ladies do to stop their tears. "I couldn't bear the thought of watching you die the way Jon did. I couldn't do that again.

Not with you, Mouse. I couldn't bear the thought of . . . that horror."

"It's okay," I said softly. "I didn't much care for it myself."

Her laughter came in a short violent burst, and that set free her tears. I rose from my chair and joined her on the sofa, collecting her in my arms while she sobbed. She felt so tiny there and her hair smelled clean and lemony.

"Get it out," I told her. "We've got a celebration to attend."

It helped that we were all there for Anna. Brian and Shawna (and Mary Ann, for that matter) were largely relieved of the problem of finding something meaningful to say at their reunion. The afternoon was strictly about Anna, so there was only a brief exchange of hugs in the lobby and a heartbreaking moment—well, heartbreaking to me—when, on our way down the hallway, Mary Ann touched Shawna's back and complimented her on her black onyx earrings. Brian, for the most part, remained stoic throughout, handling the other introductions—Ben and Jake and the flatmates—with surprising grace. He could pull it together when he wanted to.

Marguerite, as usual, provided the update:

"She's off the respirator," she told us.

I knew what that had meant in my mother's case, so I wasn't sure how to react. Was there cause for celebration or . . . cause for another type of celebration?

"What does that mean?" asked Shawna.

"She woke up briefly this morning and just yanked it off when the doctors weren't here. She's been sleeping without it."

I was frowning now. "And the doctors said that's okay?"

"Absolutely," said Selina. "Her vital signs are definitely improving." It was the longest phrase I'd heard her speak since Anna had been at the hospital, but there was something about her certainty that sounded wishful and forced.

"Is she able to talk?" asked Mary Ann.

"Just in her sleep," said Jake. "It's not makin' a lotta sense."

"Like what?" asked Brian.

"You know," said Selina, obviously putting on a brave face. "The way anybody sounds when they talk in their sleep."

Mary Ann nodded soberly, casting her eyes at Brian and Shawna.

Ben moved next to me and slipped his arm around my waist with a small but significant smile. He seemed to be telling me that we weren't out of the woods yet.

Brain damage is what I was thinking.

All seven of us were in Anna's room now. Her bed was no longer flat, but she was fast asleep. Someone—Selina or Marguerite, I presume—had made a gallant effort at making her presentable, fluffing her hair and adding color to her cheeks. Anna's eyes were closed but fluttering as she murmured unintelligibly. Brian, as already agreed upon, stood next to her and did all the talking—at least initially.

"Anna . . . if you can hear me . . . everyone's here now."

He's being the man of the family, I thought.

"It's okay if you don't want to wake up. We're just here to tell you how much we love you and appreciate everything you've—"

He was interrupted by a groan from Anna, twitching in her sleep.

"—everything you've done for us."

"Mona?" Anna murmured. "Is that you?"

My heart caught in my throat as Brian gazed toward me for guidance. I shook my head, telling him not to go there. Mary Ann caught this interaction and grimaced in confusion. *She doesn't know*, I thought. *We never even got to that.*

"It's Brian, Anna . . . and Mary Ann's here, too. She flew in all the way from Connecticut just to see you. And Selina and Marguerite are here. They're responsible for the beautiful red satin pajamas you're wearing. And Ben and Michael, of course, and Shawna, who's moving to New York next week to—"

Another moan from Anna, this one louder, more guttural.

"—to become the world's best writer. Or at least the next Susie Bright, right? And we're all very proud of her . . ."

Shawna leaned over and whispered, "Maybe this isn't a good idea."

Selina, I noticed, was already slipping out of the room, apparently shaken by Anna's failure to respond to Brian's wedding-reception-MC approach. Marguerite followed, whispering reassurances to her friend. Anna, meanwhile, was speaking again, her eyes still closed, her words slurred and cryptic.

"What's she saying?" asked Mary Ann.

Brian leaned closer. Anna's lips were moving, but I couldn't hear much of anything from where I was standing.

"It doesn't make any sense," said Brian. "It's gibberish."

"Like what?" said Shawna.

"It sounded like 'There is no . . . fisted nation.'"

"Fisted nation?" said Jake, wrinkling his nose.

Anna spoke again, apparently repeating herself, so Brian moved his ear closer to her mouth. "No," he said, looking up at us, "it's 'fifth destination.' She said, 'There is no fifth destination.'"

It took a moment, but it hit me hard. "Oh my God."

"*What?*" asked Mary Ann. "What does that mean?"

I was looking at Ben now, flabbergasted. "It's what Carlotta says."

"Who's Carlotta?" asked Brian.

"Our car," said Ben.

Mary Ann frowned. "Your car says things?"

I was still gaping at Ben, looking for the deeper meaning of this conundrum, this snake eating its tail. I remembered what Ben had said when we first heard Carlotta's stern pronouncement on the fifth destination: *If that's the answer, what is the question?* And here was Mrs. Madrigal, drifting in dreams between life and death, mumbling this phrase we'd already mocked and lovingly made our own.

Is this how she would leave, winking at us across the cosmos?

"This is the weirdest thing," I said. "I can't begin to imagine how—"

"I told her, honey." Ben was smiling gently, having burst my metaphysical bubble. "After the hula show at the Palace. We had a good laugh about it."

"Right," said Shawna. "She was vaporizing that night."

"God," said Mary Ann, "will somebody please speak English?"

The patient cleared her throat noisily. All eyes turned to the bed as Anna's eyes fluttered open. She took us in, one at a time, with a smile blooming on her face.

"Children," she said weakly.

"Yes, ma'am," said Mary Ann. "We're here."

"You'll never guess . . ." Anna's voice trailed off.

"What?" I asked. "Never guess what?"

"Where I've been," she replied.

28

This Day Alone

On the day before Thanksgiving there were already fat red berries on the holly bush at the foot of our garden. Ben and I were stretched out on our double chaise beneath a blue enamel sky, discussing our contribution to Anna's annual feast.

"What about blackberry cobbler?" I suggested.

Ben shook his head. "Brian's doing dessert. And we'll be eating it . . . by the way . . . in the Winnebago."

"You're shitting me."

"He's parking it across the street from Anna's. Says he wants our vibes in there before he leaves for Mesa Verde."

I thought for a moment. "Okay, then . . . sweet potatoes."

"Kinda boring," said Ben. "And we did that last year."

"Did we?" I had no memory of that whatsoever.

Ben smiled at me indulgently.

"Hey," I said, "some guys my age can't remember the seventies. You're getting off real easy with sweet potatoes." (Faulty memory aside, I love the fact that we're starting to repeat ourselves, settling into comfy familial rituals.)

"What about a green bean casserole?" Ben offered.

"No, wait! The brussels sprouts with maple syrup! Nobody's had that one, for sure."

"There's a reason for that," said Ben.

"Okay. Fine."

Ben leaned into me, nuzzling my neck. "Don't be hurt, honey. It was a noble effort." He threaded his fingers through mine as we gazed up at the perfect cerulean sky. "Hey . . . the nipple toys have arrived from eBay."

"And the swallows have come back to Capistrano."

He laughed. "You're gonna love 'em."

"They're from eBay? They're *used* nipple toys?"

"C'mon." Ben tugged my nipple through my polo shirt. "That would run you a whole lot more."

I chuckled. "You're right. There's probably heavy bidding on celebrity nipple toys."

"Speaking of which," said Ben. "Shawna's gonna be on *The Daily Show* next week."

I laughed sourly. "Nice segue."

"Isn't that great, though? She called all excited while

331

you were in the shower. From a bar in Chelsea. She's asked Mary Ann to be in the audience."

I felt a tinge of jealousy, I have to admit. "Has she even seen Shawna's website?"

"I would presume. Or she's boning up on it as we speak."

"It's her husband who's boning up on it."

Ben scolded me with a smile. "Don't be a fussy old uncle."

We lay there silently, watching a pair of ravens circle the old cypress in a neighbor's yard. Ben says that ravens mate for life, so it's always nice when they offer us their blessing. Looking at them, Ben gave my belly a Buddha rub, a gesture that still makes me self-conscious, as much as I love being loved in my entirety.

"You know what I'd like to do today?" he said.

"What?"

"I'd like you to take me to Barbary Lane."

"There's nothing to see, sweetie. There must be three planks left from the old house."

"I just wanna see the lane. It's a perfect day for it, and I've never even climbed those steps."

"Okay, then . . . sure. We can eat lunch in North Beach."

"Should we take Anna with us?"

I shook my head. "The steps are too much for her. And she says she'd rather remember it the way it was."

Ben took that in for a moment. "They're the same steps, though, right?"

"Actually, no. They replaced them just after I left."

"Oh."

"They look the same, though. They're almost as rickety now."

As I spoke these words I was gazing at the old cypress. It was over a century old and its limbs were elaborately trussed with steel cables to keep them from snapping in a high wind. Like a lot of the cypresses in Golden Gate Park, this one was nearing the end of its cycle. (I confess that I sometimes make bets with it as to which one of us will outlast the other, which one will remain king of the hill.)

I looked over at my husband and reminded myself for the umpteenth time that his youth was not contagious. It would certainly make the journey more pleasant, but it wouldn't save me from my destination. He had once offered me thirty years, but I'd happily settle for twenty. Hell, this day alone was enough for now.

And more than I'd ever expected.

THE END

TALES OF THE CITY
Armistead Maupin

'MAUPIN IS A RICHLY GIFTED COMIC AUTHOR'
Observer

A naïve young secretary forsakes Cleveland for San Francisco, tumbling headlong into a brave new world of laundromat Lotharios, cut throat debutantes, and Jockey Shorts dance contests. The saga that ensues is manic, romantic, tawdry, touching, and outrageous – unmistakably the handiwork of Armistead Maupin.

'A CONSUMMATE ENTERTAINER . . . IT IS MAUPIN'S DICKENSIAN GIFT TO BE ABLE TO RENDER LOVE CONVINCINGLY'
Edmund White, *The Times Literary Supplement*

'LIKE THOSE OF DICKENS AND WILKIE COLLINS, ARMISTEAD MAUPIN'S NOVELS HAVE ALL APPEARED ORIGINALLY AS SERIALS . . . IT IS THE STRENGTH OF THIS APPROACH, WITH ITS FANTASTIC ADVENTURES AND ASTONISHINGLY CONTRIVED COINCIDENCES, THAT MAKE THESE NOVELS CHARMING AND COMPELLING'
The Literary Review

'SAN FRANCISCO IS FORTUNATE IN HAVING A CHRONICLER AS WITTY AND LIKEABLE AS ARMISTEAD MAUPIN'
Independent

9780552998765

BLACK SWAN

Acknowledgments

For good company and wise counsel during the writing of this novel, I'm especially grateful to Don Bachardy, Karen Barbour, Steven Barclay, Alison Barrow, Joanna Barton, Sara Bixler, Curt Branom, Charles Busch, Alison Callahan, Jimmie Clark, Andrew Coile, Kirk Dalrymple, Gregg De Meza, Lou DiMattei, Mike Fulton, Patrick Gale, Todd Hargis, Jake Heggie, Nick Hongola, Peggy Knickerbocker, Jerry Lasley, James Lecesne, Mark Leno, Pam Ling, Laura Linney, Jean Maupin, Tony Maupin, Ian McKellen, John Cameron Mitchell, Stuart Myers, Davia Nelson, Luke Parker Bowles, Jeanette Perez, Alan Poul, Joshua Robison, Marc Schauer, Bill Scott-Kerr, David Sheff, Jim Simmons, Patrick Stettner, Amy Tan, Michael Tilson Thomas, Alicia Turner, Binky Urban, Darryl Vance, Louise Vance, Rob Waring, Colton Weeks, Mark Weigle, Judd Winick, Stephen Winter, and Jane Yates.